HE ... SIGHT OF HER . . .

Cira felt his mouth go dry as he saw her, shimmering like a misty spirit of the water. She was utterly breathtaking, raising a fearsome need in his loins. He watched her stand, face to the sun . . . Then slowly, as if in a trance, she slid long, slender fingers over her arms and breasts . . .

Pushing past the dense bushes concealing him, he rushed forward. Frozen in his tracks, barely breathing, he gazed down upon Monase's naked, glistening, sun-kissed body. He ached to touch her . . .

In a flutter, her eyes flew open. Fear and surprise melted into dark pools of desire . . .

Patricia Williams

DIAMOND BOOKS, NEW YORK

This book is a Diamond original edition,
and has never been previously published.

WARRIOR'S PRIZE

A Diamond Book / published by arrangement with
the author

PRINTING HISTORY
Diamond edition/September 1994

For information address: The Berkley Publishing Group,
200 Madison Avenue, New York, NY 10016.

ISBN: 0-7865-0040-9

Diamond Books are published by The Berkley Publishing Group,
200 Madison Avenue, New York, NY 10016.
DIAMOND and the "D" design
are trademarks belonging to Charter Communications, Inc.

PRINTED IN THE UNITED STATES OF AMERICA

10 9 8 7 6 5 4 3 2 1

To Sheila Zilar
who helped me get my dreams on paper
and
For Carrie Feron
who gave them wings.

One

TRANSVAAL, SOUTH AFRICA
DECEMBER 1818

Monase ran blindly through the forest, her tears falling freely down her cheeks. Her mother's angry words still rang harshly in her ears.

"Monase, you would think that after having seen twenty-two winters, you'd be old enough to know the damage you could have caused your father's cattle by being inside their pen. I shudder to think what your father would do if he were to find out . . . or if anyone else did; we would never be able to find a husband for you, much less one willing to pay the lobala necessary to obtain the daughter of a Great Wife."

Her mother had turned in disgust at Monase's tears, and with a grim face bid her to bathe her face before she inevitably raised questions. Monase had needed no more persuasion to dash off to the quiet, secluded embrace of the cool forest.

Monase had wanted to explain. All she had tried to do was look at the new cattle her family had received as lobala for her older sister, Sondaba. The cows were truly magnificent creatures of a pure white. She had only leaned in to get a closer look when she had lost her balance, sending her crashing into the pen. Fortunately, her mother had been the only one to see her. Her mother had averted her eyes and pulled Monase out none too gently. Half in a rage, and half in fear, her mother had dragged her back to the hut. Monase had bitten her lip and looked down at her dusty hide skirt. She knew it was taboo for women to be in the cattle pen, and that the mere shadow of a woman could cause death or illness among the cattle. She also knew that these new cows were critical for her family. With the new wife her father had obtained, and the lack of marriage-aged daughters, their too few heads of cattle indicated the wealth and status they had once enjoyed was dwindling.

These thoughts only reminded Monase that once again, she had broken her promise to herself and her parents that she would become a perfect, obedient daughter so that her betrothal would bring her family as many heads of cattle as Sondaba had brought.

Fresh, hot tears coursed down Monase's face as she remembered her mother's mocking grin at her promise. Slowing down to catch her breath, she fell to her knees on the soft loam. Clasping her thighs with her long, lean fingers, she gritted her teeth. Her mother was right. How could she ever hope to bring in half the number of cows Sondaba had? True, she was a daughter of her father's Great Wife, but she wasn't nearly as desirable as Sondaba. Sondaba was small with large melon breasts, a narrow waist, and wide hips. She was also gentle, soft-spoken, and obedient. All the things that Monase was not.

With a critical eye, Monase looked disgustedly down at her heaving breasts. Her breasts were smaller than Sondaba's, and she had a long narrow waist that swelled slightly into narrow hips. Hips, Monase thought wryly, that spoke of possible difficulty in breeding many boys to be brave impi warriors, and daughters to enrich a man's kraal. Slowly flattening the palms of her hands along her smooth thighs, she cursed her long, slim legs. All combined, she was taller than most of the men of her kraal. When she was a preadolescent, the boys and girls had teased that perhaps in making her, Umvelinquangi, "the one who is always there," had played a joke, confusing male and female. When her body changed, the taunting had stopped, but the sneers were still there when she outran and outtracked the boys.

Hugging her arms tightly across her chest, she felt the injustice of it all wash over her, rising and lumping in a burning ball in her throat. She missed Sondaba, her sister, her little foster mother. As was customary, her real mother had weaned her at three, and from that day forward, Sondaba, then seven, had been her teacher, her confidante, her caretaker. She remembered many nights sobbing into Sondaba's soft shoulder, asking why she, Monase, was so different. Sondaba would rock her slowly, crooning to her, telling her the stories of their ancestors, the Sans.

The Sans were the hunters of the great forest lands. They were quick like the cheetah, lean like the antelope, and golden like the mighty lion. They were small in stature but cunning, and none could outrun, outtrack, or outhunt them. Always at this part of the story, Sondaba stopped and smoothed Monase's brow with her cool, soothing hands. She would smile, sharing the secret that only she and Monase knew. Monase was the mysterious hunter who left small game outside their mother's hut when times were hard and their field had not produced enough. Their mother thought it was her ancestors bestowing their blessing on her, since she had not been able to bear any sons to provide for her. She would have been incensed had she known the truth. So the secret was theirs, never spoken, but creating a bond.

Sondaba's soft voice would continue, telling of the Khoikhoi "men of men," tall, strong, and black as the black Mamba, coming south from the barren desert land. The Khoikhoi were great impi warriors, and had pushed the Sans into the deep forest and mountains, taking the open plains to graze their cattle and grow their crops. After many dry winters, the wild animals began to diminish. The Sans began to come down to the open land to seek out the great Khoikhoi chiefs. The Khoikhoi impi looked favorably on the small golden Sans women. Together they bore a strong, beautiful nut-brown people. These people were the cream of the crop. They were the best hunters, grew the best crops, had the bravest impi warriors, and lived in the lands of the heavens.

Monase sighed heavily in memory. Now that Sondaba was married, Monase had no one to turn to, and that familiar burning anger and hurt reached long, searing fingers around her throat. Why, she wondered, couldn't women's merits be measured by their speed, tracking, and hunting skills? She knew she could outrun all the boys in her kraal if she were allowed to compete in the rainy-season ceremonial games. She knew she could probably best many of the impi warriors. The burning anguish crept farther down, crushing her lungs, making it hard to breathe. Monase threw back her head, wanting to release this beast of rage, willing the forest to silence her anguish, to be swallowed by the vine-covered trees. She took a deep, ragged breath. Suddenly she froze. A haunting silence surrounded her. Then she heard what had stilled the birds' and tree animals' chatter. A loud splash came from the stream just beyond the bushes.

A shiver of fear broke over Monase's flushed body. The noise was too loud to be a small animal. Maybe she should go back. Quickly, all of the dangerous wild animals it could be ran through her mind. She knew most of the large carnivorous animals drank at night. She willed her beating heart to calm so she could listen. She sniffed the air, flicking the dust with her finger to see which way the breeze was blowing. It drifted toward her, and she relaxed a little. Her human scent was going away from the stream; the animal would not smell her.

She glanced around her, quickly assessing the terrain that just moments before she had blindly passed. She gauged the closest and strongest branches to climb if the need arose. Monase the huntress emerged, erasing the angry, distraught girl. Bolder now, she crept silently toward the bushes hiding the stream. With her new bravado, she became optimistic. Perhaps, if it were a stray goat or sheep, she would bring it home. Her mother would be pleased.

Monase's eyes grew wide, and her heart thudded to a stop, then began to beat so loudly she was afraid it would give her away. There, in the middle of the stream, was the most magnificent man she had ever seen. He was naked except for the leather armbands on his massive upper arms and a necklace of sharp claws hanging upon his muscularly sculpted chest. His dark oiled locks fell to his broad shoulders.

Mesmerized, Monase watched the water glisten on his ebony skin, pooling, then sliding over rippling muscles like so many silvery snakes. Her fingers burned to reach out and touch their crystal coolness. She swallowed hard, finding her mouth unquenchably dry. This man was a giant, standing no less than six inches taller than her five-foot-eight frame. Her eyes ran up his well-defined calves to long taut thighs. She felt a blazing flush up the side of her neck and face as she gazed upon his manhood. Reluctantly, she willed her eyes to finish their journey. Narrow hips, followed by a hard, rigid stomach, then expanding outward to a massive chest and shoulders. Surely, she thought, she had wandered into the bathing grounds of a god.

She watched as he bent, scooping handfuls of cool stream water, slapping it across the smooth, black skin of his chest. Crouched in her hiding place, Monase's body tingled with heat, then washed with cold chills. Beads of perspiration formed on her upper lip and in the hollow of her neck. What was this feeling? Monase had never felt this way before. A part of her wanted to go to him, to trace the paths of the glistening water, to run her hands up his hard lean body, to feel his hands on her, to . . . Again, she felt herself flush with a longing for she knew not what. The other girls of the village played kana—"choose-the-one-you-love-the-best"—and had slyly hinted of the amorous findings in the darkened huts. She had never been chosen, so could only guess at the longings searing her body. The perspiration that had started as small beads had pooled and trickled down between her breasts. Her bent legs felt weak, and she shifted slightly. A twig cracked. The spell was broken. The bathing man halted, his chiseled face turned in her direction. His eyes were a hard, glittering topaz: a lion ready to pounce. Monase's heart jumped. Her body braced itself. Had he seen her? The man lunged toward her. Monase sprang like a wild gazelle, surefooted and swift, as she disappeared into the trees, an angry Zulu impi warrior close behind.

Two

Cira was angry at himself for getting caught off guard. His momentary musing could have cost him his life. He hadn't become head commander of the Black Shield Zulu Impi Brigade, Chief Shaka's finest warriors, by letting his thoughts wander. Damn it, he had made himself vulnerable. He had only stepped in the stream to cool off, and to wash away the weeks of dirt and grime he had collected on this last campaign. The water had felt so refreshing that he had stripped entirely and left his shield and iKlwa spear on the shore. He meant to stay only for a moment, but had begun to think of his last battle.

He had killed a worthy opponent. He had thrown the man to the ground, pinned him with his foot, his iKlwa spear tip resting in the hollow of the man's neck. The man gazed fearlessly into his eyes. Cira asked him to swear allegiance to Chief Shaka and join the Zulu army, but the man remained proud and defiant. He shouted that he was Butelezi, and would remain so in the heavens with his ancestors. Cira replied that the Zulus were, as their name said, "the people of the heavens." The man stared off silently. Reluctantly, Cira sent his iKlwa spear through him. He then ripped open the man's chest to allow the spirit to escape. Even in death the man had remained silent and proud.

Cira prayed to Umvelinquangi to accept this brave impi spirit into his midst, then withdrawing his spear, he parted from his men. Custom dictated that when an impi warrior slays another, he must cleanse himself. He must eat and sleep separately from his men until he has rid himself of death's evil spirits. He would have to clean his outer body with water and rid his inner body by releasing his seed into a woman not of his people. He planned to bathe himself, then return and choose one of the captured Butelezi maidens.

It was at this point that Cira mused pleasantly over the delectable Butelezi maidens. Chief Shaka would be pleased with his success in this last campaign and would surely give him one as a first wife. Cira smiled to himself. Yes, Shaka would be sure to have Cira choose from these new maidens. Shaka was a clever man, and had claimed that all new maidens were to join his private "UmDunkulu" and become his "sisters."

Thus, if any were married, the lobala, or dowry, would go to Shaka. A frown creased Cira's brow as he thought, Shaka may call them "sisters," but he samples each and every one of them before giving them up.

Cira then shrugged his wide shoulders. He was getting too romantic. What did it matter if his first wife was not a virgin? Maybe if he chose a wife, then the mothers in the Zulu kraal would cease their pestering for a while and stop parading their daughters before him like so many heads of cattle. The daughters had clung and simpered. He cringed at the memory. Women were a bother. Like Shaka, he felt women were good for one thing only, and wives were a hindrance to a good warrior.

One had to spend so much time and energy keeping them fed, clothed, and keeping peace between them. He would rather just have the children: beautiful daughters to cook for him and make him rich, and fearless sons to make him proud. The idea made him suck in his breath and throw back his shoulders. It was then he heard the twig snap in the bushes in front of him.

Instinctively, Cira reached to his side for his spear, then realized that it lay useless on the shore behind him with his shield. He rushed forward, cursing under his breath, ready to lunge at the beast or enemy. He was startled, and nearly fell backward, when he saw a young, beautiful, long-legged maiden spring from the bushes and disappear into the forest.

Quickly regaining his balance, Cira smiled in

amusement; then his smile faded to an angry sneer. No woman would get the better of him. Hastily he dressed, fastening his leopard umutsha around his waist. He would show that girl. He'd teach her to spy on a Zulu impi. Tucking his spear into his waistband, he smiled a lazy, sensuous smile. Yes, he's show her, cleanse himself, and leave her singing the praise of the great Zulu impi.

Running through the forest, he scanned the dappled darkness. Remembering the long, lean legs and bouncing full breasts, he felt his manhood tighten. Stopping, he turned a full circle, then paused to listen. Only silence. Even the chattering monkeys and squawking birds were silent. Squinting into the rapidly approaching darkness, Cira swallowed hard, forcing his breathing to slow down. Slowly, the forest noises began to return. A sad-eyed, gray monkey scampered in front of him, scolding him angrily. Cira kicked at the retreating monkey. He swiped the beads of perspiration from his scowling forehead.

Where had she gone? Maybe she had been a spirit. It was said that a man who had killed a foe and didn't cleanse his inner body in haste would be driven mad by the evil spirit within. Perhaps he had imagined her. The aching in his groin reminded him that she had appeared all too real. He could envision her golden-brown skin glowing in the dappled sunlight. And those legs! The flapping hide skirt exposed a firm round bottom flexing with each smooth stride. Cira slapped the sweat from the back of his neck. Cursing, he shook his head. What was happening to him? He had been celibate too damn long. He would not allow this madness to descend upon him. Taking a last long look around him, he stomped off loudly to the stream from whence he came. Aloud he muttered, "She must have been a spirit, because no mere woman could outrun me. No man could outrun me, for that matter."

Cira prided himself on the swiftness that had earned him championships in the rainy-season ceremonies for the last five—no, six—years. No one but Shaka was faster, and Shaka was already legendary.

Monase sat crouched up in the branches of the trees, willing her body to melt into the trunk she was hugging ferociously. Only when she saw the impi warrior disappear through the trees did she allow herself to breathe, but she made no other movement. Her heart was pounding so loudly she had been sure he would hear her. He had stood less than five feet directly below her. She silently thanked her ancestors that he hadn't looked up or expected a woman to run so fast.

Monase swallowed hard, gasping deep breaths, trying to calm her trembling body. The encounter had been too close. She knew that had she been caught by that impi warrior, he would no doubt have raped her, possibly even killed her. If he had let her return to her kraal, she would have been of even less value as a prospective wife than she was already. And, the spirit forbid, had he impregnated her with his child . . . She cringed to think of the what ifs. What emDletsheni man would want to raise a bastard child of a Zulu impi? She would surely be put to death.

Since the rise of Shaka to power, the fear and awe of the Zulus was at its peak. Shaka was proving to be an unconquerable leader. He had no mercy. It was said his army could cover fifty miles barefoot over rough terrain in a single day. She knew the strongest emDletsheni armies could average ten to fifteen miles a day under the best conditions, and they wore sandals. It was also rumored that the Zulu impis were invincible, and their chief Shaka would kill men, women, and children, turning a hard heart to their pleas, if their men did not swear allegiance to him. It was even said that Shaka so enjoyed killing, that after slaying a victim, he would pull his spear out of their heart and cry, "Ngadla!" (I have eaten!)

She shuddered. Every man, woman, and child in kraals all over the land had been taught to recognize a Zulu impi by the large, six-foot-or-more shield of black-and-white cow's hide and their unique iKlwa spear. She had no doubt that the bathing impi had been a Zulu. Drawing her arms across her chest, she shuddered more violently. If only half the Zulu impi were as huge as the man chasing her, then they were indeed a formidable army, and no doubt all the rumors were true. Glancing nervously around her as she climbed down the tree, she conjured up the image of the beautiful, glistening black giant: the slick hardness of his body, the tawny gold of his eyes, the high cheekbones, the sensuous mouth. Monase was stunned as she felt a hot tingling sensation wash over her body, wrapping itself around her insides and spreading down her legs, making her knees weak. Biting her lower lip, she sneered to herself, thinking, How could you? That man was an enemy. A terrible enemy.

Cautiously, Monase crept through the dark forest. All her senses and muscles were tense and alert. Fearfully, she sensed that he was still lurking in the forest somewhere. Every rustling leaf, every flapping wing made her jump. Not until she saw the welcoming fires of her kraal did she realize that her lungs were aching from lack of air, and her fingernails had cut deep crescents into her wet palms. Her first instinct was to run with all her strength to the familiar, low, hive-shaped thatched huts. But her common sense won out, demanding she slow down and think. Briefly glancing at the dark web of a forest behind her, she gazed up at the clear indigo sky. What should she tell her family?

Should she tell her father that she had encountered a Zulu impi? She really should. Her father could then tell the chief, and then her clan would be ready for a possible attack. Yes, she thought, spies could be sent out to discover the Zulu encampment, and she would be a heroine. Her parents would be proud, the young men would surely want such a woman as their wife, maybe even as their Great Wife.

Suddenly she grimaced. There would be no praise and respect for her, only incriminating questions. She would be asked why she had been out alone in the forest after dark. There would be questions concerning her virginity and, she shuddered, the chief might demand she be taken to the witch doctor to have it verified. In determined defiance, Monase threw back her shoulders and decided she would not, could not tell. With every step toward her home, the guilt steadily ate at her conscience.

Desperately, she argued aloud. "It was probably only a warrior out to cleanse himself. He was in need of a woman, and I would have been convenient."

She laughed a forced brittle laugh. "Why, the man is probably on his way home right now and has forgotten about me already."

She smirked a little at the thought of having outsmarted the handsome warrior. A heavy sigh escaped her lips as she thought that he'd really given up so easily. The familiar burning anguish started rising in her chest. Even the Zulu warrior hadn't thought she was worth the chase.

Monase dropped to her hands and knees as she entered her mother's hut. Her mother looked up sharply, scanned her face briefly, nodded, then gave her full attention to mixing the amaSi. AmaSi was a creamy mixture of mild curds and sorghum millet. Monase smiled as her stomach rumbled at the familiar welcome sight. She was glad for her mother's silence. It told her she was forgiven for the cattle-pen incident, and her father need not be involved.

Surer now of her decision not to tell of the Zulu

impi encounter, Monase happily grabbed a smooth round rock and began crushing the sorghum millet on the quern. Humming softly, she promised herself that from this moment on she would be the most obedient, most docile daughter this clan had ever seen. As long as she never saw the Zulu impi again, everything would work out all right.

Three

Monase awoke with a start. Her muscles were tense, and she was perspiring profusely. She had been dreaming. The tall, handsome warrior had caught her and was running his big, hard hands down her body. He showered her neck and shoulders with searing kisses, whispering against her flushed skin about how desirable he found her. In frustration and anger, she flung off her supple animal-skin covers. Still trembling, she crawled silently out of the hut into the chilly predawn air.

She shivered as a cool breeze embraced her damp skin. She took long, calming breaths of the cool air and watched as the first fingers of pink sunlight stroked the surrounding foothills. Gradually, the pink hues turned the rolling hills into a rich, golden green. Already, the young boy herders were sleepily taking their herds up to the hills. She turned then to look at the young men standing by the cattle-pen gates. These men no longer herded, but had been inducted into the army as apprentices and runners. By the rainy-season ceremonies, they would become full-fledged warriors. One of these young men would, she hoped, become her husband one day. Studying the men more closely, she unconsciously began comparing them with the magnificent man she had seen the day before. The men in her kraal were sturdy, with barrel chests and short, muscular legs. Their skin was a rich mahogany, not the striking ebony of the Zulu impi. She tried to imagine marriage and love with one of these men, and felt nothing. Nothing like the exciting yearning of yesterday.

"Does one appeal to you, my little gazelle?" a deep resonant voice called cheerfully.

Monase had been so deep in thought that she had not noticed Ugebula, her father, coming toward her from his hut. Blushing deeply at his term of endearment, she lowered her eyes in respect. For all her father's anger at her unwomanly behaviors, he had a soft spot for her. He often said she had inherited her fire from his beloved mother. With a soft haziness filling his eyes, he would tell her stories of his mother's bravery and determination.

Monase's favorite story was of the time her grandmother, then a young maiden, saved the chief and clan. Her grandmother's village had been attacked. As custom dictated, the men armed themselves. The chief, women, and children climbed to a nearby hill to watch. Things began to go badly. Instead of the usual barrage of insulting, pushing, and occasional killing, the attacking clan had turned truly vicious. They lunged upon the unsuspecting impi warriors, tearing at them with spears and hurling rocks. Many of the frightened men from her grandmother's tribe fled. In despair, the chief acknowledged defeat. The women and children were beginning to mourn and prepare to be captured when the crazed attackers suddenly turned to rush the hillside. Everyone was shocked. Only her grandmother stayed calm. In minutes she had organized the women and children in a line in front of the chief.

Shoulder to shoulder, with nothing more than their harvesting axes and water cabashes, they descended on the advancing enemy impi warriors. The enemy had been caught off guard. Pots and axes came raining down on the closest impi. In horror, the enemy fled. The women, now fanatical, ran after them, screaming and gnashing their teeth. The fleeing enemy impi cried out prayers to their ancestors to protect them from these bewitched evil spirits.

The chief had been elated. Although her grandmother was of low birth and only eighteen, he took her as a lower wife. Always at this point of the story, her father would turn a stern face to Monase and point out that the marriage was a rocky one, and thus it was that he was the only child she bore. He would then wag a finger in front of her nose and say, "Because my mother never learned to be obedient and submissive, she led a lonely life."

Monase would argue back that had his mother been a meek, submissive woman, her father, and perhaps the whole clan, might not be around today. Frowning and pursing his lips, he would grunt at her, but his hands always betrayed his displeasure as he drew her near and fondly stroked her cheek. If Monase's mother was around, she would glare at her husband angrily before lowering her eyes and muttering that he was only encouraging Monase's already too strong independent streak. Her father would then push Monase from him, but not without first tweaking her nose affectionately.

With these warm memories, she greeted him heartily. "Good morning, Father."

Rushing forward, she wrapped her arms around his neck and lifted her smiling face to him for a kiss. A smile touched the corners of his mouth as a scowl creased his brow. Putting strong, rough hands on her shoulders, he gently but firmly pushed her from him.

"Monase, you are not a child. You cannot hang on to my neck like one. You are a woman. Act as one!"

Monase pulled back as if slapped, the words stinging more sharply than any hand. She hung her head. She missed being a child. She didn't want to be a woman. She didn't want to marry one of those men and leave her family. Remembering her promise of yesterday, she bit her bottom lip and said, "I'm sorry, Father. I will do better."

Her father briefly hugged her to him, then as quickly released her. Looking away, he said gruffly, "Come with me. You may fuel my iron oven today."

Monase stifled a squeal of delight and nodded.

Her father was the best iron smelter around; his abilities were known far and wide and he was a great pride to the clan. His assegai spearheads were worth many sheep in trade. Monase knew that iron smelting was a difficult craft, the secrets handed down from generation to generation, and reserved only for men. She also knew that the impi warriors came to her father's ovens to have new assegai spears made, and often talked of surrounding clans, upcoming ceremonies, and battles.

Indeed, this was a wonderful treat. Quickly, she picked up her water cabash, a bundle of dried kindling, and fell into step five paces behind her father.

"Where do you think you are going?" a stern voice snapped, when they were no more than a few feet from the hut.

Her father stopped, his back rigid. Monase dared not turn around. She knew her mother was speaking to her. Monase watched her father's shoulder muscles bunch in anger as he slowly turned. His eyes were dark with rage. Slowly, in a harsh voice no louder than a whisper, he muttered through clenched teeth, "She comes with me!"

Monase felt her mother's angry eyes boring holes through her back, willing her to turn around and defy her. When she didn't, her mother lowered her voice and hissed, "You are to blame for her lack of a prospective husband and her evil ways. You treat her as a son."

Her father's dark eyes turned to smoldering black coals.

"Then beget me a son, woman, so I have an heir to carry on my trade."

Monase heard her mother painfully suck in her breath, turn, and retreat into the hut. Her father then turned and grunted, "Come."

Eagerly, she followed him. More than ever she was glad that she would not have to spend the day in the field with her mother and younger sisters. Her mother would be in a foul mood today, and her fury would undoubtedly be unleashed on her. Her father and mother rarely got along, but her father had hit a sore spot today. Monase felt sorry for her mother. As a Great Wife, she was responsible to provide an heir for her father, and in this she had failed. She had produced only four daughters. While this would add to her father's wealth when they were married, it did not provide an heir to carry on the family line and learn the secrets of iron smelting. Monase knew her mother prayed to the ancestors for a son, but she was well into her forties now, with little hope of bearing any more children. Her father's first wife had proven barren and had been traded for her sister, who so far had only been able to produce female children. Thus her father had taken a new bride, and was depending on both Sondaba's and Monase's lobala to replenish his depleted cattle pens.

It had been easy to find a husband for Sondaba. Many men, young and old, had desired her from an early age. With her curvaceous body, mild obedient manner, and strong family line, she had been promised at sixteen and had brought in a good lobala. Her mother had smiled in pride when she told the women of the tribe that Sondaba's husband had delivered fifteen cows, five of them white as the mountain snow. Although Sondaba was a first wife for her husband, and it was therefore unlikely that she would be nominated as a Great Wife, her parents had been proud, and her father's other wives were jealous.

Monase knew her father hoped that by bringing her with him to the smelting fires, she would perhaps interest one of the young warriors and thereby thwart her mother's designs of getting an older, richer man. She hoped so, too. She didn't want to marry one of the older men, who had already grown fat and lazy. She knew these men had more cattle and could more likely make her their Great Wife.

Slyly, she stole a glance at her father's profile as he stoked the fire. She knew that he wanted a young man to be the heir he might never have. Sondaba's husband was already heir to a successful hide tanner. Monase sighed heavily. Her father turned his head and snapped, "Do not make me regret my decision."

Monase didn't respond, but quickly handed her father the dry kindling. He began to blow on it with the hide bellows. Monase sat quietly with eyes downcast. She was careful not to step into the iron smelter's circle, well aware that for a woman to do so was to taint the iron and make the weapon weak. By noon, she was hot and her legs were beginning to ache from the constant standing, crouching, and walking back and forth to carry water. She didn't dare complain, but the morning had proven uneventful. There had been little talk among the men, other than their congratulations for the marriage of Sondaba and their expressions of admiration for the sizable lobala.

Monase began to think that it might perhaps have been less boring to have gone to the field with the women. The women gossiped of witchcraft, wizards, spirits, and ancestors. Often, one of the women who had joined the clan through marriage told stories of the other clans. One of Monase's favorites was the story of the woman chieftain Mjanji, who ruled over the small baPedi clan. She was said to be as big as a man, with four breasts that drooped so low that she could suckle a child on her back by swinging her breast over her shoulder. It was rumored that she was queen of the locust and could send a deluge of insects or drought against any clan that opposed her. She was believed to be immortal, and it was death to anyone not from her clan to look at her. As a result, her clan lived peacefully up in the mountains.

As Monase pondered the believability of this horrendous woman, she did not hear the approach of Jama the witch doctor. Jama was a powerful, repulsive man, second only in power to the chief. Some said he ruled the chief's spirit. Jama was almost half a foot shorter than Monase, and weighed nearly two hundred pounds. He smelled vile from the fat-and-cow-dung mixture he slathered on his body and hair to ward off evil spirits. Monase went rigid as she smelled him, and felt his fat slippery fingers run up her spine.

"What a fine, strong back. Too bad her hips are so narrow. Perhaps I could make a potion . . ."

His voice trailed off as he cupped one of her buttocks with one hand while the other slid up her spine, over her shoulder, and down to grasp her full breast possessively. Monase drew back in horror.

"Oh, but her breasts are fine—firm and full, just as they should be."

Slowly, he ran his pink tongue around his fat, flaccid lips. Monase tried hard not to shudder at his touch. She felt tears beginning to form in her eyes as she lifted them beseechingly to her father. He looked away.

Oh please, she thought desperately, not Jama. Anyone but Jama.

She knew Jama was wealthy beyond belief, due to the fact that any man accused of being bewitched was brutally killed to purge the kraal of his evil spirit. His holdings were then split between Jama and the chief. She shuddered as she recalled that every time Jama took a wife, someone inevitably had been purged of witchcraft. The lobala he'd pay would surely make her family happy, but she couldn't bear to think of his body on hers. Suddenly she could bear no more, and rocked back on her heels and rose, mumbling something about needing to get more kindling, leaving Jama's fat hand hanging in midair where her breast had been. Jama caught her eyes and again licked his puffy lips. His gaze slowly raked her body. Monase turned, this time unable to hide her shudder.

"What can I do for you today, Jama?" her father asked heartily.

Jama pulled his gaze from Monase.

"Ah, yes," Jama grunted.

Sensing a chance to escape, Monase quickly turned. Jama deftly caught her wrist, and without looking at her, he began to speak to her father.

"Chief Shaka's army is believed to be headed this way. The Zulu impi have slaughtered the Butelezi and captured their women. They let the eLangeni clan live and incorporated the young men into their army's lower ranks."

Monase's heart began to beat faster. Perhaps she should have told her father of her encounter with the Zulu impi warrior, but now it was too late. Jama slyly looked over at her. A huge grin split his face, revealing yellow, rotting teeth. Monase looked away, recalling the beautiful smile of the Zulu warrior, his even white teeth dazzling against his coal-black skin. With a sigh, she remembered the dimple on his left cheek. Jama, feeling her pulse quicken, stroked her wrist with his thumb, murmuring some question.

"Monase!" her father whispered harshly.

Only then did she realize that she had been lost in thought and that Jama had asked her a question. Turning to him with lowered eyes, she whispered softly, "I'm sorry. I did not hear your question."

Jama reached out and put his hand under her chin. Monase bravely fought her instinct to recoil from his foul-smelling hand.

"Have you heard of the Zulu impi warriors? They would enjoy a beauty such as you. They are a tall, strong people, and I hear their men are well endowed, and the captive maidens don't mind being captive at all."

Monase snatched her arm away. Blood rushed to her cheeks. Her mind was frantic. Did Jama know about her encounter with the Zulu impi? Perhaps he had spies or—her eyes grew wide with fear—maybe the spirits had told him.

In response, Jama slid the hand beneath her chin, down her neck, toying briefly with her strands of colored beads.

"I think this one needs to get a husband, and soon. She is hot with the longing for a man."

His hands continued their leisurely journey down her breastbone, lingering between her breasts. With hooded eyes, he smiled and left.

Monase turned pleading eyes to her father, but again he looked away. Hot tears blurred her eyes; her throat closed in a panic. She drew in a deep, ragged breath.

Silently she prayed, Oh please, spirits of the heavens, don't let this man marry me. Oh please, don't let my father make a contract with him. I can't, I won't become his wife.

Four

When Cira returned to his men, the Butelezi cattle were already being rounded up to begin the long journey back to Zululand. The captive women and their children were packing their few meager belongings as they, too, prepared for the journey. Cira's eyes ran searchingly over the young maidens, their nut-brown skin glowing softly and invitingly in the afternoon sun. Abruptly he turned, disgusted that he couldn't erase the vision of the lithe young woman he had encountered in the forest from his mind. Again, he saw her leaping gracefully over the bush, her lean, perspiring body gleaming.

"Stop!" he barked aloud, turning once again toward the waiting women. The single harsh syllable had caused them to start. Wide-eyed, they looked at him, some with fear and others with interest.

Squeezing the bridge of his nose with his thumb and forefinger, he shut his eyes with frustrated resignation. He must complete the cleansing ritual and bed one of these women before she became a member of the Zulu tribe. He opened his eyes, his jaw set in determination, its muscle twitching slowly as he ground his teeth. Now. He must choose one now, before the madness engulfed him. Surely his obsession with this forest spirit was a warning sign. Eyes straight ahead, shoulders back, he strode toward the women. As he crossed the distance he could sense a myriad of apprehensive eyes following him.

A petite, large-bosomed beauty stepped forward. Lowering her eyelashes coyly, she looked up at him through their sooty thickness. A dark shadow crossed his features. He crossed muscle-bound arms across his battle-scarred chest. A slight breeze tossed his long locks across his unsmiling, sensuous mouth, presenting the image of a wild, untamed, frightening, but fascinatingly dangerous animal. The small woman's eyes dilated with fear, but still she did not retreat, only swayed her hips invitingly. The line of implacable jaw softened, the corner of his mouth curved upward, dimples winked in his cheeks, lips parted to show dazzling white teeth. Throwing back his head, he laughed, grabbed her arm, and headed off toward a charred, but standing, abandoned hut. He laughed again, a soft guttural sound. Perhaps this one would make him forget.

* * *

Cira quickly released his pent-up passions, for months of warring demanded celibacy. Spent, he rolled away. Glancing at the curvaceous body pulling him to her, he felt oddly empty, devoid of desire. Experienced hands slid down the length of him, cajoling him to return to her. Just then he heard Punga, his second-in-command, call to him from outside the shelter. Rising, he wrapped his umutsha, a split-skin loincloth, around his waist. As he turned he tossed an apologetic smile over his shoulder. With a sigh, the woman, too, rose to adjust her disheveled skirt, knowing he would not return.

"I'm sorry to disturb you, Cira," Punga began, struggling to squelch a knowing grin. "But word has reached us that Chief Shaka orders us to take a battalion to find the emDletsheni tribe. He was told they have some of the finest ironsmiths, and white cattle."

Cira nodded grimly, his face a mask hiding annoyance. Punga departed to order the bulk of men to return with the captive women and cattle, while Cira selected fifty men to come with him and Punga and seek out the emDletshenis. Scowling darkly, Cira shook his head. He didn't like splitting up his men. The newly acquired cattle and women would require a lot of protection against marauding tribes and wild animals. Also, his troops were weary. They had fought well and had been away from home a long time. They wanted, and deserved, to go home. Many of them had proved valiant in battle and rightfully hoped to be awarded the permission from the chief to choose a bride.

Hunching his shoulders, Cira rolled his head back, easing the tension-knotted muscles in his neck and back. Shaka was obsessed with enlarging his pure-white herd of cattle and would not tolerate any obstacles to the fulfillment of this desire. Cira sighed resignedly. At least it would not be a total loss if they could acquire some excellent iron men. Ironsmithing was a difficult art, and the Zulus had few men who had really mastered the required skills. The ones who had were growing old, and their heirs had been drafted into Shaka's massive army and no longer had the time to learn the tricky melding techniques. He just hoped that this mission wouldn't take more than his fifty impis, and that it could be completed with a peaceful surrender. For all his fierceness as a Zulu warrior, he loathed unnecessary bloodshed.

Raising a rigid arm above his head, Cira gave the signal for the waiting caravan of people to begin their journey. The remaining men watched them go—bare feet, sandals, and hooves creating swirling clouds of dust around their retreating backs. As he squinted at the bright sun a hint of sadness clouded Cira's weary eyes. He regretted that there had been no new recruits to increase his battalion. Again he remembered the defiant warrior he had slain. He admired men with fierce pride and courage. Shaking his head, he tried to rid himself of that memory physically, and the one that had followed.

Then lowering his large frame, he sat on his haunches, beckoning his remaining men to gather around him. Picking up a small stick, he began drawing his military strategies in the rich, red dirt.

* * *

Late the next afternoon, Cira's band reached the stream where he had encountered the young woman or spirit. Cira carefully looked around, jabbing his spear into the surrounding bushes. His men watched silently, shaking their heads in wonder, yet not one questioned his actions. His men liked and respected him. He never asked a man to do something he himself would not or could not do. He was firm but fair. He always gave the opponent the opportunity to swear allegiance to Chief Shaka and King Dingoswayo. Cira, too, liked and admired his men. They were the best. They could travel fifty-plus miles in a day and move silently and gracefully as dancers. They could sneak up unsuspected on an enemy while they slept, capturing the whole tribe with a negligible amount of bloodshed.

Assured that no maidens or spirits lurked in the surrounding brush, Cira signaled for five scouts to go ahead in order to gauge the remaining distance and the number of able-bodied impi in the tribe. The rest moved silently to set up camp.

In a short time two men returned. They told Cira that the emDletsheni village was just beyond the forest, down in a shallow valley. Cira nodded, ordering the men to seek out their chief and arrange to talk or do battle.

Then, returning to his men, he eyed the bushes suspiciously once more.

It had been two days since Jama had come to her father's fire. Monase had barely been able to eat or sleep and had spoken very little since then. Dark smudges stained the delicate skin below her eyes.

Her mother had nodded approvingly at her apparently docile manner. Her father had avoided her, not inviting her to work with him again. Sickening possibilities loomed ominously before her. Fear squeezed icy fingers around her heart as she thought of her father drawing up a marriage contract with that evil, loathsome Jama. Never had a man shown any lustful inclination toward her. What had drawn Jama?

Shudders of revulsion shimmied down her body as she recalled the horrible stories of Jama's perverted and exotic tastes. She wished she could relieve herself with tears, but her eyes had been wrung dry. Hugging her arms to her chest, she tried to console herself that Jama would surely tire of her. Then she would be able to remain in her kraal and not have to leave her family and familiar surroundings to marry a man in a faraway, strange kraal. Comfort escaped her as she drew within herself, singing in a low, whispering voice, allowing herself to be lost in the melody's sweet sadness.

"Monase! Monase! Hurry! Mama will surely kill you if she finds you sitting here."

Mkabuyi, Monase's younger sister and charge, shook her shoulders. When Monase refused to answer, she burst into tears. Unable to bear the anguish in her little sister's sobs, Monase dragged herself from self-pity. In a placating gesture, she kissed Mkabuyi's damp cheek. A bright smile of relief wreathed the childlike face.

"Oh, Monase, come with me now, before Mama finds you are not in the field. I shall tell you a wonderful new story I have just learned."

Mkabuyi jumped up, tugging at Monase's lifeless limbs. Monase gazed up in wonder at the incredible resilience in the girl. Mkabuyi was as unpredictable as the spring weather: one minute dark, ominous, threatening to release a downpour, only to have a breeze reveal a shining sun in the next.

Drawing in a deep, fortifying breath, Monase rose to her feet and docilely followed Mkabuyi's figure as she skipped merrily through the trampled grass to a field behind their hut.

Every wife was allotted a field large enough to provide for herself and her children. Together, mothers and daughters worked the spot. Monase and Mkabuyi's mother demanded that each daughter, no matter how young, earn her keep and learn that life was hard, affording no holiday. Most days were spent from sunup to sundown toiling in the hot, blistering sun.

Today, as the sun began a downward arch in the azure-blue sky, Monase rose to straighten her cramped back. Lowering her harvesting ax, she raised her water basket to cool her parched throat. Hours earlier, Mkabuyi had grown tired of her older sister's sullen silence and had drifted off to chatter with her other sisters while pulling weeds from between the rows of maize.

Drinking of the water's refreshing sweetness, Monase thoughtfully scanned the rolling hillside. A deep longing filled her eyes as they reached the dark, shadowed forest. She let her mind drift to the magnificent man she had seen bathing in the stream. No sooner had she remembered him than she experienced a familiar tightening in her loins.

Suddenly she let out an explosive rush of air, surprised to realize she had been holding her breath. Grief washed over her anew. If only Jama could conjure up some magic to give him the appearance of that splendid Zulu warrior, then she would rush into his arms gladly, bearing at least a dozen or more children.

Realizing the direction of her thoughts, she blushed, embarrassed at her wanton, shallow fantasies. Why, she admonished herself, she had never even been kissed, and here she was dreaming of throwing herself into the arms of a dangerous stranger. The slow smile died on her lips as her eyes widened in disbelief. Without changing her stance, she stared hard at the dark cobweb of branches forming the forest. She had seen a flash of white moving behind the trees. Her heart pounded against the constraining walls of her chest. In absolute horror, she counted three—no five—men. Her mind reluctantly registered the meaning of their hidden, tall, dark, barefoot forms. The white she had seen was the unmistakable cow's-tail band around arms and legs.

Dear ancestors in heaven, the Zulu impis had returned!

Guilt and fear threatened to force a warning howl from deep within her. Clenching her teeth, she willed herself to regain her composure. Her mind raced frantically; her father's new prized herd was grazing close to the tangle of trees. Dropping her water basket, she ran to her father's fire. As she gasped deep gulps of air the words tumbled forth.

"Zulu warriors . . . in the forest . . . five, maybe more."

A silence fell over the men, then in a clatter of confusion, they grabbed their long-handled assegai spears and headed for the forest.

The riotous disorder set the children to crying, the women to screaming, and the confused grazing animals to mournful lowing. Monase rushed to the field with the other women to scoop the frightened children up into their arms and retire to the hillside to watch the upcoming battle. The old withered chief followed, with Jama close at his heels. The crowd fell silent as their warriors brought forth the five unmistakable Zulu warriors. Uneasiness hung tangibly upon the hillside as one tall, dark Zulu warrior stepped forward, directing his loud, booming voice to the assembly on the hillside.

"The choice is yours. We are emissaries of Chief Shaka, chosen of King Dingoswayo."

A murmur rippled through the throng. Ignoring the unrest, the warrior continued.

"Join us and swear allegiance to his greatness, Chief Shaka, or perish. Our army waits beyond the forest, a thousand strong."

With these words echoing over the hillside, all eyes turned to the chief. Suddenly he appeared old and faded. His regal shoulders slumped. Waving a weary hand, he beckoned the Zulu emissary to approach.

"Come. Be my guests. Eat of our food; sit at our fires."

Tense excitement buzzed through the group. The ancestors had said only members of one's tribe might eat of the same food at the family fire. Had the chief turned his allegiance to Shaka?

Swiftly and silently, the women filed down the

hillside. Even the children were silent, knowing that something important was poised to descend on their village. The stunned emDletsheni impi straggled back to the village, mumbling among themselves, several fingers pointing at the Zulu's bare, callused feet. At some time during the chief's descent, Jama had appointed Monase's mother, Niamani, to help the chief's wives prepare the feast.

"Monase, come get your sister Mkabuyi. We are to help prepare the meal," Niamani whispered in breathless excitement. "Hurry, hurry! Get more water." She sucked in her breath with an impatient hiss. Grabbing several large water cabashes, Monase thrust them into Mkabuyi's arms, pulling the thunderstruck girl behind her.

As they slipped into the forest the setting sun sent soft, golden rays through the branches, dappling the lush undergrowth with brilliant spatters of fire. Flinging her head back, Mkabuyi spun in circles of delight.

"Oh, Monase, this is magical."

A distant nightjar confirmed her cry by issuing forth a beautiful string of notes.

"Mkabuyi, please stop this nonsense!" Monase cried insistently.

The girl stopped briefly, smiled adoringly into Monase's eyes, then began to spin again. Annoyance vibrated in Monase's voice as she dragged the dizzy child forward, trying hard to stay stern. She knew she couldn't, at least not where Mkabuyi was concerned. She loved this little sister with a passion. Where Sondaba had been her rock, safe and secure, Mkabuyi was the sunshine, the laughter, all that was free and innocent. A naive beauty radiated from her. She knew no stranger; she trusted everyone. Her father had encouraged Monase's fierce protectiveness, warning her to watch over Mkabuyi carefully. Unaware of the dangers that lurked even now in the approaching darkness, Mkabuyi saw only beauty.

"Monase, you are so terribly unimaginative. Where is your spirit of adventure? Weren't those Zulu warriors glorious?"

On and on Mkabuyi chattered, drowning out the warning silences of the forest, which was usually so alive with sound. Suddenly the exuberant girl stopped, her eyes deep, bottomless pools of fear. Grabbing Monase's arm, she clung to her.

Monase felt the small hairs on her neck rise as a cold chill whispered down her spine. Pulling Mkabuyi behind her, she turned to face more than forty towering Zulu warriors.

Five

A lean, leering Zulu warrior stepped forward, pulling Mkabuyi from behind Monase. Slowly, he ran a long finger down Mkabuyi's arm.

"This one would make a fine partner for Ukuhlobonga."

At her baffled, trembling look, he explained, "Sexual love play, my little dove."

A maternal, protective outrage, as old as time, rose like a hurricane, wrapping Monase in its swirling fury.

"Leave her, you filthy beast. She is just a child!"

She tore Mkabuyi from his grasp, enveloping her in her arms. Slowly, she began backing up, holding her sister tightly.

"Let us be. We must return to my husband. He is a powerful medicine man."

Her voice quavered slightly at the lie, her eyes never leaving the offending warrior as she continued her retreat.

"My husband would not look kindly on—"

Her breath left her lungs in a whoosh as she slammed into a hard, unyielding surface with a bone-jarring force.

"Kindly on what?" a deep voice rumbled in amusement.

The sound seemed to reverberate through every nerve in Monase's body, and she turned reluctantly. Dark amber eyes burned down on her, devouring her with their magnetic force. Her pupils dilated fearfully. Fire coursed through her veins like molten lava, her knees threatened to buckle, but a pitiful whimper from the sobbing Mkabuyi pulled her back to reality. Jutting her chin out in angry defiance, she narrowed challenging eyes at the giant from her fantasies.

Cira raked a bold appraising stare over her, his eyes locked with hers.

"She is indeed a little temptress, although a most innocent-looking one. I doubt such a powerful medicine man would send such a treasure out in the dark to do such a dangerous task as . . . "

Cira's eyes strayed to the abandoned water baskets. His mouth curved in a wide grin as his eyes locked again with Monase's.

Pure, undiluted outrage emanated from every pore in Monase's body. Seething, she released Mkabuyi, and hands on her hips, she advanced toward Cira. He, too, stepped forward, closing the gap between them. Monase gasped as his warm chest grazed her nipples. Cira laughed a low, seductive laugh.

"I doubt she even has a husband," one of the surrounding warriors cried, and the others roared with glee.

Embarrassment and wounded pride revived Monase's dissolving anger. She squared her shoulders to lessen the terrible intimidation Cira's six-and-a-half-foot frame made her feel.

"How dare you contradict me! What my husband chooses for me to do is his choice, and if you so much as touch my little sister, I'll—"

"It's not your sister I'm thinking of touching."

The low timbre of his voice reached out and caressed her just as surely as if he had run the callused tips of his fingers over her naked flesh. Monase suppressed a shiver mixed with fear and delight as she stepped back, breaking the contact of their warm bared skin. Regaining her senses, she bent down, picking up a sharp stone. Cira's gaze flickered to the rock and returned, his full sensual lips twitching, his dark eyes smoldering, threatening to ignite.

So it wasn't a spirit who had fled from him the other day . . . or perhaps the wicked wizards had sent her back to taunt him more, and taunt him she did, standing so close, with her large, dark nipples erect with fear and yearning, luscious ripe fruit waiting to be tasted. His Adam's apple bobbed painfully as he swallowed, remembering their grating brush against his chest. He liked the fierce courage and innocence that emanated from this woman-child.

Abruptly he brought his thoughts up short. It scarcely mattered what he liked. When the scouts returned, she would return, and he would probably never see her again. Brushing past her, he felt a strange unnerving pang of sadness.

"Enough. Return to your duties!" Cira snapped in annoyance as the men made way for him to pass.

Punga stepped forward, a gentle giant of a man. "What of the woman and the girl?" he asked in a voice gentle with concern.

"Some woman," Cira snorted as he raked an insolent gaze over Monase. He doubted, from the look in her embarrassed yearning eyes, that she had extensive knowledge of men. This thought aroused him, causing him to curse under his breath. He whipped his fiery glare to Punga. "The girls shall be, shall I say, our guests for—"

Before he could finish, Monase screamed in outrage, "I will return with my sister to my kraal!"

Spitting on the ground before her, she grabbed her sister's upper arm, and in a socket-wrenching pull, she turned to leave. Rough, determined hands seized her, whirling her around to face those tawny, incensed eyes. In a low, icily calm voice that belied the look in those ardent flaming orbs, Cira continued as if she hadn't interrupted.

"—as long as I deem necessary. By force, if need be."

These last words were more a threatening question than a statement; and their condescending tone grated unbearably against Monase's bruised and battered pride. She struggled hopelessly, much to the surrounding warriors' enjoyment.

A voice called out between deep, masculine chuckles.

"She's neither woman nor girl, but a wildcat, if you ask me."

This sent a roar of laughter through the men. When Cira did not join in, their laughter died to an embarrassed silence. With a sign from Punga, they scattered to return to the tasks previously assigned them. Only Punga remained. He watched Cira pull Monase toward him, then lower his face within inches of hers, the cold threat barely whispered.

"Must I bind you?"

Suddenly Cira flinched, as if he'd been dealt a blow, when he saw the proud defiance in Monase's eyes melt into wide pools of terror. He dropped her arms in disgust. Here he was threatening to harm her, when every nerve in his body cried out to wrap her in his strong, protective embrace.

"I doubt you would want to be separated from that clinging little sister of yours," he said in a defeated, weary voice, and walked away without a single backward glance.

Punga struggled to decide what exactly Cira had ordered him to do. Confused, he drew his hand in frustration across the back of his neck. He was baffled. Cira was always so calm, so confident. He rarely exhibited his anger, but here this mere wisp of a girl had forced him to lose his temper. Looking up, he saw the two girls huddling together, their eyes wide and terrified. Punga shifted uneasily. He could not tie them up. He'd have to take his chances; he would have to leave them unbound with an appointed guard. Well, he thought as he ran an admiring glance over Mkabuyi's sweet face, he might even guard them himself. After all, they were their guests.

Determinedly, he walked over to where Monase and her sister stood rooted and bowed to them graciously, as if they were royalty. Gently, he took Mkabuyi's trembling hand and led her to a small fire the men had lit a short distance from the camp's main fire. With a secure grasp on her sister's arm, Monase followed.

As they passed the men, now busy at their assorted jobs of sharpening spears, refilling water bags, and making ready the evening meal, she spotted the man the warriors had called Cira. As if feeling her presence, he turned, his hooded eyes glittering gold in the dancing firelight. Monase held her breath as the now familiar tingle of fear, excitement, and something else flickered like a wildfire through her body. What was this man doing to her? His face was dangerously sensual. Her eyes traced the lean contours, the perfect full lips, the rich dark skin setting off gleaming, even teeth. The men of her tribe seemed mere adolescents next to him. Startled, she realized that he, too, was appraising her, his gaze running heatedly over the contours of her body.

He started to rise from his position by the fire. She stumbled. In one long stride, his strong arms caught her around her waist. He pulled her against his fire-warmed chest. Panic swept through Monase's body as she felt herself melt willingly into that warmth. With a strength born of desperation, she pushed away from him at the same instant he released her.

The force sent her sprawling on the ground. Her skin skirt flapped open, revealing a long, lean leg bared to the hip. In horror, she looked up to see Cira looking through hooded eyes at her exposed leg. Like a deer caught in the sights of a hunter's deadly weapon, she could not move. His eyes, the tawny gold of the mighty lion, flared. She couldn't miss the ardent desire burning there.

Suddenly an idea fluttered across her mind. What possible degradation and horror lay in the night ahead for her sister and herself she didn't know. But this man certainly wanted her, and if she played it right, perhaps she could barter for their release, or at least her sister's. Her mother had told her often enough that men were arrogant fools, territorial animals who would fight like the hideous hyena to win and keep what they felt was theirs all to themselves. Silently begging her ancestors to give her strength and cunning, she lowered her eyelashes, letting them flutter like the restive wings of a captured bird. Looking up under the thick shadow of her lashes, she ran a pink tongue slowly over her bottom lip.

"Cira?" she began in a throaty whisper. His only response was a muscle twitching rapidly along the ridge of his jaw and a barely perceptible nod of his head. The eyes did not change or waver. Monase swallowed hard as she lifted a limp hand toward him. Still, he did not move.

"I wish to speak to you . . . alone"—the last word dipping to a deep husky rush of breath.

The muscle ceased working in his jaw. He turned and walked in the direction of the distant fire toward which Punga had led her and her sister.

Smoothing her skirt with stiff fingers, Monase tried to raise herself gracefully. The man was insufferable. Wincing, she dusted off her bruised buttocks, grabbed her sister's hand, and stalked off after him.

Arriving at the fire, she gently bade Mkabuyi to warm herself. Turning, she walked over to the shadows of the trees, out of Mkabuyi's view. Swaying her hips slightly, she hoped Cira was following her. Turning, she ruefully saw that her hope had been fulfilled. Her throat suddenly went dry as she thought about the seduction she was going to attempt. Maybe she could plead, beg, or cry instead. For a brief minute she had the feeling that she was drifting into perilous waters. Maybe for once she was straying out of her depths. Shaking off these menacing thoughts, she slowly began loosening her skirt. Her fingers grew clumsy, but she managed to untie it.

"You don't need my little sister. Let her go."

The hide slipped heavily to the dirt.

"Perhaps we could spend a little time together, then I could go, too. You wouldn't have to share."

Her arms dropped nervously across his rigid shoulders.

"I could be all yours."

Cira didn't move, didn't dare to move, as she stood before him in all her splendor, adorned only in a twisted string of beads around her neck and a bronze band on her upper arm. He hated the fire that seared through his loins. Ikunata, how he wanted this woman, as he had never wanted a woman before. Every nerve in his body screamed to accept her wanton invitation. But he was a Zulu impi on a campaign. He owed it to his chief and his men to uphold the most sacred of the warrior's oaths, that of celibacy. He had cleansed himself already. He could not permit himself to break his vow. With a great effort, he bent. Retrieving her skirt, he thrust it at her.

"Dress yourself, woman. Do not parade your wicked ways before my men, or I won't be held responsible for the consequences."

His eyes drifted involuntarily to her fumbling hands. A strained smile twitched at his lips as he brought surprisingly amused eyes to her face.

"I'm sure your illustrious husband would find your lack of modesty very . . . disturbing."

A cry of embarrassment and shame escaped Monase's lips. A sick, sinking feeling filled her as she saw her only chance drifting out of reach. She had misread his desire. He had refused her, and now she could only hope that believing her to be so loose, he would not throw her to his women-starved men. Hot tears burned her eyes. How could she have allowed herself to be so humiliated? She squeezed her eyes shut tightly, and a single tear escaped, sliding down her cheek.

Cira's warm, rough fingertips blocked its descent. She looked up and saw his face looming close above her own. Gentle concern etched his brow. Softly, he took her face into his hands, his thumb stroking her damp cheek. Monase closed her tear-laden lashes. She felt his tender, warm mouth kiss her brow, the bridge of her nose, working its way down to claim her moist, waiting lips. She stood on tiptoe, entwining her fingers in his hair, as she pressed the length of her body against his, all thoughts overwhelmed by this burning, all-consuming desire.

A moan rose to her lips as his head bent to her neck. Without warning, his back went rigid, and he wrenched himself from her embrace, once again sending her sprawling. Monase's head spun as she tried to recover from the humiliation that had not once, but twice, knocked her to the ground. As she rose on shaky knees her mind sought desperately for something to hang on to. His last ironic words echoed in a mad rush through her ears: ". . . your illustrious husband . . ."

"At least my husband is man enough to satisfy my desires!" she fairly screeched.

For a rage-blinding second Cira whirled on her, advancing a step. He spoke softly, but his voice had enough of an edge to it to cause Monase to take a wary step backward.

"Go sit by the fire, and bother me no more."

He turned toward the fire, halting as he stooped over the now sleeping Mkabuyi, and every maternal instinct surged through the outraged Monase's veins. This beast, this monster, had not only refused her, but was now going to attack her sleeping little sister.

With a bloodcurdling scream, she leaped through the air, flinging herself upon his bent back. She felt the strong cords of muscle tighten under her as he tumbled forward. Rolling dangerously near the flames, they struggled: he, to be free of her, she to inflict any injury she could. Eyes closed, she clawed blindly, viciously. Her back smacked solidly against the hard ground, the wind rushed from her lungs, and her eyes flew open. For long, anguishing moments she stared into Cira's unreadable gaze.

Then, suddenly, he released her, his hand flying wide as if burned. He staggered to his knees, his face a mask of disbelieving horror. Flinging back his head, he roared a hauntingly desperate cry for Punga.

Hardly a moment passed before the man rushed forward, his face terrified, unable to believe that such a cry could have come from his leader.

"Watch them closely," Cira whispered in a ragged, hoarse voice.

Punga nodded, his eyes concerned and a little frightened as they watched Cira's retreating shadow.

Monase, too, stared after him. Had she dissuaded him from ravishing her sister? Perhaps he feared her supposed husband's magical powers. The sound of a nervous giggle tore her gaze from the shadows that had engulfed Cira, and she saw that Mkabuyi was smiling at the giant of a man called Punga, her eyelashes coyly lowered.

Monase grabbed her sister's wrist, biting her nails into the soft flesh. "Come!" she hissed in anger.

Large, quivering tears welled in Mkabuyi's doe eyes. Monase looked away in disgust. Mkabuyi had no idea what had almost befallen her. Monase suppressed a sudden shiver.

Punga's deep mellow voice broke into her thoughts. "Please stay here," the kindly giant told her.

Monase was taken aback at the gentle, almost pleading words and grudgingly released Mkabuyi's wrist, hunkering down to huddle abjectly by a large rock.

Punga smiled thankfully and began to talk to Mkabuyi again. The sound of the sweet, gentle prattle between the two soothed Monase. Leaning back, she became all too aware of her aching muscles, her hopeless situation. Nodding slightly, she jerked her head upright, but again it lolled, her chin nestling in the hollow at the base of her neck. The last thing she heard was Punga's deep voice telling Mkabuyi of the extraordinary beauty of his home, Zululand, the land of the heavens.

Six

Dreams, or rather nightmares, swirled around Monase, dragging her down. Cira's warm lips upon her forehead, her cheeks, suddenly turning into fierce fangs, slicing into her skin. The beast turned into Jama, laughing a ghastly laugh as he turned into a yawning viper, trying to swallow her whole. She struggled to run, but his coils wrapped tightly around her shoulders. Flailing, she tossed the covers from her, the cold air striking her body in a frigid rush.

Suddenly she bolted upright. Raising a hand to her cheek, she felt the deep impression of the rock on which she had been sleeping. Still sleep-dazed, she glanced around her, getting her bearings. Mkabuyi slept peacefully, her lips curved in a contented smile. In the distance, she could make out the figures of Punga, Cira, and a number of his impi leaning intently toward some drawings that Cira drew in the dirt. The welcoming smell of roasted meat wafted through the night air. Monase's stomach rumbled.

She tried to push the thoughts of hunger from her mind. She had to concentrate. The time for her to escape had arrived. Sorrowfully, she gazed at her sister. If she awakened Mkabuyi to come with her, they would never make it. Again her eyes flickered to the absorbed impis. Obviously, tonight they had no plans for their captives. Perhaps if she hurried, she could get to her father and return with some of their impi to demand Mkabuyi's release before they noticed her escape. Daring not to kiss Mkabuyi's sweet face lest she awaken, Monase bundled her discarded covers into a mound to look like a sleeping form and slipped off into the darkness.

Running along the familiar trail, she was glad for her years of practice tracking with the herd boys. They had let her play, because she was strong and fast and was an advantage for their team. That had all changed when she entered puberty. Her ears had been pierced, and life had become a daily battle of wills with her mother. She had continued to practice on her own, unbeknownst to anyone save Sondaba. As a result, she now moved through the forest with skilled silence, her bare feet careful of every leaf and twig.

When she heard Cira's resounding laughter echo through the branches, she stopped. Anger thrummed through her blood. He was probably telling the men how she had thrown herself at him. Suddenly a cool revenging thought flowed over her as she smiled into the dark night's embrace. *Let's see who's laughing when you find I have escaped and thwarted your plans.* Her spirits rising, she rushed through the tangled web of darkness.

Monase ran swiftly through the darkness, not slowing until she had reached the fence surrounding her kraal. She slipped through the gate. Instinctively, she headed for her mother's hut. Her breath coming in great gasps, her blood pounding in her ears, she didn't hear the distant revelry. Dropping to her knees, she entered, and was greeted by a cold emptiness. Halting in the doorway, she felt a shiver of trepidation slide over her. It was as she was backing out that she heard the tinkle of laughter, the soft music floating in delicious, melodious waves over the village.

Drawing closer to the bright fires, Monase hesitated. She hung in the dark shadows just outside the fire's blaze. A deep loneliness momentarily emerged from the depths of her being, overshadowing her earlier urgency. No one had even missed her. No one even cared. Angrily, she chastised herself. What had she expected? A tear-stained mother waiting with open arms? Yes, she had. Sondaba would have been frantic. She would have cared, and now she was gone. Suddenly Mkabuyi's sleep-softened image rose up before her. Monase plunged into the fire's glow.

"The Zulus . . . they've captured her . . . I escaped. Please help her!"

The words sputtered forth as Monase splayed her fingers before her in a pleading gesture. Her eyes turned beseechingly from face to face. They froze as they met those of the Zulu emissary. The impact of what she had done hit her with a force that nearly caused her to double over. Her chief turned hard condemning eyes to her father. Ugebula rose, dragging Monase away with an urgent pull. Concern, disgust, and a shade of disbelief clouded his dark eyes.

"Monase, we have now sworn our allegiance to Chief Shaka. You have embarrassed our tribe with your outburst. The impis you encountered are with this Zulu emissary."

"But what of Mkabuyi, her safety, her virtue?" Monase cried.

Her father ran a weary hand over his eyes. "You should not have gone. Her safety is now in the hands of their leader, Cira."

Monase gasped. She watched as her father returned to the fire. He bent to whisper in the ear of one of the Zulu impi. The man's eyes turned to her as he shook his head, a deep scowl creasing his brow. The impi then spoke to another warrior and rose to leave. Passing by Monase, he paused.

"Cira is not a man to cross. He will not be pleased to find you have escaped."

He shook his head as he hurried off toward the forest.

Monase backed up slowly, wishing to melt into the obscure darkness. Hot tears of humiliation stained her cheeks. Once again she had been the fool. Her mother would kill her. She was turning to run away when her senses were assaulted by an all-too-familiar stench.

"Did the Zulu impi admire your beauty, my little . . . gazelle?"

Jama's oily voice oozed over her. She shuddered at the use of her father's term of endearment. A wicked, knowing smile spread slowly over the witch doctor's face. An evil smell of decay and disease issued forth from his mouth as he laughed a bloodcurdling laugh, a laugh that was identical to the one in her dreams. Monase stepped back, releasing her arm from his slimy grip.

"I must be going . . . my mother . . . my hut . . . I . . ."

Her voice floated aimlessly behind her as she fled. Running, she could not escape the numbing fear that Jama knew all, even the hastily spoken lie she had told about being his wife.

Seven

It was indeed an angry Cira who stood above the cowering Mkabuyi and a heap of empty coverings. Kicking the hides with unleashed fury, he muttered a string of curses. Stalking over to Punga, he ordered him to get the now sobbing girl out of his sight. When Punga didn't move, but waited for further instructions, Cira cursed again.

"Get her out of here! Bring her back to her kraal. I don't want to lay eyes on her or her sister again. Do you hear me? Move!"

Punga hastened off, again bewildered by Cira's uncharacteristic display of anger.

The impi scout who had returned late that night was also baffled. He had expected hearty congratulations from Cira. Bloodshed had been avoided.

The emDletsheni chief had offered five young recruits, fifteen pure-white cows, thirty spotted ones, and his finest ironsmith as a tribute to Shaka's beneficent rule. Cira had barely acknowledged his message. Instead, his eyes had turned a flat hazy gold when he was told of the girl Monase's reappearance at her kraal. Without a word, he strode over to the empty coverings, his fist clenching and unclenching against his thighs.

Small, trembling hands grasped Cira's arm as weak sobs echoed in his ears.

"Where is my sister? Why has she abandoned me?"

The small plaintive cry stirred something in Cira, a memory of another small voice crying out that same question years ago. The words echoed painfully around the chambers of his heart, a heart that he had supposed had grown hard and callused. For a brief moment the barriers he had built around himself wavered, crumbling as he took the small, cold hands into his large, warm ones.

"Do not worry, little one, you are safe. We will return you to your home—and your sister."

The last word was uttered in a hard, rigid tone of voice; the barricade around his heart remained intact. His hands dropped, but still her hand clung to him like a lost child. Turning, she followed him, sending a wistful, telling smile to a blushing Punga.

In silence, they trudged through the trees. The branches gleamed with a faint lunar glow, the leaves rustled gently, the eerie flutter of bats' wings endowing the night with mystery. Mkabuyi drew close to Cira, her voice cracked with nervous apprehension.

"Do not be angry with Punga for letting my sister escape. No one can make my sister do anything she doesn't want to do. She has always been headstrong and disobedient. That is why my mother says it will be nigh impossible to find a husband for her. She thinks Jama, the witch doctor, may be interested in her. Would he be a catch! He's as rich as a chief and very powerful. I hope so, too, on the account that Monase is so tall and bony. The men of our tribe like their women smaller than they themselves are, and docile. Do Zulu men like such women, too?"

The question was uttered with more earnestness than Cira noted. He smiled slightly.

"Some do." He chuckled.

He had been right. Monase wasn't married, and from the sound of it, she was not a favorite among the men of her tribe either. But this Jama. What of him? A scowl creased his forehead.

"I was just thinking about your sister's medicine man . . . husband? I think I will have to speak to him about her, er, presumptions."

Eyes wide in sickening horror, Mkabuyi tugged at his hand until Cira stopped and faced her.

"You can't! You mustn't!" she pleaded. "She was only trying to protect me. Jama would be so very angry, you might ruin her chances—"

Cira cut her off brusquely. A sudden irrational jealousy seized him as he realized that he had thought the medicine man was a complete invention on Monase's part. Tightening his grip on Mkabuyi's hand, he increased his pace. She struggled to keep up with his long-legged strides; all fears of he surrounding darkness vanished. She peeked up into Cira's intensely preoccupied face, amused to see the possessive, jealous mask there. She knew that look. She had seen it before, on the boys vying for her attention.

Mkabuyi smiled. She liked these handsome Zulu impi, especially the gentle giant Punga. Maybe Punga would ask for her as a bride, and if she talked to Monase, and Monase were to be a little less fierce toward this man, then maybe if Jama refused her, Cira would ask for Monase to be his bride. Surely a man so tall wouldn't mind such a tall wife. After all, it surely looked as if he wanted her.

The following morning, Cira and his men stood outside the emDletsheni chief's hut. It was a large building, his kraal perhaps a quarter mile in diameter. As Cira stooped to enter he recalled the magnitude of Shaka's royal amakhanda. His kraal was over a mile in diameter. His hut filled with the finest wares from the surrounding region. Ivory and bronze carvings graced the entryway, and the floor was covered with vividly colored animal hides and feathers.

As the Zulu's eyes adjusted to the dark smoke-filled interior, he glanced around. While more austere, the trappings spoke of another type of wealth. Hanging from wooden hooks secured several feet off the ground was an array of amazing masks, tools and weapons of copper, iron, and bronze. Drawn to the assegai spears, Cira moved near them to feel their sharpness.

Upon seeing his interest, the chief introduced

him to his finest ironsmith, Ugebula. The men began an earnest discussion about the extraction of the iron ore and its melding.

Cira was so engrossed in the conversation that he didn't notice the entrance of the other man until the pungent smell pierced the aromatic smoke of the sandalwood branches burning on the hearth. Drawing his head back with a grimace, he turned offended eyes to stare at Jama. Immediately he knew by his garb that this man was a witch doctor. Disbelieving shock sapped his face of its calm when introductions were made. This was the man Monase wanted as a husband? Cira recoiled at the very image of her young flesh against this monstrosity.

As he regained his composure bitter understanding told him that she was like most women: hungry for power and wealth, no matter the cost. With dismissing eyes, he returned his attention to Ugebula.

Ugebula was flattered. This bright young man had ignored Jama, preferring to listen to him tell of his love, his work. Ugebula quickly began to entertain the possibility of marrying off one of his daughters to this handsome and strong warrior. If a deal could be made, then perhaps when Cira retired from the army in a couple of years, he could become Ugebula's apprentice . . . his heir. This exciting prospect sent a thrill through the ironsmith. Since the chief had already promised to send him and his family with this man to Zululand, why not broach the subject now? he thought.

"My family and I look forward to returning to your home." He hesitated, forming the next words carefully in his mind before speaking. "I thank you for returning my daughter safely. I hope she was not too much of an inconvenience."

Surprise again widened Cira's eyes as he realized this ironsmith was Monase's father.

"No, *Mkabuyi* caused me no trouble," was all he said in reply.

The emphasis on Mkabuyi's name, and the unspoken name of Monase, caused Ugebula to look away. He knew all too well that Cira was alluding to the fact that Monase had caused trouble. Drawing in a deep fortifying breath, he returned his eyes to Cira's.

"She is a beauty, my little one, is she not?"

Misunderstanding this reference to Mkabuyi because of his own thoughts of Monase, Cira returned a heated stare, muttering "yes" in a deeply felt whisper. The implication was not lost on Jama; the witch doctor's eyes narrowed in shrewdness as Cira rose, silently excusing himself.

Ugebula was pleased. Mkabuyi was still young, but with the right pressure, and a little time . . . He looked again at Cira and smiled. Life could be very good. Cira would make a good husband for Mkabuyi. As the men dispersed, Ugebula hurried home to prepare his cattle and family for the journey.

"Tomorrow!" Niamani screeched in disbelief when her husband told her of the impending journey in the morning. "We can't possibly be ready by then. My fields, the weaving . . ."

Ugebula sought to dismiss her words with a weary wave of his hand. Pulling her toward him, he brought her out into the moon-bright night. Unbeknownst to him, Monase sat huddled in the shadows alongside the hut.

"Listen, woman. For once, just listen." He sighed in exasperation. "The Zulu warrior, the leader Cira, he fancies our Mkabuyi."

Niamani's eyes brightened hopefully in the moonlight. "Then what are you wasting my time for? I have a lot of work to do."

Turning, she scuttled back into the hut. A pleased smile wreathed Ugebula's face. He rarely pleased his wife, and as much as he was loath to admit it, it bothered him greatly. Triumphant, he turned to go. Suddenly he noticed Monase's crouching figure. He opened his mouth to admonish her for eavesdropping when he saw the silvery tears streaking her face. The lonely, pitiful aura around her struck a deep piercing blow to his heart. Unwanted, she had no one. Jama had not offered for her yet. Perhaps she would always be alone, so beautiful, but so unruly.

With a heavy heart, he turned and left.

The morning arrived all too soon. As the orange-gold light of dawn filtered in over the sleepy mist-filled valley, Monase rubbed her eyes. She yawned and stretched. She was tired and out of sorts. She had ended up doing most of the packing, as the other daughters and wives gathered eagerly about Mkabuyi to listen to her tales of the handsome Zulu impi. Mkabuyi wove the events of the night before into a magical, mysterious adventure. During the narration, wide eyes of horror and admiration turned intermittently to Monase. Turning in her bed, Monase now felt a vague shiver of uneasiness and apprehension at the memories.

By the time Cira and his men arrived, the sun was well above the trees, the mountains a purple haze in the distance. The Zulu looked about him. He nodded his approval at the prompt efficiency of the small band of people. The chief stood solemnly by his amakhanda. Several women came forward to embrace Ugebula's wives and daughters. One young widow approached Ugebula, her trembling hands extending a beautifully beaded belt, its bright beads woven into a tale of love, sorrow, and hope.

Monase turned heartfelt eyes on the woman's face. The woman had hoped to become another of Ugebula's wives, after a lobala was collected for Monase. A solitary tear of sympathy rolled down Monase's cheek.

"Sorry to be leaving your illustrious lover?" Cira's voice sneered into her ear.

She jumped, startled at his nearness. Her face was dark with fear and confusion as she gazed into his golden eyes. Cursing her innocent face, he brushed aside any tender feelings she had evoked.

"Perhaps the powerful Jama will come and take you away . . . if the price is right. Zulu brides are not cheap. Then you can have your large hut and bronze anklets for your beautiful arms and legs."

Monase gasped at the harsh note in his voice. What did he mean? Was he planning to strike a deal with Jama? Could he do that? She had hoped to escape Jama, but now . . . Her eyes glanced frantically around for her father, but he was deep in conversation with the chief. Again she scanned the kraal.

"Is Jama here? Did he ask for me?"

A cruel sneer curled Cira's lip as his eyes narrowed to dark, unreadable slits.

"I should have known a beauty like you would have a price so high that she would sell her spirit to the umkovu to obtain her material desires." His lips twisted in disgust as he continued, "Even at the cost of surrendering to that baboon."

His cruel, assuming way irritated Monase's already stretched and frazzled nerves. Throwing her head back haughtily, she glared back at him with unbridled ferocity.

"If my father so wishes it, I would marry him. He would bring great honor and cattle to my family."

Cira snorted, a crass derogatory sound, and stomped off to the front of the caravan.

Almost as rapidly as the blood had surged through her in angry defiance, it receded, leaving her feeling weak and despondent. What had she hoped for? To go to Zululand and marry a tall, handsome Zulu impi? No, her fate had been sealed. Cira was planning on seeing her married off to Jama. He would probably arrange to get a cut of the lobala. Depression settled heavily on her shoulders as the caravan began its long, dusty journey up the hillside, across the bushland to their new home.

Eight

The journey seemed endless, and the December sun beat down unmercifully on the straining beasts and burdened people. The rich, red clay crumbled to a fine pink powder that tainted their skin, clothing, and food. Water was scarce, and so the water baskets and bladder bags were treasured as if they were gold. Every day, in the hazy light before dawn, Cira sent his scouts out to follow the large nocturnal predators to find their watering hole. Often those holes had dried up to mere puddles, guarded jealously by the wild beasts. Tempers were short, and Monase dreamed of the cool, refreshing rains of June.

At night her family would ease themselves down, removing their sandals to rub their raw, blistered feet. As always, they wondered in amazement at the bare, tough, callused feet of the Zulus. Later they would sit chewing on leathery biltong, listening in silent admiration to the elegant poetry of the Zulu warriors. The men would tell of their ancestors, their voices rising in pride as they sang the praises of their king and chief.

On the eighth morning, the parched, travel-worn group came upon a wide, placid river. The children dashed forward, the blistered and cracked soles of their feet slapping noisily in the shallow waters along the shore. Suddenly Cira came bounding down the grassy bank to where the children played. At first Monase imagined he had gone to join in their frolicking. She had seen in the past week how, when he was surrounded by children, his face softened and his demeanor became gentle. Oftentimes, in the golden hours before sunset, he would pretend to be the mighty lion, stalking the little girls. They in turn would throw their harmless reed spears at him in mock challenge, running away, squealing with delight as he tumbled them gently in the long grass.

Now she was smiling as he splashed loudly through the water, scooping her youngest sister in his arms when suddenly a grayish-green crocodile opened its yawning jaws. A scream died unheard in Monase's throat as she rushed forward to catch the child he threw toward the bank. The calm water came alive. Large, thrashing tails sliced through the murky water. Punga jumped to Cira's aid, the struggling men stabbing again and again at the persistent onslaught of teeth and scales. Monase cradled the sobbing child against her, watching in horrible fascination the nightmare before her. The river in her old home had been a small trickling stream, the only fear an occasional night animal or snake. Here, the waters were alive with huge monsters that seemed to rise from its swirling depths.

Just as suddenly as it had started, the turbulent water grew calm again, the remaining crocodiles sliding off gracefully through the water, submerging to disappear among concealing reeds. Cira and Punga struggled to haul a huge dead crocodile from the water, its almond-shaped yellow eyes revealing a black, slitted-diamond pupil. Its jaw curved in what looked like a wicked smile as sharp teeth glittered against its muted scaly skin.

Monase shuddered, pulling the child closer, as the men flopped the offending reptile belly-up at her feet. For the first time since the journey began, she allowed her eyes to meet Cira's. With a trembling smile, she mouthed the words *thank you* to him. His eyes clouded, and for that moment a strange vulnerability shone from them. Hastily, he dropped his gaze as he knelt to slit the great beast's stomach.

The meat had a strange, bitter taste, but was a welcome change from the tough biltong. That night, Cira warned the travelers of the new dangers they would encounter in the upcoming bush. He told them that for now they would rest and graze the cattle for several days before they ventured on to the low, vine-tangled forest called the bush. As if reinforcing the ominous warning Cira uttered about the dark, threatening place, a zebra emitted a shrill, querulous yelp. The silence that followed was broken by a chorus of hyenas baying melodiously in answer, their cries growing fainter with the distance until the silence settled in again, heavy and mysteriously dangerous.

Shivering at the unearthly sounds, Monase stole a glance at Cira, his back rigid, his profile haloed in the firelight. He turned briefly in her direction, his eyes reflecting a haunted sadness. He did not see her, but seemed to focus inwardly on some dark image that caused his lips to thin with a hidden torment. Monase suppressed an aching desire to go to him, to caress him, to soothe his wounded spirit, but she resisted this impulse, knowing that his male pride would never allow him to be coddled, and looked on helplessly.

The following morning, Punga led the women upstream to a narrow belt of rapid water. It flowed invitingly over large rocks into shallow pools. In earnest, the women began the daunting task of cleaning their clothes and bodies of the ever-present red dust.

As they slowed down their work to enjoy their baths, Monase stepped off to a secluded spot just a little farther upstream. There, she loosened her skirt, stepping into the inviting cool water. From a small hide pouch fastened to her belt, she removed a bone-colored block. In slow, lingering movements, she rubbed the solidified mixture of animal oils, herbs, and berries over her dry, grimy skin. The lather instantly turned a creamy pink as the water washed the red dust and perspiration from her body. The water was shallow, affording safety from the frightening crocodiles, but forcing

Monase to hunker down to dip below the surface to rinse herself clean. Rising slowly, she inhaled sharply as a subtle breeze brushed past her dampened skin. The feeling was exquisite, sending tingling sensations rippling over her. Sighing, she stepped from the water to stretch out on a sun-warmed rock.

Cira hadn't meant to spy on her, but had only gone to warn her not to stray from the others. He felt his mouth go dry as he saw her emerge, shimmering like a misty spirit of the water. She was utterly breathtaking, raising a fearsome need in his loins. He watched her stand, face to the sun, while its rays danced brilliantly on the water, reflecting a rainbow of colors off the surface of her skin. Then slowly, as if in a trance-induced dance, she slid long, slender fingers over her arms and breasts. Unable to look away, Cira watched as she turned toward him, eyes so gentle and faraway that he forced his lips tight to constrain the rush of a groan rising from his lungs. When she advanced toward him, he stiffened, wondering if she'd seen him and was going to offer herself again. He squeezed his eyes tightly. This time he knew he would not have the strength to refuse her. A whispered moan escaped his now parted lips.

When at last he opened his eyes, resigned to his fate, he blinked. She had vanished. Pushing past the dense bushes concealing him, he rushed forward, his eyes darting about wildly. Frozen in his tracks, not moving, barely breathing, he gazed down upon Monase's naked, glistening, sun-kissed body. Half in wonder, half in relief, he lowered himself to one knee, his hand outstretched, hovering above her. He ached to touch her, to verify her reality. In a flutter, her eyes flew open. Fear and surprise melted into dark pools of desire. A deep moan of surrender ripped through Cira's lungs as he poised above her.

As he drew in deep, measured breaths Monase could sense him struggling to leash the passions building within him. Shrill warnings echoed through her, but the blood roaring in her ears drowned out their plaintive cries. All reason left her; she only knew she wanted this man. Her arm circled around his neck, drawing him downward. Closing her eyes, she offered her lips to him in surrender. She wanted him to kiss her, to take her, to brand her forever as his before reason could return her to her senses.

Cira slipped a strong arm under her shoulders, pulling her toward his heaving chest. He crushed his lips hungrily to hers. Chills of delight rippled across her still-damp skin. His free hand cupped her breast, molding it to his callused, demanding palm, his fingertips pausing, then gentle as they brushed against her swollen nipples, leaving her breathless. Another groan escaped his lips as he lowered them to taste the tender straining morsels. The hot, wet flick of his tongue was electric, a lightning bolt searing to the very center of her passion. The pleasure was painfully intense, causing her unconsciously to pull away.

Cira's head snapped up, his eyes suddenly dark and wary. His arm released her, lowering her back to the ground. The dark glimmer of betrayal faded to hard, flat, despising eyes.

"Afraid I might spoil you for your medicine man?"

Before she could respond, he rose, anger quivering in every muscle as he departed. When he had gotten several feet away, he stopped.

"Dress yourself, and so help me, if I ever again see you parading yourself about naked before me, I will not be so . . . gallant about your virtue."

Then he was gone.

For several long minutes Monase lay there, shaken, still trembling from his touch. What had gone wrong? Shame flushed her cheeks as she felt the urge to run after him and beg him to satisfy this yearning she didn't understand. Then she recalled his bitter words. Frustration, laced with despair, closed in upon her. It could never be. He had wanted her, but he was afraid of Jama's power. Never had she been so sure that the only man she wanted to touch her again would be the man she'd call her husband. Her mind refused even to consider Jama for this title and the privileges it granted. Bitter tears threatened to blind her, when out of the darkness a ray of hope pierced her grief-clouded mind.

A husband . . . Jama was not her husband yet. Cira may have been frightened of Jama's power, but he had desired her. Maybe another Zulu man might find her attractive as well. Surely not all the Zulu men would know of Jama's intent to wed her. Perhaps she could seduce a Zulu man into marrying her. Bolstered by this knowledge of her newly discovered feminine power, she felt strong enough to rise and face the future. A future without Jama.

A small voice whispered in the corner of her mind, *Without Cira.*

Monase was relieved when Cira decided to move on to Zululand. Since that day by the stream, she often found him staring at her, his eyes an unnerving magnetic force pulling her toward him. Always, a cruel knowing smile curved his sensuous lips before he turned away.

Again at night, the Zulu impi would recite their poems of bravery and valor as the fire's flame danced high in the cloud-shrouded sky. Over the days, Punga told them the story of Shaka, the poor rejected and abused boy. It seemed his start in life had been shaky at best. His mother, Nandi, as a young maiden, had seen and lusted after Shaka's father, Senzangakona, chief of the then tiny Zulu tribe. Nandi seduced Senzangakona while she bathed. In his lust, Senzangakona impregnated her. At this point in the narrative, Cira turned a hot, accusing glare Monase's way. Unaware, Punga continued the story.

"When Nandi's people, the eLangeni, discovered Nandi was unwed with child, they sent word to Senzangakona that he needed to do the honorable thing and make her his wife. At first, Senzangakona refused, saying it was only the Ishaka beetle that caused women's monthly bleeding to cease. When, nine months later, Nandi bore a son, Senzangakona could no longer deny her claims, and sent for her and her infant son, Shaka."

A sigh escaped Monase's lips at this apparently happy ending, for it was close to her wishes for herself. She leaned forward in earnest as Punga continued his tale.

"Senzangakona's wives were incensed. Although Nandi was not a first wife or a Great Wife, her beauty drew him to her hut night after night. In a short time, she delivered a beautiful baby girl. The other wives tore their hair in grief. Only Nandi had borne Senzangakona both a son and a daughter. They vowed that this bastard child would not be the heir to the Zulu chieftainship.

"Although Senzangakona desired Nandi's beautiful face and body, he was angered by her stubborn outspoken ways. One day little Shaka, a boy of no more than six or seven winters, was watching the herds of cattle and sheep when a wild dog leaped from the forest and stole a new lamb. Shaka ran after the vicious dog, throwing the little clay cows he had made at it, but the lamb was dead. Sullenly, he returned to tell his father."

At this point, Punga paused, a teasing smile on his lips, and rose, excusing himself to retire for the night. The women and children sent up a plea of such magnitude that he was forced to relent and tell a little more. The moon weaved softly throughout the clouds as the family huddled closer, straining to hear the engrossing story of their new chief.

"Senzangakona was infuriated and ordered Shaka punished. Nandi, wrapping her arms around the small boy, refused to allow this, defying the chief in front of the whole tribe. Senzangakona, urged on by his other wives, banished Nandi and her children from the Zulu kraal, forcing her to return to her own people, abandoned and ashamed."

Monase shifted uneasily on the hard ground. She didn't like the direction this tale was taking. This

Nandi sounded too much like herself, and the consequences of her behavior had been dire. Her discomfort grew when Punga told how badly the returning Nandi and her children were treated. They were ostracized; the boys of the eLangeni tribe teased and tormented poor Shaka. His mother was his only consolation. At night she would rock him, telling him that one day he would prevail and avenge himself. She told him of her dream that one day he would be a great and powerful chief. Shaka never doubted her word, and began to prepare himself for greatness.

Monase let her mind wander. Wouldn't it be wonderful to have a mother who could tell you what your future held? She let her eyes wander to her mother's intent face. Once she had been gentle and loving, but that had all changed after the stillbirth of her only son. For days afterward Niamani had been left to bleed slowly in an isolated shelter. The medicine man and the herbalist had sought in vain to stop it. They had tied elephant-tail bracelets and necklaces about her to ward off the illness, but still she bled. Afraid the smell of fresh blood would attract the wild animals of the night, they left her alone after dark.

With a shiver, Monase remembered her mother's fervent cries, calling for her, for anyone, to help her. Then, miraculously, the bleeding stopped. Niamani emerged from the shelter a prematurely aged, hardened woman. She no longer sang; she no longer coddled her children. With dark, haunted eyes, she would tell her daughters that she had been punished for her vain and haughty ways. Monase had been twelve at the time, and had been terrified when a year later she began her menstrual flow. When she informed her mother of this, Niamani had laughed, a dry brittle laugh, telling her to rue this day forever. She had offered no comfort, no instruction. Monase had fled to the stream, scrubbing herself with a vengeance, willing to wash away every trace of this curse. Still the blood ran down her legs. Sondaba, her gentle sister, had found her curled in a fetal ball, sobbing hysterically. Rocking her gently, Sondaba had shushed her, telling her not to worry; it was natural; nature was preparing her body to become a woman. The words had not soothed Monase; her mother had warned her that womanhood was not to be desired.

By the firelight, her mother looked young, as eager as a child, but this softening of her habitual demeanor was not of long duration. Suddenly the harshness returned to her face and she clucked her tongue in disgust. Monase turned her attention back to the story in order to discover what had caused her mother's disapproval. Punga was telling of Shaka's family being outcast from the tribe during the great drought Madlatule ("eat what you can and say nothing"). Nandi had turned to a man in the Qunabes tribe. He had taken her and her children in—taken Nandi as his woman. From years of training at the hands of her mother, Monase shuddered at the disgrace of their future chief's mother, but couldn't help but wonder what she herself might have done if faced with the same circumstances.

Sighing heavily, she realized the great responsibility that came with bringing children into the world. What sacrifices would have to be made if the father refused to claim and protect the mother and child. She knew she could never risk such a thing.

Punga spread his large hands before the fire, pausing to let his audience realize fully the extent of the suffering Shaka had borne and overcome. Then, in his deep baritone voice, he continued in a lighter tone to describe the following years of happiness Shaka had known. Nandi and her children's painful past was forgotten. Shaka's ignoble beginning no longer mattered. For once, he was accepted; his mother's status ceased to reflect on him. He was bigger and stronger than the other boys of his age, and his self-taught skill with his assegai spears won him respect and admiration. At fifteen, he was chosen to be the leader—"itNtanga"—of the boys his age, a great honor.

Punga then went on to tell of Shaka's many accomplishments. One event in particular thrilled Monase, and she begged him to repeat it in detail. In her excitement, she was unaware that her mother cast a suspicious glance her way. Monase had been fascinated by the story of Shaka, as a young boy, and a spotted tree leopard. Remembering his earlier disgrace, when he had failed to protect his herd, he rushed to stand between his cow and the leopard, which crouched overhead in a tree. Knowing he was no match for the leopard's strength, he had held his spear up, the handle resting against his chest. When the leopard pounced, the assegai's blade plunged deep into the animal's heart, the impact of the blow knocking Shaka to the ground.

Monase smiled to herself. Always the huntress,

she filed the clever strategy away. She wondered, now that she was going to a tribe as large as the Zulus, if she would ever have a chance to challenge large game, or any game at all for that matter.

Her musings were interrupted by the gentle, lilting voice of her sister Mkabuyi asking Punga to move on with the story. Then Mkabuyi's voice dropped to a whisper, asking shyly if Shaka had ever fallen in love and married. Hearing this, Ugebula's younger wives giggled nervously, making it obvious that they, too, had wondered the same. At the sound of their laughter, Monase's mother let her breath out in a huff and marched off from the fire. Surprised, Monase watched her father's eyes trail after Niamani's retreating back. She noticed that when he turned back to the firelight, he looked old and tired. Monase suddenly realized how much younger her father's other wives were, barely older than her twenty-two years. After he had traded in his first wife for Ona, her younger sister, only Niamani remained as a companion, someone nearer in age to him. But her parents' constant battles had left deep scars, and they both were lonely.

Suddenly Monase wondered if her parents had ever felt the way she had felt when she was with Cira. She glanced around the intently listening faces; his was not there. She turned to look at the rest of the men smoking small wooden pipes a short distance away. He was absent there as well. A stiff uneasiness settled around her. Unbidden images of the crocodile's yawning jaws snapping at Cira whirled in her mind. Where was he? Obviously, no one had seen him leave. Perhaps he had wandered off and been injured. Silently she rose, muttering something about finding her mother to the unlistening gathering.

As she moved away from the bright fire its flames cast long, eerie shadows, elongating the trees and rocks into mysterious shapes. The top of her head tingled, the feeling reaching down her spine and arms. As she moved farther from the camp Cira's name swelled within her throat. Suddenly she couldn't bear the thought of losing this frightening but gentle man. She pictured him laughing with the children, helping her father when he had stumbled, twisting his ankle, remembered his gruff but concerned warnings to her when she had nearly stepped on a coiled poisonous adder. She searched for the hatred, the angry defiance she threw at him when he had tried to help her, but it was gone. Only a sinking dread wound about her heart as the darkness loomed before her.

She caught her breath in an inaudible gasp when she saw him sitting beneath a small, aromatic umsinsi tree. He was still, only his hands moving, as he twirled a deep crimson blossom from the tree between his fingers. His eyes stared unseeing at the vivid petals, a heart-wrenching sadness enveloping him, making him appear young and vulnerable. Again, Monase felt the urge to go to him. She crept silently forward, hesitating before she finally lowered herself beside him. If he heard, he gave no indication. Tentatively, she reached out her hand, paused, then laid it tenderly on his arm. Immediately he ceased twirling the flower, but made no other acknowledgment of her presence.

The heady smell of umsinsi blossoms wafted through the warm night. The moonlight slipped through the leafy branches, illuminating the pool of vivid red flowers surrounding them. Monase leaned forward, picking up a fragile velvet petal, crushing it between her fingers; then bringing it to her nose, she inhaled deeply.

"My mother loved these blooms," Cira began. "My father would bring armfuls of them to shower upon her. . . ."

His voice was strained. It cracked on the word *mother*. Monase remained silent, unmoving, afraid he'd say no more. Her silence was rewarded as his voice came from far away.

"After they were gone, Shaka took me under his wing; he made me his uDibi to carry his supplies in battle. I was barely seven."

Cira raised his head. A strange light shone from his eyes.

"When I came of age, he inducted me into the Haze, his favorite corps."

Then, just as suddenly, a dark memory passed over him like a cloud; it almost seemed to obscure the silvery moon that hovered above. His voice became low and ragged.

"The men, they became my family."

The night around them, at first silent, grew louder as it accepted these sullen human intruders in its midst. An imbulu lizard let out an agonizing moan from a nearby rock. From a greater distance, a chorus of frogs added a deeper, calmer note to the harmony. Again Monase waited, feeling that there was more. She wanted to ask what had happened to Cira's parents, but wisely waited.

"Shaka was my mentor. He was our leader. He taught us a new way to fight; he created a new spear."

Cira's hand absentmindedly touched the short-handled spear that was always at his side. Monase recalled her father's interest in it. She had listened while the Zulu impis told him of its superiority in battle. While most warriors carried the traditional handful of six-foot wood assegai spears topped with a six-inch iron tip, Shaka's men had only their one, shorter swordlike spear, called an iKlwa. They had explained that while their enemies threw the assegai spears at them in a haphazard manner, losing their precious weapons, the Zulu impi used their one to push aside all shields and then to plunge into the enemy's unprotected torso.

Cira continued, in a trancelike state, to tell how Shaka's new weapon and fighting techniques had won him the admiration of King Dingoswayo. As he warmed to his subject a smile traced his lips and his chest swelled with pride.

"Once Shaka defeated a great warrior, who challenged the king. Shaka displayed his new methods and weapons, defeating the man, when all others had failed. King Dingoswayo honored Shaka with many cattle and, upon Shaka's father's death, made him chief of the Zulu tribe. Since that time, Chief Shaka has increased the Zululands a hundredfold. King Dingoswayo, the 'Great One,' has named him his heir. Shaka will be a good king. He is fair, and he rewards his warriors handsomely by splitting the booty from the campaigns with them."

At these words, Monase stiffened. Did he consider her "booty"? Was that why he would have the right to sell her to the highest bidder? To Jama? She glanced fearfully at his profile. But still he looked out, as if no one was with him. Dropping the flower, he lowered his head to his hands and began massaging his brow. A wry smile touched his lips.

"Yes, I have gained a great many warrior's prizes. I have all a man could want."

The last words, uttered in a bitter tone of voice, seemed to Monase to hover oppressively above him.

Unable to contain herself any longer, she pushed aside her earlier fears and whispered, "Do you?"

As if stung by a poisonous viper, Cira snatched his arm from beneath her hand. His eyes narrowed distrustfully, as if he had just noticed her beside him. The earlier vulnerability vanished, covered by a shroud of suspicion. She reached forward, as if to catch and retain the fleeting trust of a few moments before.

"What happened to your parents? Your family?"

The suspicion in his eyes deepened. She watched the swirling golden depths turn dark with anger and shame and saw the pain that his earlier admission had cost him. She saw him retreat, not wanting his grief to be known. She bet that Cira had let many people come close to his body, but none near that battered, lonely heart.

"They are gone. And between what I inherited and my prizes, I am a wealthy man."

The last words were a brutal sneer that plunged like an iKlwa spear, piercing her exposed heart. She staggered back on her heels, well aware of what he implied. She braced her hands on the ground to raise herself and flee, but his strong fingers grasped her wrist, stopping her.

Cira didn't know why he had stopped her, but he did know why she had sought him; her questions concerning his wealth made that obvious. Didn't they? His doubt angered him, causing him to tighten his grip. A small whimper of pain from Monase caused him to release her. Yet still she lingered, when moments ago she had been ready to escape. Gazing into her eyes, he was hurt by the fear there. Damn, what did he expect? He was always grasping her roughly, showering her with cruelty. But she didn't deserve more. She was trying to batten down the tough barriers he had built around him, to take everything he had.

"Run, damn it, run!" he wanted to scream into those innocent pools of hope staring at him.

But instead, it was he who rose to leave, he who ran away. Running away from a hope that threatened to shatter his world, to make him see the empty, lonely shell he called life. She would destroy him, wanting everything. Then she, too, would abandon him. Like his father before him, he would shrivel up and blow away.

Monase was still crouched, hands beside her on the ground, when Jurin, Cira's uDibi—assistant—approached her. She smiled a weak smile that did not reach her eyes when he lent a hand to help her. She could still see that last, desperate, heart-wrenching look Cira had given her. What had he been trying to say? Frustrations burned in a tight knot in her throat, making it hard to speak. Instead, she nodded her thanks to Jurin, following him, deep in thought, to the camp.

* * *

The following day Cira avoided her altogether, and at the evening meal he was nowhere to be seen. When she timidly inquired as to his whereabouts from Punga, she was informed that he and some men had gone out to hunt for fresh meat for the remaining journey. The men returned at noon with a huge wildebeest carcass slung over the backs of two of the largest impi. The men and women of the caravan hurried forward as the animal was lowered to the ground. While some of the impi began skinning the animal others were cutting down branches from nearby trees and making a mat of clean fresh twigs and leaves. Monase, Mkabuyi, and their mother stepped back while Punga peeled the hide back from the body on one side, loosening it clear to the backbone. The women then moved forward to pull out the exposed meat, holding it taut, while Punga rolled the animal back, exposing the other side for the other wives to work on. Again, the hide was peeled back, and in a short time the animal was skinned and clean. This completed, six of the impi immediately withdrew their spears, slicing through the joints, cutting the meat, while the women carried it off on the mats to cook and dry for biltong.

When most of the work was completed, Monase allowed her gaze to wander about the camp, searching for Cira. She looked among the Zulu impi who were squatting down to scoop up handfuls of the hot blood that filled the stripped cavity of the beast. They drank it with relish as they recounted the hunt for their compatriots. Cira was not there. Monase turned to look at the women who were fastening the large joints of meat on the spit above the fire. Punga and a few men were sitting just beyond it, cleaning their blood-encrusted blades. For an instant their eyes met, and Monase looked away, embarrassed. She was sure Punga knew for whom she was searching.

A sharp laugh erupted beyond a clump of trees near the river. Monase turned to see two warriors gleefully tossing a white object between them. They then turned to present the object to Cira. He scowled, pressing the object back into the hand of the giver. The two warriors hooted in amusement. A smile tickled the left side of Cira's mouth, flashing that charming dimple.

At the sight, relief flooded Monase. Why she had been concerned she did not know. Now curiosity followed in its wake. Mkabuyi's voice brushed softly against her neck.

"It's a rhinoceros horn. Punga says the men found it while hunting. They told Cira they should mix it in with the food tonight and play a little kana with us older girls."

Monase knew that the rhinoceros horn was a potent aphrodisiac. Although she had never tried any, she was afraid that its rumored potency might be just what was needed to break her weak resolve concerning Cira. Mkabuyi's next words caused her to feel welcome relief, tinged with shameful regret.

"Cira says there are too many of them, and not enough of us. So they insisted he take it as a gift, but he refused, saying he's not interested. See, still they tease him." Mkabuyi sighed. "I wouldn't mind slipping off to the tall grasses with Punga."

A sharp look from Monase silenced her, but only momentarily.

"Would you mind Cira so much?" she suddenly asked.

Monase stomped off, afraid that her desire would reveal itself to her sister. It was Monase's responsibility to set a good example for Mkabuyi, and searching out Cira every minute was not living up to it.

The next day dawned hot and steamy, a warning of the changing season. Hour by hour, the terrain grew into a dense tangle of dry, thorny brambles and heavy vines. The trees wound together, covered with thick moss and parasitic vegetation, blocking out the azure skies. The caravan was silent as they fought to avoid the sharp, tearing thorns and snakes lounging in the branches. At midday, they came upon a sleeping rhinoceros. The crowd huddled as the massive animal staggered to its feet at the scent of them. It turned, hesitated, then sniffed for more information. It seemed to be getting ready to charge.

Seeing the enormous animal, Monase searched the branches above for a secure roost. Then, as if it had forgotten which direction to go, the rhinoceros ambled off into the surrounding bush. Whispering nervously among themselves, Monase's family was startled when Jurin let out a triumphant cry. All eyes turned to him as he revealed an unnoticed termite hill swarming with the bugs. Hungry for a change, forgetting the frightening, gray wrinkled beast, they advanced upon the hill. Jabbing the insects with branches, they forced the winged termites onto their sticks and into their mouths. The children crunched happily as the women ground handfuls of bugs into a pulverized meal, stashing them in their depleted hip pouches.

When they had finished with the termites, the tired troop reluctantly moved on, suddenly coming upon a wide expanse of yellow waving grass, dotted by sturdy, gnarled, flat-topped trees. A group of parched-skinned, long-tusked elephants stood in the distance, gleaning the few scattered leaves from the trees. Monase and her family skirted the gathering, giving the animals a wide berth. Suddenly, without provocation, one old bull lifted his head back, tusks curving skyward without a sound. He opened his ears into large, fanning palms, extended his trunk, and trumpeted furiously. Cira and his men spread out in front of the elephants, bracing for a charge. Then, unexpectedly, the giant beasts turned in unison and disappeared, crashing through the bush. Cursing, the men returned to hacking the bush. Evidently, they had hoped to return to their chief with the additional prize of ivory tusks.

The days were long, but the nights grew intolerably longer. The women-starved warriors were growing restless. Cira and Punga began sleeping a watchful sleep around Ugebula's women. The proximity of Cira's body to Monase's bed was unsettling, and she longed to be home, undisturbed as she had been before that fateful encounter at the stream.

The following morning, a new group of impi went ahead to scout out the trail and clear the undergrowth. Suddenly joyous whoops swept through the air. As if their joy were contagious, the remaining impi surrounding Monase and her family joined in the sonorous racket. The cries echoed through the animal-silent bush.

"Home. We have arrived. 'The land of the heavens.'"

Crashing through the undergrowth, heedless of the sharp thorns tearing gashes in their legs, the warriors rushed forward. Swept up in the enthusiasm, the women and children followed, anxious to see their new home.

Monase caught her breath as she stared down the hillside. Everything was suspended, as if in a dream. The air vibrated with heat around her, causing the scene to tremble like a mirage. Tall grasses shimmered golden as a gentle breeze ran skimming fingers through them. Millions of flowers sparkled like so many jewels around the perimeter of the magnificently large village below. Lush ceiba, sandalwood, and umsinsi trees clustered around a gushing waterfall. In the distance, the misty purple mountains parted to reveal the glimmering indigo ocean, embraced by silvery white beaches. Never in her wildest dreams had she imagined a land so breathtakingly beautiful. Focusing her gaze on the sprawling village, she recognized the familiar hive-shaped huts gathered in circular family kraals, each with its entrance facing east toward the water and a fenced cattle pen in its center. She continued to survey the Zulu kingdom as the caravan was urged down the hillside.

Cries of welcome rushed up the hill to greet the returning warriors. Several sentries by the thick, tree-woven fence surrounding the village rushed off to inform their chief of the caravan's arrival. The other guards parted to allow Cira and his following to enter. Throngs of Zulus rushed forward to greet their long-awaited men and to glance curiously at the new arrivals.

Suddenly Monase felt lonely as she and her family were paraded down a long, wide avenue. The tribe stared openly, assessing them. She paused. Something was missing. There were no young men. All the gawkers were either women, children, or older men. Only Cira and his fifty warriors were young males. She knew that the young boys were probably up in the hills herding, but was this all the eligible young men? Where were the other impis? Where was Shaka's daunting army of men? Where was a possible future husband? She fought down a rising feeling of panic. Just then, the crowd parted to let the parade turn toward a large platform in the center of the town. Upon the slightly raised stage, over two hundred men moved gracefully in a silent dance, their bare feet falling soundlessly on the dirt-packed, split-tree surface. Their skin gleamed with perspiration as again and again they raised their spears and lunged forward. A deep voice at her ear startled her.

"These men are only a portion of Shaka's great army. The rest are housed in separate barracks a short distance from the family kraals. Chief Shaka demands that his men be celibate while on campaign."

Monase turned to stare openmouthed at Cira. Vivid images of the wild, carousing young impi in her old village raced through her mind. Yet these

Zulu men were so disciplined. Embarrassed at her boldness, she respectfully lowered her eyes. A hot flush crept steadily up her cheek when Cira continued to speak in a stern tone, as if admonishing a child.

"Therefore, now that my men are home, I would watch your . . . overtly friendly behavior."

He fixed meaningful eyes on her downcast visage. Monase felt the flush creep higher, burning her ears. When she finally had the courage to look up, Cira was gone. She watched his long, smooth strides as he moved to the head of the caravan.

Slowly the crowd began to disperse. Cira's men led the cattle off to Shaka's pen. Cira continued to lead Monase's family toward a huge palisade made of trees planted in the ground. Two fully armed guards stood to either side. Cira called out a greeting from outside the entrance. He then handed his spear and shield to Jurin, who remained outside. Cira threw himself on the ground, his nose touching the dirt. He then moved through the entrance, crawling on his belly. Punga instructed the members of Monase's family to do likewise.

Ugebula, his wives, and daughters entered, stooping, then lying prone, while Cira crawled to the middle of the vast court.

"Bayete!" he called.

He then sang a praise song in a deep chanting voice. The song he sang told of the greatness of Dingoswayo and Shaka, the cattle and Zululands. When he had ended, he touched his forehead to the ground. Shaka raised his hand in greeting. Monase dared to peek up at this legendary man. Like Cira, he was tall, dark, and handsome. His feet were bare, his muscular legs and arms encircled with leather bands fringed with white cow tails. He wore his hair closely cropped, a long blue feather dipped gracefully from a fiber circlet woven into it. His broad chest was also covered with white cow tails suspended from a beautifully beaded breastplate. His lower body was covered with a golden kilt made from civet fur. A large white shield with one black spot in the center rested against his knee. As Monase's gaze strayed up his body she was mortified to find his eyes trained on her, their magnetic force making it impossible to look away. Abruptly, Shaka turned his eyes back to Cira, freeing Monase to return hers to the ground. Rising, Shaka dismissed Ugebula and his family and Cira.

Praying fervently that her parents hadn't seen the visual contact between the great chief and herself, she followed them out of the large building. Monase listened distractedly to Mkabuyi's excited chatter as they constructed their new hut. While Ugebula and some of the impi built the hemp-and-branch central cattle pen, Monase's mother, in her role as Great Wife, marked out a large spot at the far end of the pen's gates. Nomtomba, Ugebula's new wife, quickly moved to Monase's mother's left side once Niamani had demarcated her hut's foundation. Monase knew Nomtomba hoped to bear her father a son and earn the honor of being nominated as substitute Great Wife. Thus, she would be able to move her hut to Niamani's right-hand side, a place of greater strength and honor.

Monase's fingers worked nimbly as they wove the supple sapling branches together while Mkabuyi and her mother thatched it with the long, dried grasses. The two younger girls stood giggling in the middle of the marked circle, holding the center supporting pole. Every time Nomtomba threw Niamani a dirty, envious look, the young girls burst into another peal of laughter.

As the sun began its rapid descent along the horizon, Monase moved to the eastern side of the hut to weave the flap for the small, low entrance. She smelled her mother's approach before she turned and saw her. Niamani dragged a mat loaded with the traditional mixture of clay and cow dung for the hut's floor. Grabbing handfuls of the lumpy paste, the girls spread it evenly over the ground, rubbing it until it shone a lustrous green. As the last rays of golden sunlight slipped over the tangled bush, Monase's mother started a small, smoky fire on the hearth in the center of the hut. Soon, the smoky wood smell of the fire extinguished the new floor's pungent odor. Monase stretched her weary muscles as she watched her sister mix the last of the millet and termite meal with water. Their father wouldn't be bringing any milk until tomorrow.

Turning to scoop up her small bundle of belongings, Monase untied it. Gently, she shook out her few precious possessions. She touched each piece, loving its familiar feel. She removed her wooden bowl. Only after she had rolled out her woven-grass sleeping mat and hung her hide bag containing another wooden bowl, two wooden combs, and the treasured thin gold bracelet her father had brought back from an iron-ore exploration, did she finally feel that this place was home. She then began hanging her sisters' and mother's belongings on the remaining wooden hooks scattered around the upper half of the thatched hut's perimeter.

When she finished the unpacking, she joined Niamani and her sisters around the glowing hearth to eat the mush Mkabuyi had prepared. Without the milk flavor, the mixture was bland. It clung to her fingers and teeth; the roof of her mouth became gummy and sticky. Her appetite lost, she felt her eyes close wearily. The past week's upsets, and the strenuous journey, seemed finally to have caught up with her. Her head nodded forward. The hut was warm and comfortable; outside, the cool night air rushed up from the ocean, whipping about the shelter. The crashing of the waterfall, muted and distant, echoed soothingly. It was all too much. Without a word, Monase gratefully crawled off to snuggle between her hide covers. Her fingers stroked the familiar, worn skins. In a short time she drifted off into a dreamless sleep.

Nine

By the time Cira reached his barracks, he was in a foul mood. Deep lines creased his forehead. Propping his iKlwa spear and shield by the door, he cupped his hands around the back of his neck. His thumbs massaged the tight, knotted muscles of his shoulders. With irrational irritation, he noticed his men lounging about the vast shelter. They had been talking eagerly about the upcoming Incwala ceremony, where Chief Shaka would give the bravest men his permission to take a bride. The men who had escorted the Butelezi women back were discussing their attributes and wondering if Shaka would charge the standard ten-head-of-cattle lobala for one of his new "sisters." There was laughter mixed with admiration at Shaka's clever arrangement. He would certainly be a wealthy "older brother."

Soon the talk moved on to how many heads they would each be awarded, then to the new ironsmith and his daughters. At the mention of Mkabuyi, there were grunts of approval, which sparked a few lurid comments, until Punga growled a deep warning of displeasure. A few masculine chuckles followed. Then one man mentioned Monase. The name was followed by falsetto moans of fear and uproarious laughter.

"You mean that wild demon cat?" one man called out.

"Ah, yes. But what a pleasure to tame," another answered.

The discussion dissolved into graphic accounts of taming methods when Cira, no longer able to remain silent, stormed into their midst.

"Enough! These are the daughters of our new ironsmith. They deserve our respect. Ugebula is an important man."

The silence that followed was fraught with tension. Punga looked over at his leader and friend. He shook his head in true astonishment. Cira, whose name meant "the mountain," cool and distant, was threatening to become a volcano. And Punga did not want to be around when he erupted. That maiden, Monase, had most certainly bewitched him. Punga again shook his head in wonder. He couldn't understand Cira's attraction to her. Admittedly she was beautiful, long-legged, with a lean, leopardlike grace. But like a leopard, to tangle with her could be lethal. Monase was wild, unpredictable. Now, Mkabuyi—there was a maiden a man would want for his own. Another four or five years and she would be of marriageable age. She was the daughter of an ironsmith, descendant of a chief, and from the womb of a Great Wife.

He smiled to himself as Mkabuyi's laughing face appeared before him. She would be expensive. Better not to have her as a first wife . . . perhaps a Great Wife. He would have to check out the possibilities. She certainly seemed willing. He would have to talk to Cira to help arrange a contract. He looked over at his brooding friend.

Cira was now seated on his sleeping mat, angrily pulling long thorns from the instep of his foot. As his heated curses vibrated through the now almost empty barracks, Punga decided his questions could wait. For now he would try to pacify his irate friend. Perhaps some food and millet beer. Before Punga could reach Cira's side, Cira's young uDibi, Jurin, arrived. The boy announced that Chief Shaka wished to see Cira in his royal palace immediately. Cira rose instantly, the thorns forgotten. He followed Jurin out of the barracks, with Punga following at a discreet distance. Perhaps now was the time to slip a hint to Cira about getting Shaka's permission to approach Ugebula about Mkabuyi.

Cira sat before Shaka, his head bowed, the formal greetings completed. With a royal wave of his hand, Shaka dismissed his ever-present guards. Only then did Cira raise his eyes to Shaka, his chief, his mentor, and his friend. His gaze was met by eyes crinkled in humorous pleasure. Mischief twinkled in their black depths.

"So tell me, loyal friend, what has transpired over your long absence . . . and please leave nothing out." Shaka's voice barely concealed amused laughter.

Warily, Cira began a dry, detailed account of the smooth transition of the emDletsheni, of the cattle, especially the pure-white ones, his eyes not leaving Shaka's, but searching them for a clue to Shaka's amusement. With all of the chief's spies, Cira was sure Shaka was already aware of all the information he was imparting. Undoubtedly, Shaka had already been out to inspect the cattle and ensure that they had been securely tucked into his own cattle pen. Cira talked with glowing praise of Ugebula's talents, presenting Shaka with six assegai tips and a dozen copper bracelets for his mother, Nandi. Shaka had never married, and worshiped the ground his mother walked on. The gift for his mother pleased him greatly, and his eyes were bright with delight. Cira was glad he had told Ugebula to include them among his gifts. When his account was finished, Cira fell silent.

Shaka piled the articles before him in a small mound. Picking up one of the shiny bangles, he studied Cira.

"Is that all you have to tell me, your old friend?" he asked.

Cira squirmed uneasily, aware of the heat rising in his face. What was Shaka driving at? A nagging voice in the back of his mind warned him that the chief might know of his torrid encounters with Monase, and an indescribable anger surged through him. He would kill Monase; he'd kill whoever had informed Shaka. What had they said? His

Zulu impi pledge had not been breached. Who had dared to mar his name and reputation? His back straight and his chin forward, he waited.

Finally unable to contain his mirth, Shaka released a short bark of laughter. His eyes danced roguishly. Twirling the copper bracelet between his thumbs and forefingers, he cocked his head to one side.

"I believe you discovered a couple of maidens wandering into your camp outside the emDletsheni village . . ." he prompted.

Cira nodded in agreement, but added no information. Shaka flung back his head and roared with laughter. Cira watched the long, blue feather in Shaka's headband bob vigorously.

"Let me see. I think I was told that one of the women—no, I believe the term was *wild cat*, threw herself at you, and when you refused, she escaped." Again the chief howled with delight. Wiping tears of laughter out of his eyes, he continued, "My mighty impi could not even keep a young girl."

Cira felt his body quiver with rage and embarrassment as he struggled to leash his temper. He was being made sport of, and that was unforgivable. Someone would pay dearly. Monase would rue the day she crossed his path.

Shaka eyed Cira's trembling, rigid frame. Could Cira finally have met his match? he mused. A woman had finally made Cira look twice. He recalled the bold girl, how her impudent eyes had met his when the caravan entered the village. At that moment he had been reminded of his mother as a young woman. Turning serious eyes toward Cira's silent form, he spoke.

"She is brazen, but courageous. I like that. But beware of those kinds of women, they are dangerous with their wily ways. They will stop at nothing to attain what they want."

Immediately a picture of the grotesque witch doctor flashed before Cira's eyes.

"I'm not what she is after."

Shaka's eyes narrowed to dark slits. "Do not be so sure. But enough now of women. The rainy season is approaching. The Incwala ceremony must be arranged. What men are to be rewarded with brides? What men can we afford to lose to the ranks of the married?"

Cira knew that to permit a man to marry meant that he had less time for training, and his dedication would waver. Taking deep, even breaths, he willed his body to remain calm. He needed a clear head. He was deciding the fates of *his men*.

Reluctantly, he ticked off the men he felt should be rewarded with brides. Once they were married, they would cease to be in Shaka's elite uFasimba battalion. They would serve in another troop, under another leader. In a low voice, devoid of emotion, he began listing the men and their deeds. After several hours of discussion, Cira mentioned Punga's name. He smiled inwardly as he recalled his friend's last-minute, whispered request for Mkabuyi's hand. He told Shaka of Punga's desire for one of the new ironsmith's daughters. A dark scowl crossed Shaka's forehead.

"Not your woman?" he demanded.

"No," Cira responded, his voice vibrating in annoyance at Shaka's implication that Monase belonged to him. "It is the younger one. She is only fifteen or sixteen at best. I think that to grant him permission to draw up a contract with her father has merit. You would be rewarding his bravery, yet as one of my most valued warriors, I could retain him for another five years."

Here Cira paused. A smile played along his lips. "And I can vouch for his unwavering loyalty and dedication. He is quite smitten, and nearly begged me to get your permission to mark her now, before she should be taken. He wouldn't want to risk losing her."

Shaka screwed up his lips in reflection. But try as he might, he was unable to recall this Mkabuyi in his pavilion that morning. With a shrug, he nodded his approval. Stretching his arms toward the ceiling, the chief leaned back into a plush mound of striped and spotted pelts. Cira bowed and made to leave.

"Wait. There is one more impi," Shaka said, propping himself up on his elbows, his eyes bright.

Cira pursed his lips in thought. He again ran through the list of men in his brain and came up empty. His eyes returned to Shaka's, a quizzical glint reflecting off their gold surface.

"You, my valiant warrior, what prize would you have? You already have many cattle. Are you maybe willing to part with a few to lay claim to a bride? The ironsmith's older daughter perhaps?" An insolent grin wreathed Shaka's face.

"No!" Cira shouted.

Shaka drew back in mock horror, a knowing smile still fixed upon his lips. Cira instantly apologized for his outburst, hurrying to say, "To serve you well is honor enough." And in an effort to somehow modify the forcefulness of his original answer, he added, "I think I will keep my cattle for a while. They are much less trouble than women."

Shaka again laughed, pulling himself upright to place a hand on each of Cira's shoulders.

"So true, but not"—he waved a hand in the air above his head, as if grasping for the words—"not as pleasing on a cold, dark night." He interrupted himself with a snorting laugh. "Or anytime the blood is hot, eh?"

Cira nodded lamely in response and took his leave. As Shaka watched his retreating back he clapped his hands loudly. A young messenger scurried out of the far corner of the shadows. With a wickedly impish smile, the chief sent him to bring the man Ugebula to him.

"You shall have your prize, my reluctant warrior," Shaka whispered into the now surrounding emptiness.

Cira was obviously distracted by this woman. It was time.

Outside Shaka's doorway, Cira nodded stiffly to the guards who were posted there. Straightening his broad shoulders, he scanned the darkening village. The air had turned chilly; the faint glow of fires shone brightly, welcoming family members home. A deep loneliness welled up inside Cira, an ache for the home that had been so brutally snatched from him so many years ago. His fists clenched and unclenched as he fought to bury the lonely little boy within.

A soft rustling of the dry grass behind him made him turn. Punga stood before him, a questioning, hopeful look filling his eyes. Relief flooded Cira's mind. The abandoned child within him retreated into the dark corners of his heart, and dropping an arm around his companion's shoulder, he smiled. Grateful for the diversion, he began to tell Punga of Shaka's consent.

Cira had his men. He didn't need another family.

Early the next morning, Monase was digging holes with a stick in her mother's new field, her thoughts on the almost ripe melons and maize she had left behind in her old home. As her mind drifted off, the dirt swirled up about her. A breathless Mkabuyi skidded to a stop beside her.

"Hurry, Monase! Father wants to talk to us. Last night after we went to sleep, Chief Shaka summoned him."

Monase's heart skipped a beat as she rose, carefully dusting off her knees. What had the chief wanted? What did it have to do with her? Leaving her stick in the dirt, she ran to catch up with the rapidly disappearing Mkabuyi.

Outside the hut's entrance, Ugebula stood impatiently tapping his feet, his arms folded tightly across his chest. Niamani scurried about excitedly, trying to find something to occupy her frenetic hands while waiting for the children to gather. With an odd, delighted smile, Ugebula stepped toward Monase. Grasping her chin gently in his outstretched hand, he turned her face back and forth, as if studying it. His eyes traced the lean contours, a look of wistfulness misting over them. Releasing her, he turned to enter her mother's hut. Niamani followed, then Monase, Mkabuyi, and their younger sister.

Inside, the women seated themselves respectfully to the left of Ugebula, who perched on a small wooden stool. He stretched out his short, wiry legs as he leaned back to tap his empty pipe on his palm. With a frustrated swish of her skirt, Monase's mother reached above her to grab a bag of tobacco hanging on a hook. She neatly rammed the leafy substance into the hollow bowl of the pipe. Ugebula lit the pipe and sighed, obviously enjoying the "hurry up and wait" game he had initiated.

For once, Monase did not share in his enjoyment of testing her mother's notoriously short patience. With a sharp tingle of dread, she knew his news concerned her, and would probably not be to her liking. Unable to wait a moment more, she opened her mouth to speak. With a scowling nod, her father cut off the words that would have spilled out.

"As you know, Chief Shaka called me to the palisade last night." Ugebula took a long draw on his pipe, his eyes closing as he held in the acrid smoke. When he released his breath, the smoke poured out of his mouth in a billowy rush. "He wanted to talk to me of marriage contracts."

Monase's heart stood still. She had heard rumors from Mkabuyi that Jama had entered the village several days ago astride a great white bull, his massive bulk slipping precariously over its back. At that time she had brushed her sister's words away as cruel teasing, but now she wanted to ask if they were indeed true. A look at Mkabuyi's wide-eyed, openmouthed glance was all the confirmation she needed. With a heart filled with trepidation, she turned her attention back to her father, but his eyes were on Mkabuyi as he continued.

"The Zulu impi Punga has requested the promise of Mkabuyi as his bride four rainy seasons hence."

Mkabuyi looked stunned, then her face dissolved into a beatific smile, and she clasped her hands before her, as if to hold this precious moment forever.

"He has offered three cows a year in the interim, with two more on the day of the wedding."

Now Niamani gasped in delight. She hadn't hoped for anything more than the customary ten cows. And what a windfall to receive them so far in advance. Surely, the ancestors blessed her this day. The great value of her daughters could not fail to put her in good standing among the women of the tribe. Monase had turned in relief to embrace the exuberant Mkabuyi when her father spoke again.

"But that is not all. He spoke to me of another marriage contract."

For a brief moment Monase thought he was going to tell her that she, too, was to marry Punga—to be his first wife while the more valuable Mkabuyi would be his Great Wife. But this thought soon fled.

"A contract was made for Monase. Niamani and I had hoped to have this man as a son before we left our old tribe."

The floor rose up before Monase, and darkness swirled about her, threatening to engulf her. She heard her mother's cry of delight, and her stomach churned and roiled. Jama's ugly, repugnant visage swam before her mind's eye. His vile stench filled her nostrils. His laughing face, yellow rotting teeth, the thick slobbery tongue flicking across his puffy lips . . .

Unable to stand any more, she rushed from the hut, wings to her heels, and ran. Blindly she fled, the fragrant dew-wet grass entangling her feet. She stumbled, but still she ran, fleeing her father's unspoken words.

Hours later, disheveled, and with red-rimmed but now dry eyes, Monase returned to the field. Mkabuyi was singing and haphazardly swinging the harvest ax. Upon seeing Monase, she rushed to her, dropping the ax, her arms held out to embrace her sister. Monase abruptly turned her back. Mkabuyi faltered, halting behind her.

"I don't understand. Surely it is not that bad," her puzzled, plaintive voice cried.

Monase braced her shoulders as a new onslaught of grief flooded over her.

"Congratulations, Mkabuyi," she replied in a cold, tense voice. Bending to retrieve her digging stick, which she had abandoned earlier that morning, Monase refused to face the baffled girl. "I believe we have a lot of work to do. So, if you don't mind . . ."

She began digging with a fierce vengeance, not pausing until she heard Mkabuyi's sobbing, choked departure. A small wave of regret washed over Monase. Poor Mkabuyi. She had only wanted to share her happiness. But right now Monase had no sympathy for anyone else. She needed to wallow in self-pity. She began to sing a low, sorrowful song. Her rich, beautiful voice surrounded her like a cloak, protecting her, at least momentarily, from the harsh reality of her future.

Monase hadn't seen her mother since the morning family conference and registered only slight surprise when, at dinner, the hearth was cold and there was no meal. Mixing some borrowed millet and fresh milk, she heated some food for her little sisters. Squashing some winter berries into a thick paste, she stirred it into the lumpy mixture. Mechanically, she scooped the untasted food into her mouth. Silent, her eyes staring hard at the empty walls, she willed her mind to remain blissfully blank. Like a dying woman, she wrestled to deny what she knew was inevitable. She couldn't accept the horrible reality. At least not yet.

Late that night, as she huddled in her covers, seeking unsuccessfully to warm herself, she heard slurred words and laughter outside the hut. A sharp blast of cool night air gushed through the low entryway as her mother and father crawled through it. As her parents stumbled past her Niamani giggled. A strong, liquor-scented breath fanned over her. Her parents had been drinking. She had seen her father drunk before, but never her mother. Suddenly the meaning of the now writhing covers in the far recesses of the darkened hut dawned upon her. She could barely remember the last time her father had stayed the night with her mother. A sharp gasp, followed by a deep moan, echoed through the darkness.

Monase rolled onto her side, trying to force herself to sleep. When the moaning and thrashing continued, she rolled onto her back and stared at the invisible ceiling. With every cry of pleasure, the dark, unknown fears and questions came flooding back into her mind. How could she . . . with Jama? What strange perverted things would he make her do? She tried to push all the rumors she had heard of his peculiar likes and dislikes from her mind, but like evil two-headed demons, they slithered in, wrapping long, disgusting tentacles around her. She tried to reason with her terror, accusing herself of being selfish. But once again, tears overcame her. In the dark, early hours of the morning, she finally succumbed to a restless sleep.

The next morning Niamani was like a young girl, humming and skipping about the hut. The girls had awakened to find their father sprawled out on their mother's mat, snoring loudly. Evidently, their mother had not had as much to drink as he had, and she was now singing happily outside. When Nomtomba, their father's first wife, realized what was happening, she stomped off to her own field, throwing dark glowering looks over her shoulder, much to Niamani's obvious delight.

The bright morning light slashed painfully at Monase's strained, puffy eyes. Her head was pounding ferociously as she bent to splash some water on her face from the basket outside the door. Her stomach felt tight and dull. She attempted to swallow a handful of the now congealed mush her mother had set out for her, but gave up, returning the thick, pulpy mixture to the pot near the door. Lifting her harvest ax across her shoulder, she set out to a far corner of the field.

At her arrival, Mkabuyi, who was already at work, turned to her, a happy, expectant smile on her face. The smile faded rapidly as Monase sidestepped her, turning a cold shoulder. To Monase's relief, the morning passed in blessed silence. Neither her mother nor her sisters approached her. Monase forced her mind on the task before her, thrusting her ax into the rich, dark earth with a feral intensity.

At noon, Niamani shooed her two youngest off to fetch water. She then made her way toward her older daughter. Monase halted her swings, wiping a dirty arm across her sweat-streaked brow. She watched her mother's approach with a strange detachment, as if her spirit had somehow taken leave of her body. A smile crinkled in the corners of Niamani's mouth and eyes. Monase studied this unusual configuration of her face. Niamani placed her strong, work-worn hands on her daughter's shoulders, pulling her toward her. Monase, who was several inches taller, stooped to receive the awkward dry kiss her mother placed on her cheek. Niamani pulled away slowly, not releasing her shoulders. Her tired, happy eyes studied her daughter's face with a wistful sadness.

"He is a good man. He will take good care of you." When Monase showed no response, Niamani released a heavy sigh, her hands sliding down her daughter's arms. Briefly, she squeezed Monase's hands, then turned and walked away.

Unmoving, Monase watched her go. A small voice inside her cried out, *Mama, hold me! I'm scared!* But the voice went unheeded, and Monase bent to continue her tilling.

The long, hot days grew shorter and shorter as the rainy season approached. Day after day Monase drew deeper into herself. Her family and the other women had ceased trying to entice her into conversation. Mostly she worked off by herself, a blank, emotionless numbness enveloping her. She clung to its folds of blissful oblivion, wrapping them tightly around her to ward off the cold, harsh reality of the approaching rainy season and its ceremonies . . . her wedding. As the day grew closer she drew the cloak tighter; even her singing ceased to give her comfort. She refused all pleas for her to join in the preparation of songs for the upcoming events.

In another part of the kraal, Cira seethed in anger at the cruel jest fate had played on him. The days since he had learned of Shaka's prize for him were filled with mindless anger. He pushed his men to their limits, forcing them to train from before the sun rose to well after sunset. He was brutal—unforgiving of any mistakes. He slashed viciously during the drills, frightening his men with his savage fury. At the infrequent breaks Cira allowed, the men pleaded with Punga to talk to him.

This morning, as the sun crested over the water, Punga dismissed the man Cira had engaged in a mock battle. Cira narrowed his eyes to dark slits as Punga took the man's place. Cira had brushed off all previous attempts to talk to him, saying there was no time for such matters. Punga now looked with deep concern at his friend. His joy over his own betrothal was overshadowed by Cira's vehement anger at his own.

As he readied himself for combat Punga moved cautiously, dancing in a small half circle around his opponent. Cira, too, moved warily, stealthily, muscles coiled, ready to pounce. Then Punga slipped, making the unforgivable error of looking into his opponent's eyes, losing track of his own hands and feet. Cira grabbed the opportunity and lunged, all his savage energy surging into his spear. Punga moved too late; the spear slashed a deep crimson gash in his right biceps, and he staggered backward, disbelief widening his eyes and slackening his jaw. The men around them froze, watching in horror, as Cira drew back his spear to thrust again.

Suddenly, with an all but audible snap, Cira's eyes came back into focus. A jolt raced through his body; his hand, clenching the spear, relaxed. The weapon fell to the ground, the metal tip ringing out loudly as it contacted the wooden floor. The men watched it roll, then lie in silence. Punga and Cira's eyes locked, neither one moving. Cira dropped to one knee, his face drained of color. His hand reached out to touch the bloodied wound. He stared in horror at the dark red stain on his fingers, shaking his head slowly. Punga reached out a trembling hand, covering Cira's.

"Help a wounded man up?" he asked. Still, Cira stared at the large hand on his. "It's nothing. A superficial wound." Punga's voice was laced with pain.

Slowly, as he raised his eyes to his friend's, Cira's face was filled with horror.

"Come on now, help me back to the barracks.

You can be my nursemaid . . . although I'd prefer one more . . . curvaceous, and less violent."

At this quip, the surrounding impi chuckled with relief. In a daze, Cira helped the fallen Punga to his feet. Wrapping his arm around the wounded man's waist, he half led, and was half led himself, back to the barracks. The men remained behind, adjusting their shields, returning to their practice.

When they reached the barracks, Cira lowered Punga gently to the ground. Small beads of perspiration dotted Punga's upper lip and forehead. Drawing in deep, measured breaths, he squeezed his eyes shut, refusing to let Cira see the pain he had inflicted. Wringing out a small wet hide, Cira bent to examine the wound.

"Punga . . . I can't believe . . . I don't know what . . . I'm sorry, so very sorry."

Punga winced as Cira dabbed the tender place with the cloth.

"Jurin!" Cira shouted. The boy appeared out of nowhere. "Fetch an inyanga and a witch doctor."

The boy left as quickly as he had appeared.

"I'm sure the inyanga can mix up a poultice to stop the bleeding."

Punga nodded silently. As Cira wrapped a tourniquet around his arm Punga opened his eyes. "Cira, what is it? Am I wrong? Do you not want the ironsmith's older daughter, Monase?"

At these words, Cira pulled the bandage tight with an angry jerk. Punga recoiled.

"I'm sorry." Cira's eyes stilled blazed with the anger, but his voice was gentle. "It is just that I'm confused. Sometimes I want her so badly that I ache, but I will not have a woman who longs for another."

Punga raised a questioning eyebrow, and Cira continued, his shoulders sagging forward. "The witch doctor, Jama. She told me herself that she would marry him, that he would bring much wealth and honor to her family." He rubbed his eyes with his hand, then pushed it back through his hair. "I don't want a wife, especially one who doesn't want me. Why would Shaka do this to me? I have served him well. I made it clear to him I had no desire for this woman. Now I will lose all this."

His hand stretched in an arch before him, encompassing the room. "My men, they will no longer be my . . ." The words died with a catch in his throat. His eyes shifted to the barren walls, his voice barely a whisper. "I need no other family, I will not be abandoned again."

Punga struggled to sit up, to hear these last words. "Cira, surely she does not desire that fat old man over you? The man Jama is here. If indeed he is so powerful and wealthy, why did her father not make a contract with him?"

Cira shook his head, his long, dark locks gently slapping his cheeks and neck. "Perhaps he doesn't want her."

Punga leaned back, exhausted. A heavy gush of air rushed out of his mouth as his back hit the ground. "No, that is not so. The witch doctor is furious. He has offered twenty-five cows for her. Ugebula refused, saying it is both his chief and daughter's wish for the union with you."

Cira sat up sharply, his eyes mere slits of burnished gold. "Where did you hear such rumors?"

He continued, not waiting for an answer: "What is that witch up to now?"

Alarm spread across Punga's face. "Surely you do not believe *her* to be a witch?" He knew the fate of witches, and as much as he desired Mkabuyi, he would have to think twice before consenting to marry the sister of a witch.

Cira lay a gentle hand on his shoulder. "No, my friend, but she has most certainly bewitched me, the chief, the witch doctor, and her father. What man would give consideration to the preferences of his daughter, especially at the cost of five head of cattle? The contract Shaka established for me only offered twenty head."

Punga gulped loudly at the extravagant number of cows. Cira chuckled, a low mirthless sound. "But, what is her design? I was unaware of her part in this." Punga shrugged his shoulders. Cira smiled a smile that didn't quite reach his eyes. "Trust me, friend, I have every intention of finding out. I will not be a puppet in her play."

Punga waved him away. "Go then, resolve this thing. Return to us the man and leader you were before. I'm fine; the medicine man will soon be here." His words were interrupted by the entrance of several men following Jurin.

Cira paused as he watched a now familiar jowl-wobbling face enter the low doorway. Cira and Jama's eyes locked for a moment, the fat man's loathing and hatred almost tangible in the space between them. Slowly, a wicked, unearthly smile spread across Jama's bloated face.

Cira looked away in disgust. "I will return shortly, Punga." Turning his gaze to the Zulu witch doctor, he said, "Mend him well. He is one of my best soldiers." Avoiding Jama's eyes, he slipped from the barracks.

Cira found Monase at the river with the other women, washing clothes and weaving reeds into baskets. She was sitting a short distance from the crowd. Her head bent over nimble fingers, she wound the supple reeds together. Although she appeared aloof, she was listening intently to a story being told by an old woman who smoked a long wooden pipe and sat cross-legged upon a large rock.

The woman had been brought to Zululand from a land far away. She had been a young bride when she left her homeland in the heart of the continent. She had since been captured and transported to six different villages. She spoke of her birthplace, somewhere north of Zululand, as a land where the mountains breathed with fire. Her name was Tika. A favorite storyteller of the people, she was often invited into the inner sanctums of Shaka and Nandi's home. This alone placed her in a position of high esteem and would have made her welcome anywhere. But it was not to win honor that she told her tales; she truly enjoyed recounting her life to all who would listen, providing her with a little tobacco for her pipe. This innate modesty endeared her to the tribe.

She sat peacefully upon the rock like a wrinkled lizard, the smoke swirling thickly about her head. Taking a deep, practiced draw from her pipe, she spoke in a rough, gravelly voice.

"Long, long ago, my ancestors lived below a beautiful mountain called Naka. Ah, Naka was a most haughty and powerful mountain. She rumbled and smoked at all that displeased her. But she was good to her people, for they pleased her greatly. They sang her praises and lavished many gifts upon her." Closing her eyes, Tika paused, drawing again on the intricately carved pipe. "Then, one dark, moonless night, Naka was disturbed. She rumbled loudly. Her people grew concerned by her agitation. They were used to her occasional snores, but now she seemed to be awakening. The people were frightened, and they hid among the bushes surrounding their kraals. The earth grew silent, then the ancestors' spirits inhabited the trees, speaking with the voice of the wind. Oh, how they moaned, telling of Naka's anger."

The basket forgotten, Monase leaned closer. She could almost hear the ancestors calling their warning. Small bumps prickled along her arms. She could feel the cold winds whistling through the trees.

The old woman's eyes became bright. "Then Naka spoke in a voice of thunder, the sound splitting the earth, spitting out fire. . . ."

Monase gasped as a strong hand gripped her arm. She struggled, afraid that the ancestors had come to claim her. She swung around to come face-to-face with Cira, and her heart rammed up against her ribs. She had kept her distance from him for so long, going weeks without catching a glimpse of him, that she had felt sure she was over him. But now that all faded away, as if it had been only yesterday that he had kissed her by the stream. Her eyes traced the lean contours of his face, the sensual curve of his lips, lips that were sweet with the promise of pleasures she had barely tasted. She watched the tight muscle in his jaw twitching rapidly, the straining muscles standing out along his neck, and closed her eyes, drinking in the warm, musky, masculine scent of his skin.

The group of surrounding women grew quiet, and old Tika's voice paused. Monase opened her eyes, staring into Cira's rich amber ones. She shivered at the molten gold sparks shooting from their depths. As always, he seemed to be angry at her. Turning, he pulled her to her feet. Monase could hear the women's subtle tittering, and then the gruff voice of Tika finishing her story. Docilely, she followed Cira, having no will to fight. The effect he had on her was unexpected and unnerving. She was to marry another man in less than a week, and here she was panting after this Zulu warrior. He dragged her off deeper into the forest, until the women's voices were no more than the whisper of a breeze rustling through the leaves.

Then, without warning, Cira flung her around to face him. His thumbs pressed deeply into the veins at her wrists, and her pupils dilated with fear. Cira muttered a curse under his breath, released her, and turned his head away. Instinctively, Monase recoiled from him, rubbing her bruised wrists. Catching her backward movement out of the corner of his eye, Cira turned to her, taking a step closer, his eyes pounding down upon her, riveting her to the spot where she stood. She released a small, plaintive whimper. Cira sneered, his skin pulling taut against his forehead, his eyes slits of fire. Again he reached out to grab her. She stumbled backward, her hands, palms out, a barrier between them.

"No, don't touch me," she whispered.

Cira's strong arms encircled her narrow waist, crushing her to him. A heartless laugh rumbled deep inside his chest. "Don't touch you? Is this more than you bargained for?" His lips slanted downward, grinding the tender skin of her lips against her teeth.

She pressed violently against him, her hands caught between them. She struggled, wanting to protest against this brutal, loveless onslaught, but his tongue pierced her lips, swallowing all sound, and finally all resistance. She leaned heavily into him, his unshaven stubble scraping her sensitive skin. The hand on her waist slid upward, pausing beneath her breast, as his thumb, rough and callused, ran teasingly across her hardened nipple. As his kiss deepened he bent her backward, his other hand slipping down her back. His hand stroked, then cupped her firm buttocks, pressing her pliant body against his hard, unyielding flesh. Gently, but firmly, his knee slid between her thighs. She felt his hard heat burn through her skirt, singeing the skin on her thigh. His demanding lips moved over her cheeks, her temple, her ears, then down the long cords of her throat, pausing only as a groan escaped her lips, then again making their exquisitely sensual descent. He paused again at the hollow of her neck as a shudder racked her body.

Monase felt her knees weaken, threatening to give way. Her breath came in short, quick rasps. Her heart was pounding, pumping hot, surging blood through her veins, roaring in her ears. Her mind clouded; she couldn't think clearly. This was wrong, so wrong, but she couldn't and didn't want to break free. Surrendering, she wound her fingers in his long, coiled locks. She flung her head back, giving him clear access to her throat and breast. His mouth grew more urgent, and his hand pushed up her skirt, sliding up her quivering thigh, kneading and stroking as it went ever upward. Gently, he lowered her to the ground, pulling his head away slightly, his eyes hooded with passion, his legs twining with hers. His breath, warm and sweet, brushed against her skin. She pulled him close, arching her body into his, demanding him not to stop. Cira's deep husky voice vibrated against the sensitive skin below her ear, caressing and titillating.

"My Monase, you were made to be loved by a real man, not a grotesque excuse of a man like Jama."

Warning calls screeched through her mind. *Jama, Jama.* She would be ruined. Not even Jama would have her. She struggled to get free, her hands frantic, pulling, pushing at his unyielding weight. Cira only chuckled, a deep rumble against her chest.

"Please," she whispered.

Cira only rolled on top of her, pinning her with a deeper thrust of his knee between her legs. Monase fought the overwhelming desire to melt back into his inviting embrace, to let him carry her away to the delicious bliss he promised. In desperation, she sharply raised a knee, cringing as she felt contact with his hard throbbing manhood. When Cira rolled away with a groan of real pain, she scrambled to her feet. Regret swept over her—for what she'd done, and for what she'd missed. But she couldn't let this man ruin her only chance at marriage, no matter how repulsive the bridegroom. It all seemed so clear to her now, away from his hypnotic eyes and disarming touch. He had probably been informed that he would not receive any part of her lobala, and he meant to deflower her, to gain his vengeance on Jama and her father.

Had he even given any consideration to the fact that once he did so, Jama would reject her and her father would be disgraced? She felt hysterical rage rising in her chest. Her father was a good man, he deserved all the lobala she could bring. She stared down at Cira with naked hatred. Throwing back her shoulders, she straightened her skirt and pulled the grass and debris from her hair. She opened her mouth to spit a curse at the still-moaning Cira, but could only gather enough moisture in her mouth to emit a weak hiss. Whirling, she stalked off toward her kraal.

Cira lay on the ground, his groin aching. But this pain was rivaled by another much more poignant one in his heart. Never had such hatred and loathing been directed at him. Even the impi he had defeated in battle did not reveal such unadulterated hate. Slowly raising himself on one knee, he studied Monase's retreating figure. She had responded with such unrestrained passion; she had been enjoying herself. He had begun to believe his assumption about her had been wrong, that perhaps she wanted him as he did her. With a grimace, he pulled himself to his feet. No, she had tricked him once again. He didn't know what her game was, but he was not going to be her dupe again.

He'd marry her, because he had to. He would not insult Shaka's gift to him, but he'd be damned before he'd touch her again. She could experience the humiliating shame of being an unwanted, untouched wife. He would take many women, flaunt them before her. But he would kill any man she sought out, witch doctor or chief. She was his woman, his property. She would crawl to him, begging for his touch.

Yes, that was how he'd teach her, Cira thought, tossing his unruly mane, drawing his mouth in a tight line. He must resist her; she would bewitch him no more. Slowly a sly smile curved his lips. He would make her crawl to him. She would offer him her body, her heart—his smile grew wider—she'd offer her very spirit—

Suddenly his smile wilted as he realized with irritation that he would settle for nothing less than *her* spirit . . . since she already had a firm hold on his.

Ten

Northeasterly winds swept through the Zululand valley, bringing with them the promise of much-longed-for rains. In the early evenings, the thunder rumbled in the distance as dark, ominous clouds rimmed in gold and pink hung over the mountains. An occasional eerie greenish light would enshroud the surrounding bush and ocean, hushing the wildlife for its duration.

Monase found herself jumping in fearful anticipation at the sound of every male voice. Since her last encounter with Cira, he had not sought her out. She tried to keep her mind and hands occupied with the enormous task of preparing for the impending rainy-season ceremony. Everywhere, the village was alive with excitement. Her father worked diligently on a new cattle pen for the pledged lobala cattle. Her mother sewed tirelessly on an intricately beaded belt, necklace, and hat for Monase's wedding. Niamani had long ago given up trying to persuade Monase to join her in this work. Instead she allowed her daughter to do the more difficult labor in the field. Every afternoon, Mkabuyi pleaded with Monase to lend her beautiful voice to the chorus of women rehearsing for the impi honors awards. Monase always refused, seeking to stay as far away from the festivities, and their painful reminder of her upcoming nuptials. Instead, when she finished her labors in her own field, she would offer her help in the other fields.

One afternoon, as she worked in a field close to the palisade, she heard the faint notes of the practicing women, their voices rising and falling with songs about the deeds of Shaka's brave warriors. Unconsciously, Monase began to hum the tune, her ax rising and falling with the beat of the drums. Unable to hear the exact words, she began to make up her own.

Suddenly, like a dam whose logs have given way, the solace of song flooded through her. At first her words were an echo of the backbreaking labor in the field. Then the words assumed a life of their own. She sang of the drudgery of day-to-day living, the hope for tomorrow. The dream of happiness, love, and children. Then her voice rose in sorrow, and she sang a heart-piercing song of lost love and innocence. Monase was unaware of the other women in the fields stopping to stare at her and listen. One elderly woman sighed a deep sigh, which seemed to be dragged up from the depths of her being. She joined her voice with Monase's in a soft lilting harmony of nonsensical words, sounding like the fall of a gentle rain. Monase turned toward the woman without halting, rewarding her with a tearful sad smile. Hesitantly, the other women began to add their voices to the song. The song brought the rehearsing women from the palisade. They, too, joined in the chorus, slapping their thighs softly in time. Monase raised her voice to the sky.

The singing drifted hauntingly across the field, slipping through the open doorways of the closest hut, drawing the inhabitants outside. Still, Monase sang, her voice strong and clear. She was so wrapped up in her song that she did not see the crowd gathering. The people whispered in approval. They asked why such an exquisite voice had not been heard before this, and wondered if she was going to sing for the ceremonies.

Meanwhile, Punga found yet another excuse to visit Ugebula's kraal. He hemmed and hawed over some idea for a new tip for a spear. Cira smiled as he nodded his permission, knowing full well that his old friend was hoping to run into Mkabuyi. Once his request had been granted, Punga nearly ran from the barracks, afraid that Cira might change his mind. He was arrested by the sad, beautiful singing rising from the fields. He swerved from his path, catching sight of the large crowd. With his enormous height, he was able to see clearly over the heads of the group.

His mouth dropped open as he beheld the women encircling the lone figure of Monase. She stood with her face to the sky, her outreaching hands, palms up, fingers curled, beseeching the heavens. He noticed the fat tears rolling down her cheeks. He paused to listen, the song twisting uncomfortably in his chest. Then he turned and ran back to the barracks, Mkabuyi forgotten.

"Cira, come quickly." He didn't know why he felt Cira should see and hear Monase, and didn't pause to think that perhaps it was a mistake. All Punga knew was that what he had witnessed was something beautiful and moving, that its source was Cira's betrothed, and that Cira should experience it himself.

Cira moved rapidly after Punga, the unasked question halted by the odd disturbed look on Punga's face. He knew he had to follow. Breathless, they stopped at the outskirts of an ever-growing crowd. Cira heard the music, wafting over him. The melancholy words stirred something deep within. He felt the thick scarred walls around his heart begin to crumble as memories of the same deep sadness and loss ripped through his chest. Clutching his heart, he brusquely shouldered his way through the audience. The pain deepened, twisting sharply, unmercifully, as his eyes fell on the now kneeling figure of Monase. Again his senses were assaulted by the naked torment of her words and pose.

He caught his breath. Had he truly caused her such sorrow? Her words of lost innocence, of the abandoned happiness of childhood, were more than he could bear.

Fight them though he might, the memories swirled about him, of Cira the small boy crying out the same hopelessly desperate plea as his struggling mother was dragged from the hut in the fierce jaw of a hyena. She had been small, barely more than eight stones. Her cries of pleading terror had ripped through the stunned silence. "It carries me. It has put me down." Even in her hour of desperation, she had remembered to recite the chant, to let any follower know when the beast rested, and was most vulnerable. But no one had dared to follow. The animal had been hideously large, and hungry. A few who had heard the cries had banged loudly on drums, hoping to scare off the animal. Cira had tried to run after her outstretched arms. He could envision her face. The eyes round with pain and horror. Her mouth a deep dark hole, twisted, screaming. Hands had held him back. Helpless, he watched.

Then his father had come. His father had cried out in anguish and followed after the vicious thief. Relief had momentarily calmed him. His father would save her. Surely his father would save her. He had not. Days later, his father had returned, alone. He was dirty, ragged, hopeless. He had aged a hundred years. His shoulders slumped dejectedly, his hands clutched a bloody tattered piece of hide. He looked with hollow eyes past his only son. Neither of his parents ever really returned. His father was just a shell of the man he had once been. Cira watched him shrivel up and die before his young eyes. Day after day his father sat in the dark cold hut, smoking a strange, sweet, intoxicating substance in his wooden pipe. He drank little, and ate even less, his lost love, and loneliness, eating him slowly like a growing cancer.

From this time onward, Cira, no more than six seasons, grew up fast. He hunted, and fended for himself, and his father. At night he would crouch down in the cold, damp, fireless hovel and swear he would never love anyone again. He would not allow anyone to abandon him again. Then, one night, his father had disappeared. He had just gotten up and left, like a wounded animal gone off alone to die. He never came back. The new sense of loss had washed over Cira afresh. He had wanted to die, too, but his healthy young body refused to die of a broken heart. Instead he grew strong, hard, and distant. They had called him "the mountain." Only Shaka had recognized the tortured child, so like himself. He had saved him, made him strong . . . helped him bury the past.

But now the past had come back to haunt him. This time he was strong, a full-grown man. He could not ignore this woman, his love, his future wife's desperate plea for help. He broke free of the huddled crowd. His eyes trained on Monase. The afternoon sky roiled about her, threatening clouds of purple and gray. In the distance, thunder rumbled. A wind tossed the golden sheaves of maize about her. A single ray of sun sliced through the clouds, highlighting Monase's forlorn profile. She didn't turn, didn't move. Cira swept her dejected, spent body into his arms. She lay there limp, beyond caring, as he carried her through the parted crowd.

Cira walked with his eyes straight ahead, not daring to look at her. Confusion and doubt gnawed at his mind. He would think about what he was doing later. Sometimes a man had to do what his gut told him to do, no matter the consequences. And now this hurting woman needed him. He couldn't think about his promise, not now. Not while the hyenas were so close.

The stunned crowd suddenly broke into applause. Men hooted, and the women clacked their tongues, urging them on. A shrill challenging voice called after them.

"Choose, choose, the one you love the best." The group roared in appreciative laughter. Amusement rippled through the happy people as they returned to their recently abandoned jobs. Punga stood scratching his head, then turned to find Ugebula and Mkabuyi.

The loud cries had shaken Monase from her reverie. She felt a hot flush of embarrassment and excitement flow through her body, enflaming her cheeks. She was shocked that the tribe had encouraged Cira to take her away to play kana when in less than two days she was to become another man's bride. Shyly she raised her eyes to Cira's strong chin. Twice before she had been in his strong arms, and she had rebuked him. She had fought the strange exciting feelings he evoked in her. But now, oddly, she felt safe. His strong muscular arms held her high above the lapping flames of tomorrow. She knew that whatever he wanted, this time she would not refuse him. No matter the consequences, she could resist him no more.

Lowering Monase's feet to the ground, Cira entwined his fingers with hers. Without looking at her, he dropped to the ground and entered a large, unfamiliar hut. Nervously, Monase sought to untangle her fingers from his. In response, he tightened his grip. As he crawled through the entrance, his voice was low and strained, lending it a vulnerable quality.

"Do not resist me this time . . . please." Monase followed him meekly, amazed and shaken by the gentle words. With a single turn of her head, she gazed around, a tight knot of fear in her stomach. She did not see Jama. Closing her eyes, she entered the dark cool shadow of the doorway.

Tentatively, she opened one eye, then the other. She shivered and wrapped her arms around her body. Afraid of what she might see in Cira's eyes, she let her eyes wander around the unadorned hut. The walls were bare; only a few wooden pegs dotted the periphery. The thatch of the walls smelled new, fresh, free of smoke. Her mind unconsciously registered these things, but her main focus was on her fearful anticipation of what would come next. Squaring her shoulders for an onslaught of abuse, she wondered which was more formidable: an enraged powerful witch doctor, or a vengeful truculent impi.

As the silence persisted she searched about for something to say. Her eyes lit on the lavish, plush furs that lined the floor. Stroking a satiny leopard skin, she caught her bottom lip between her teeth and raised her eyes to Cira's.

"The floor is covered with fine furs?" The question hung awkwardly, drifting, then falling flat in the silence. Monase continued making small circular motions through the furs. She watched as Cira stooped to light a fire in the hearth. He fanned the small sparks with his hand, causing his muscles to ripple. The flames outlined his creased brow, the small twitch in his jaw, but left his eyes shadowed, unreadable. The silence stretched between them. Several times Monase opened her mouth to speak, to ease the strain, but instead, she swallowed unsteadily, lost for words. Suddenly Cira released a deep chuckle. Monase's eyes darted to his face. Still, he toyed with the fire.

"They are the finest. Go on, stretch out on them, feel their softness." His voice was soft, low, inviting. Monase ceased stroking the fur, wariness tightening the skin about her eyes. Again his low voice sounded. Softer, but determined.

"Lie down."

The familiar tingle of excitement and fear surged through her. She remained seated. Cira glanced over at her, then returned to the fire.

"I won't touch you, I promise . . . not until you want me to." His words had a hard resigned edge to them.

Monase hesitated, then shook her head. "I'm fine. Maybe I'd better go."

Cira now turned, his full attention on her. "No." Silence; then: "We need to talk." He moved closer.

Monase felt her heart race. Her adrenaline flowed like fire through her veins. Yet she sat frozen, like a small animal waiting for the kill.

Cira stopped, his voice weary, anguished. "Do you hate me then so very much?"

Monase blinked her eyes hard several times, willing her tears to stay at bay. A single tear shimmered down her cheek, catching at the corner of her nose. She raised her hand to brush it away, but it was stopped by Cira's. Catching her wrist gently in his fist, he ran the rough callused pad of his forefinger along the silvered tear track. His thumb hooked under her chin, drawing her gaze up to meet his. His finger pivoted, sliding down her cheek and across her chin, down her jawline. Slowly, seductively, he ran his thumb along the stretched cords of her throat. She closed her eyes, letting the hypnotic motion calm her fears. She swayed slightly, lifting her chin higher. He released her wrist and began a slow methodical stroking of her temple, stopping occasionally to trace the outline of her ear, her jaw, her lips. His voice flowed over her like warm oil.

"Who has hurt you, little one?" His voice broke. "Have I caused you so much pain?"

Monase opened her eyes, stunned by the grief and distress pouring from his. She raised her hands, capturing his wrists. His hands stilled. She released a deep ragged sigh and leaned forward, resting her forehead against his chest. She shuddered as he drew her into his warm embrace. She shook her head no, unable to form words to answer his questions.

"Then why the tears? Why the sorrow, and the sad song?" One large hand stroked her spine, sending familiar tingles vibrating through every nerve in her body. The other hand rested lightly on her hip, making small circles in the hollow there. Softly, he kissed the top of her head. With a voice that belied her true feelings, Monase placed a hand upon his chest, separating their warm skin.

"This is not right." Her voice was nothing more than a plaintive whisper.

Cira pulled her tighter as he kissed her cheekbone, then her eyelid. His breath was warm upon her skin, his voice tickling her.

"The wedding night is only two nights away."

He pulled back. "Is that what is bothering you?" His eyes burned bright with tentative hope.

Monase gasped, the tears no longer in check. Savage sobs racked her body. The tenuous light in Cira's eyes shattered, falling into dark pools of dismal rejection. Still he held her. A strange feeling wrapped around him. This time he was not angry, just tired, bone-tired. He cradled her trembling body against him, attempting to ease her sadness, to stave off the dark despair welling inside of himself. He had lost, been abandoned before ever being really found. He'd taken a chance, and lost. He had hoped her refusal stemmed from her fear of impropriety, not from a desire for the status Jama offered. Silently, he cursed his weak resolve. Unable to break away, he simply held her.

Monase relaxed against him, drinking in the warm security of his embrace, her eyelids heavy with unshed tears, and with the weight of weeks of sleepless nights. She turned her head, her cheek resting against the steady beating of his heart. The sound, and the gentle unthreatening movements of his hands, lulled her into a dreamless slumber.

As the dappled shadows of evening melted into the long blue silhouettes of moonlight, Cira continued to hold her, and let her sleep. The small flame on the hearth sputtered and died. A cold breeze whistled in through the partially open doorway. Pressing one last kiss on Monase's sleeping brow, he laid her down upon the furs. She murmured softly in her sleep. Cira ran his gaze down her lean supple body before drawing a large brown hide over her. Pulling away, he lingered, wondering at his actions.

What had come over him? Here he was being a nursemaid to a woman, his future wife. She should be waiting on him. He pushed the irritation, and the thought that had provoked it, from his mind, unwilling to break the spell just yet. At this moment he felt content, even happy. There was no denying the fact that he still desired her, ached to feel her body writhing beneath his. But there was more. He wanted this. To just hold her, to protect her, to make her happy. He dropped his head into his hands. But how could he make her happy when she thought only of that medicine man? Slowly he rubbed his long fingers along his temples, massaging the flesh, willing the motion to give him some answers.

Why did she want Jama? He was repulsive by anyone's standards. His overpowering evil was at odds with Monase's sweet innocence. Yes, he was powerful, rich, and any wife would enjoy great status. But still, Cira wondered. When he really looked at the situation, he could not see Monase as such a shallow creature, interested only in material wealth. Bending over the hearth, he stoked the glowing embers, tossing a few fragrant sandalwood branches on the growing flames. Turning his head, he watched the firelight flicker across Monase's peaceful visage. Crawling closer, he chuckled at her sleep-slack mouth, her lips making a round pink "O." Her lashes were thick and sooty, elongated by the shadows. He touched a finger on the dried salty tear track alongside her nose.

Monase twitched her nose, her hand moving ineffectually beneath the hide, as if to brush away a pest.

Cira's eyes darkened as he followed the movement. Inadvertently, her hand had dislodged the covers, revealing the generous curve of a breast. He leaned toward her, his eyes following the arch, squinting into the folds to see it dome to a barely revealed dark crest. As he drew in a deep breath and held it, he was conscious of the growing demand within his body. His hand lingered above her, aching to capture that soft enticing dome. Monase tossed restlessly, flinging the hide about her.

"Jama?"

Cira snatched back his hand as if he had been burned. Even in her sleep she thought of him. His throat constricted, making it painful to swallow. With eyes narrowed, he fell back on his haunches. She had destroyed the peace. He must leave. Silently he turned and exited, not hearing her last whispered cries for him.

Several hours later Monase awoke with a start. The fire had died down again. Only the warm scent of sandalwood remained. Sometime during the hours she had slept, the wind had picked up, beating severely against the sturdy hut.

Instinctively, Monase drew her coverings closer. Lying very still, she tried to clear her sleep-fogged mind. Where was she? Whose home was this? Slowly, the petals of realization unfurled before her, releasing the memories of the day, waving them clearly before her eyes. She bolted upright, in a panic. Frenzied terror gripped her chest.

What had she done? She remembered Cira's embrace. His lazy seductive strokes. She whipped the blanket from her, gazing in relief at her intact skirt. The relief was quickly replaced by shameful disappointment. She remembered her wanton submission to Cira's desire for her. Yet now it seemed that he had rejected her. Her brow creased in confusion. Why?

She had had a fitful sleep, her slumber besieged by nightmares. She dreamed that Jama had found her in Cira's embrace. He had screamed in rage, threatening terrible punishment for both of them. Cira had been blown across the hut, writhing in agony, his face a gruesome mask of pain, then had curled into a fetal ball, dissolving into a slimy dark substance, staining the earthen floor. . . .

Cira, where was he? The seeming reality of the dream surrounded her again. She must find him. She must assure herself he was okay. She recalled the pain in his eyes when he had asked her about her sorrow. She must explain to him, if she could, why she could not see him anymore. She no longer believed his intentions were malicious. But, most of all, she had to know why he had denied her this time. It would not be an easy question to ask, and probably best left unspoken, but she had to know.

Monase crept out into the starless night. The wind whipped across her face as the clouds scuttled across the misty moon. A fine drizzle sprinkled down on her. With a hasty movement of the back of her hand, she wiped the collecting moisture from her eyes. The kraal was silent. Only gentle plumes of smoke could be seen rising from the hive-shaped huts. In the distance, under the covered palisade, she saw a weak fire flicker beneath the misting rain. As a moth drawn to a flame, she headed to the light.

As she approached she saw the silent training impis. In the darkness, their eyes and teeth gleamed brightly, reflecting the wavering flame. Mesmerized, she watched their graceful bodies move in sync, their muscles rolling smoothly beneath their sweat-glistened ebony skin. Their feet thudded in unison against the wooden surface as they turned together, leaped as one. There must be at least fifty warriors here. Running her eyes along their straining bodies, she recognized Punga, then some of the other men who had escorted her family on the journey from her old home. This was Shaka's Haze, his corps. His chosen ones. Cira's men.

As if in answer to her searching eyes, Cira appeared from behind the company, clad only in a short leopard pelt that hung just below his manhood. Momentarily their eyes met. A tight knot of apprehension and desire contorted within her stomach. Folding her fingers into a fist, she tried to maintain her resolve and wait. She moved closer to the fire and the slight overhang.

With a great rush of exhaled breath, the warriors finished their last exercise. With nothing further to detain him, Cira strode toward her. His eyes were dull, devoid of any emotion. Monase inwardly cringed at his distant expressionless gaze. The air around them was filled with the muted chatter of the men, who splashed water from wooden troughs upon their sweat-drenched skin. Cira stood unmoving before her, his feet wide apart, his brawny arms folded across his chest. Monase was staring, speechless, into his eyes when she heard the sound of harsh laughter erupt behind him. Glad for an excuse to break away from his unnerving blank stare, she flicked her eyes over his shoulder. The men began to chuckle, murmuring knowingly and nodding their heads toward her and Cira. One man called out to Cira.

"She came for more already? Not willing to wait for the marriage bed, eh?"

A hot flush deluged her cheeks. She brought her eyes back to Cira's. His expression had not changed. Monase steeled herself against the need to flee. Her nails pierced the tender skin of her palms, and she swallowed past the immovable lump in her throat. Her mind was racing, searching wildly for a way to begin, when Cira's frigid voice ripped the awkward silence.

"You have words for me, woman?"

Monase stepped back stunned, as if he had directed a blow to her stomach. She had not expected this. She had expected anger, hoped for a trace of the gentleness he had displayed a few hours ago, but not this cold, haughty man.

"I would . . . I'd like to . . . Why?" She stumbled, halted. The words hung in the silence. He offered no assistance. She swallowed hard, and started again. "Why did you leave?" Her hands fluttered restlessly about her, betraying her attempt at composure. Her voice dropped to a low whisper as she began again. "Why didn't you . . ."

The words died as his iron grip wrapped around

her upper arms, pulling her away from his all-too-attentive men. Shocked, Monase continued to stare at his long fingers encasing her arms.

"I thought you'd be relieved, that I respected your virtuous wish to wait until the wedding night." His voice no more than a whisper, hammered against her ears. Her eyes snapped to his. "But make no mistake, you are to be my wife. Although I cannot stop you from dreaming of . . . Jama"—he spat the name in disgust—"I will not stand for any mention of his name from your lips."

Monase's knees buckled beneath her. Only his strong grip kept her from falling. Brief surprise registered in his eyes, before they resumed their lackluster glare.

Then, abruptly, he turned on his heels and strolled back to his waiting men.

Monase stood rooted, unable to move. Could it possibly be true? Everything she had wanted had been within her grasp? But she had thrown it all away. All the pieces now fell into place. She had been a blind fool.

She cried out, "Cira." A forlorn plea floating through the night.

Cira halted, not turning, then resumed his determined stride. Monase looked hopelessly at his departing back. She raised a limp hand, getting only as far as her waist before it dropped back to dangle uselessly at her side. She turned, then turned back. Her mouth moved, but no words issued forth. Blindly, she stumbled away, unaware that the skies had opened, sending a deluge of rain. A crack of lightning illuminated the night.

Feigning nonchalance, Cira glanced back over his shoulder toward her soaked figure silhouetted by the streaks of light in the sky. He noticed her slumped, dejected shoulders, her aimless progress. Silently, he berated himself for the tender concern he felt stirring for her in his chest. Still, he could not shake this feeling that something was not right. The look in her eyes, her silence . . . the tone in her voice when she had called to him just now. This time she had not fought him with the angry indignation that he had expected. She had not resisted his embrace as he had held her.

He squinted again into the darkness. He could barely make out her outline in the steadily slanting rain. He caught his breath, saw her stumble, then go down. When she did not rise, Cira's heart slammed against his chest. Growling a low curse beneath his breath, he grabbed his fur cape and started after her.

Monase felt the sodden earth beneath her fingers. She watched the rich red clay ooze over them. The rain streamed down her face, gluing her long lashes to her cheeks. *You've lost him. You've lost him.* The words rang heartlessly over and over in her head. A dry sob seized her chest, squeezing, unrelenting. Turning her face to the torrent of rain, she gasped for air, for relief from this unbearable pressure mounting inside of her.

Suddenly out of the darkness, as if in answer to her unformed prayers, strong sturdy arms swept her up and pressed her against a warm familiar chest. Cira hastily wrapped his fur cape around her trembling body. Monase clung to him. The tears that had eluded her before came in a downpour. Her lips moved wordlessly against his rain-slick chest. Cira clutched her to him, carrying her with long purposeful strides to their new home.

They entered the dark cold hut, and Monase shivered beneath Cira's drenched cape. Huddling, she watched him stoke the fire, bringing it to life once more. She sniffed softly as her teeth began to chatter.

"You'd better get out of those wet things and cover up with some dry hides." His voice was gruff with concern as the words floated over his shoulders to her.

Wordlessly Monase obeyed. She continued to watch his intense preoccupation with the fire. His movements were slow, determined. The silence remained, broken only by the crackle of the flames and the snap of dry twigs beneath his strong fingers.

After what seemed an interminably long time, he turned to face her. His eyes were dark, unreadable. Monase lowered her eyes and began stroking the soft hide wrapped around her shoulders. Intently, she studied the dark ridges her movements made. Cira stared silently at her for a long time. Then she heard his weight shift. Daring to look up only as far as his legs, she saw him settle on a small wooden three-legged stool by the wall. Grunting, he sprawled his long muscular legs before him, his toes barely touching the edge of the fur where she sat. Monase nibbled lightly at the inside of her lip as she allowed her gaze to continue traveling up over the long rugged length of him. His arms were folded loosely over his burly chest, a barrier between them. Hesitating, she forced her eyes to meet his. They caught, and held. His voice came simply and softly.

"Tell me."

Monase turned her head to look away, but still their eyes held fast. She opened her mouth to speak, but instead swallowed a gulp of the smoky air. Running her open palm down her face, she sought to break the magnetic hold his eyes had on her. But again, they were riveted on his.

"I thought I was to wed—" She paused. He nodded, urging her on. She continued. "To wed Jama." The words were low and soft, but they echoed harshly in the stillness. Cira waited in silent expectation. Monase's brown eyes flickered rapidly from one tawny eye to another, trying to read what lay there. What more did he want her to say? "I am to marry you?"

Cira nodded yes, in answer to her question.

"I did not know . . . I did not believe . . . In my clan, my old clan, no man wanted me." She looked down, embarrassed at this admission. "No one but Jama." Suddenly her eyes looked up imploring. "I will be a good wife . . . I will obey . . . I don't know much." Her hand gestured toward the furs about her. "Please don't turn me away . . . to become Jama's wife."

Cira leaned forward, his eyes narrow slits of amber. If she was lying, she was good, damn good.

"You mean to tell me you have no desire to marry the medicine man?"

Monase shook her head vigorously, the precariously perched tears flying free. One landed on Cira's folded forearm. He bent his head to look at it. Slowly unwinding his arms, he gathered the sparkling drop on his finger. With a slow deliberateness, he rubbed it between his thumb and forefinger. When he raised his head again, his eyes glinted at her with suspicion. "Why then did you refuse me?"

Monase felt the blood rush to her cheeks, as she lowered her eyes. "It would not be right."

Cira responded with a curt disbelieving laugh. "Surely you don't expect me to believe that you have never engaged in kana."

The mirthless sound sent a shiver down her spine. Still she refused to meet his eyes. She only shook her head, tears of humiliation sliding down her cheeks. The silence that ensued was deafening. Suddenly a creak in the wood of the stool told her that Cira had shifted. The small hairs on the nape of her neck rose as she felt his warm breath caress her there.

"With your beauty, I'm sure you must have had many willing partners choose you for love play." His voice was low and husky, sending rampant flames through her already heated blood. She gripped her hands together, wringing them until the knuckles turned white.

"No, never," she croaked, her mouth exceedingly dry. Slowly, she raised her eyes to see his widen appreciatively. He reached out to touch the hide wrapped around her shoulder.

"You are telling me," Cira began as he held her chin with one hand and peeled the hide back across her shoulder with the other, "no man has ever caressed this golden skin?" He ran a finger from the nape of her neck to her shoulder, her skin feeling seared by his touch. She sucked in her breath, holding it, and shook her head from side to side. He drew nearer, his eyes lazy, seductive. Her heart hammered against her breastbone. Cira's left hand dragged slowly, sensuously back across her shoulder, dipping down into the shadowed valley between her breasts.

"No man before me has fondled these breasts, to drink of their sweetness?" Her nipples hardened in response to the gentle fingers that encircled them. His questions now became an exquisite torment as she arched toward him. His eyes became burning embers beneath his hooded lids. He pulled her toward him, catching her breast up high in his splayed hand. His mouth descended moist and warm upon her parted willing lips. His words were muffled in the embrace.

"No man has drunk of . . ." His tongue plunged inside, meeting her tongue, tasting, exploring, demanding. His right hand slid from her chin, running the length of her back, pressing her deeper against him.

A small moan escaped Monase's lips as Cira lowered his searching mouth to her straining nipples. His tongue made small wet circles around the dark areolas, then gently touched the tip of the erect nipples. He blew softly on their damp surface, enticing them to grow harder, to seek the warmth of his mouth. With a low, deep chuckle, Cira drew back his tongue, running his teeth delicately along the rim of her nipples. Monase whimpered. Cupping her hands behind his head, she pushed him against her. Relenting, Cira pulled the whole demanding nipple into his mouth, suckling hungrily.

There would be no stopping now. Monase lowered her hands, grasping his broad shoulders, sinking her nails into the hard muscles beneath. Cira groaned, lowering her, pressing her back into the plush fur. The hide slipped away as he ground his throbbing manhood into her naked hip. Only the thin pelt of his loincloth separated their heated flesh. As his mouth descended down her ribs to her flat stomach, she lost her grip on his shoulders, instead immersing her fingers in his hair.

His tongue made delicious circles around her navel, then moved onward, making her body quiver with undeniable need. She heard Cira's soft chuckle warm against the skin of her abdomen as his hands slid up her inner thighs, separating them, preparing her for him. As his tongue lashed across the swollen lips of her womanhood, she bucked upward, his touch electrifying. Cira grasped her buttocks, keeping her hips high, draping her legs around his shoulders. His mouth drained her, making her wriggle in ecstasy. She tossed her head from side to side in wild abandon. She had never imagined this. When she could stand no more, she tugged viciously at his locks, forcing him to cease his exquisite torture.

Teasingly, he rose slowly, his kisses ascending, leaving a burning trail in their wake. Then he paused, and his rough scratchy cheek rested upon her breasts. Again, with his finger he drew lazy circles around their circumference. As her nipples hardened he raised his head to look into her eyes. He watched her face as he rolled the nub between his forefinger and thumb, a wickedly mischievous smile curving his lips. Rolling to his side, he propped his head upon his other hand. His eyes never left hers as his fingers ran lightly over the trail his kisses had just made. She gasped as they rounded the dark nest of her feminine hair. Briefly he toyed with the black curls, then his palm cupped the moist triangle. Slowly he rotated the heel of his hand, and Monase arched upward to greet him. His smile deepened, his hooded eyes crinkling at the corners. One, then two fingers slid into her dark moist womanhood.

Monase released a strangled cry as she crimped her eyes closed. Delirious pleasure washed over her, but still she yearned for more. She opened her eyes, staring questioningly into Cira's. His hand left her as he pulled her close. His voice was gruff, yet tender, when he spoke.

"Yes, little one, there is more. . . . Do you want me to wait until the wedding night?"

Monase hugged him tight in response. Her hand gliding downward, timid at first, then bolder. She wrapped her hand around him, amazed at his size.

Now Cira gasped, his voice broken, husky. "Oh, Monase, my sweet Monase. How long I have wanted you. I will try not to hurt you." He pushed her gently away, looking deep into her yearning eyes. "Stop me if I hurt you."

She nodded silently as he gathered her again in his strong embrace. Releasing her, he wedged his knee between her legs, moving them apart. Willingly, she let him, her heart beating rapidly in anticipation. Kneeling between her spread legs, he traced the outline of her full breast, her flat belly, her rounded hips. Lovingly, he stroked the inside of her thighs. She shuddered. Gently he lowered himself upon her, his manhood gliding smoothly over the moist surface of her upper thigh. Slowly, he entered. She fixed her eyes on his, fingers gripping his rib cage. He panted above her, struggling to contain the longing and passion bursting inside of him. He kissed her softly, then more hungrily, as he slid the whole length of himself within her.

She momentarily froze as she felt her maidenhood give way. The pain ripped through her, causing her fingers to dig deeply into his flesh, pressing against the bone. Cira began to withdraw. Monase, the initial sharp pain receding, clung to him. She wrapped her long lean legs around his waist, refusing to let him go. He plunged into her again; this time there was no pain, only the beginning of a burning, all-consuming fire. Again and again he rose and fell, the friction igniting a flame that scorched and exhilarated them. She rose higher, higher, finally bursting in an explosion of light and sound.

Somewhere amid her cries, Cira stiffened, and throwing back his head in exultation, he matched her cries, spilling his seeds within her. Spent, exhausted, their bodies intimately entwined, they slept. Monase's spirits soared as she thought of the lifetime of such nights ahead of her.

When Monase awoke, it was another gray dismal day, but she felt like singing. Cira had already left for the training grounds, and she gently rubbed the crushed furs where his body had lain next to hers. With a sigh, she stretched out, luxuriating on the soft pelts. In her mind, she spread the treasured memories of last night before her. Again she sighed as she tossed her covers to the side. Humming, she splashed some rainwater on her face from a clay pot outside. Turning her face to the dreary sky, she smiled, hugging herself. In less than two days she would officially be Cira's wife. She whirled around, unable to contain her glee. She happily raced over to her mother's hut to help with the finishing touches on her wedding garb. She wanted to be absolutely beautiful for Cira.

As Monase rounded the corner, whistling, her kneeling mother looked up in surprise.

"And where would a single maiden have spent a whole night away from her mother's watchful eye?"

A blush crept up Monase's shining cheeks at her mother's words.

"I see. It would seem our reluctant bride has abandoned her wailing for the days of innocence." Her mother clicked her tongue in playful admonishment. Monase smiled, falling to her knees to hug her tenderly. Niamani pulled back, suddenly uncomfortable with this unusually bold display of affection. But her smile remained as she rose to balance the pots, full of the night rain, on her head.

"Come, join us in the preparations for the festivities." With a smile, Monase picked up another pot and followed her mother.

The other women were surprised to see Monase and whispered among themselves. As the day wore on they were delighted to find this previously sullen girl talkative and friendly. By midafternoon, one woman ventured to ask if the gifted girl would join in the singing for the ceremonies, and perhaps even create her own song. Monase astonished the women by avidly agreeing. The day flew by, its moments filled with the delicate golden glow of her happiness. Her only regret was that she didn't catch a glimpse of Cira.

Later that evening Monase hovered outside the training field, anxious to see Cira again. A warm tingle skittered up her spine as two familiar arms wrapped around her from behind. She turned in his embrace, her eyes sparkling with delight.

"I didn't get to see you all day," she cried with a false pout.

Cira, laughing, crushed her to his chest. She smiled, the deep rumble tickling her cheek where it rested upon his skin. Releasing her, he placed a chaste kiss upon her brow.

"I must stay away from you, if I am to honor your virtuous nature and wait until we are wed."

Monase dropped her eyes, blushing, as she dug one of her toes into the soft dirt. Again Cira laughed. Reaching out, he lifted the colorful beads around her neck. His fingers fluttered suggestively against the skin below her collarbone. Flashing her a brilliant smile, he released them and hurried off to join his men. Monase watched him go. Clutching the beads which were still warm from his touch, she felt as if her heart would burst with happiness.

The morning before the long-awaited day dawned with an ominous red sky. The elders of the tribe whispered among themselves that it was a warning from the ancestors. Monase refused to let the unrest destroy her joyful mood.

"Come," she called to Mkabuyi. "Help me bring my belongings to my new home." Together they crossed the wide main avenue Shaka had built to parade his prized white cattle and brave impi. Happily they chatted, excited about the upcoming ceremonies and nuptials.

As they approached the hut Mkabuyi cried out, "Oh, Monase, what a beautiful hut." She waved her arms around her. "You even have sandalwood trees right outside your door." She paused, crouching just beyond the entrance. "Oh, what beautiful flowers. Cira has left you a basket full of the most beautiful, fragrant red blossoms. I wonder what they are?"

Tears of disbelieving happiness welled up in Monase's eyes. "They are umsinsi blossoms," she whispered.

Mkabuyi halted, a bloom halfway to her nose. "Is everything all right?"

Monase nodded, a tear rolling down her cheek. "It couldn't be righter," she responded with feeling.

Mkabuyi smiled, shaking her head in wonder at her sister's ever-changing moods.

Lifting the basket, Monase bent to enter the doorway. She froze. The basket dropped from her hands, spilling the ruby flowers across the floor. Her hand flew to her mouth, barring a scream that would have escaped. On the hearth lay a large pale snake, its silvery scales gleaming eerily in the darkness. Mkabuyi ducked her head in the opening, trying to see what had rendered her sister speechless. Monase's voice was hollow as she backed away.

"It is an ancestor come to warn us. But why my bridal home?" She wrung her hands as she turned pleading eyes to her sister. "Why? What do you think it has to say?"

Mkabuyi wrapped a gentle arm around her sister's shoulder, drawing her from the hut. "Perhaps he has come to bless your marriage bed." The words sounded false, empty. Both women were silent as they remembered another silver snake upon another hearth.

Just such a snake had slithered across the threshold of her mother's hut when she was heavy with her unborn son. For two days her sisters, mother, and Monase herself had stayed outside the hut, awaiting the ancestor's departure. As was custom, no human being was permitted to share the same shelter with an ancestor. When the all-seeing isangoma arrived, she had placed a hand on Niamani's swollen belly, her eyes grave, as she shook her head sadly. Niamani, whispering like a wounded animal, wrapped her arms protectively around her burgeoning middle, her tears rolling down the deep creases alongside her nose and mouth. The next day her son was born dead. The baby had been buried, and at last the snake departed.

Picking up Monase's scattered belongings, Mkabuyi turned to lay a gentle hand on her rigid shoulder. "Come now. We will get Mother, she will know what to do."

In a trance, Monase followed her. Over and over she repeated the falsely hopeful words Mkabuyi had offered. She willed herself to believe that the omen was positive, but a deep-rooted dread spread dark shadows of foreboding.

Sadly, Niamani was unable to offer any relief to Monase's growing fears. When told about the appearances of the snake, she, too, had grown pale, urging Monase to come with her to the Zulu isangoma. Suddenly the day seemed intolerably cold and dark. The awful snake that had turned her mother to a hard bitter woman had now returned to darken her daughter's future as well. Bowing her head, Monase feverishly prayed to the spirit of her grandmother to help her remain calm as she faced this threatening calamity.

The isangoma was an old woman, over seventy seasons. Upon hearing Niamani's account of the snake's visitations, she bent slowly to gather a few carved sticks and a worn leather pouch. Placing a gnarled hand at the base of her spine, she straightened, waving her hand in front of her, motioning for Monase to lead the way.

It seemed an eternity to Monase, her mother, and her sister, as they waited outside the hut while the woman communicated with the snake. On the threshold of the doorway, the old woman sprinkled some finely ground powder. Then her fingers tightened on the intricately carved sticks she held in her hands, and she shook them. Next, crouching down, she opened her hand to let the sticks roll off her flattened palm. As they fell to the ground she called out in a low monotone voice to the ancestors of old. In the silence that followed her words, Monase heard the breeze ruffle through the few remaining sandalwood leaves above her head.

Then all was still, and the woman rose to face them. Her wrinkled face showed no expression, hopeful or fearful, but her dark eyes glittered dangerously. Without a word, the isangoma moved forward, touching Monase's cheek with a dry brittle finger. The finger slid across her young fresh skin, then curled into a hook, beckoning the girl to follow. Monase shuddered, fear flickering through her mind. They all rose to follow the woman, her heart heavy with foreboding.

Monase crossed the distance to Shaka's great house, which was called Ndhlunkula. As she walked, her hands unconsciously twisted the beads at her throat, fighting down the fear and anxiety that threatened to reduce her to hysteria. She'd been through too much already; this waiting was unbearable. She wanted to scream out, *"Tell me what it all means."*

Monase was so lost in thought that she failed even to notice when they had stopped outside of Ndhlunkula. Niamani gasped in horror at the significance of their presence here: the great Chief Shaka was being involved in her family's personal affairs. At the sound of her mother, Monase snapped out of her deep reverie and saw the chief leaving his great house. She knew the name of his hut meant "forbidden ground." One of the first things she had learned upon arriving in Zululand was that few people entered Ndhlunkulu, and among those, even fewer left it alive. Even now, in the broad light of the day, ten fierce-looking impi patrolled its perimeter, fully armed.

The isangoma crossed the short distance to Shaka, her eyes respectfully lowered. Shaka stood towering above her hunched figure, his eyes straight ahead, unseeing. The woman approached a guard. The man leaned close as she muttered a few words. The impi pulled back, shock etched in his face. On bent knee, he bowed before Shaka. No words passed between the men. Shaka studied the man's face, nodded, and then turned to enter the rear entrance of the great meeting palisade.

After this mysterious exchange, the old woman hastened to the palisade's formal entrance. Shaken, Monase hesitated, her eyes wandering to the long row of huts that snaked out from the back of

Shaka's great house. She had not been so close to the palace since that first day, and then she had been too exhausted to pay much attention. In the shadows beside the huts, beautiful young girls with frightened doe eyes gazed out at her, a wistful sadness in their eyes.

As if reading Monase's thoughts, Mkabuyi moved closer to her, gripping her arm. She, too, was watching these beautiful "sisters" of Shaka. Monase turned tender eyes to her cowering sister. A feather of surprise tickled her mind as she realized that even in her innocence, Mkabuyi was aware of the sad plight of these poor captive maidens. How easily she or Mkabuyi could have been among their numbers. Although Shaka claimed them to be sisters, too revered for sexual intimacy with him it was well known that he visited these huts nightly. The most beautiful of the girls were rarely given permission to marry, and when they passed their prime, they where given to Shaka's counselors, like scraps of meat thrown to wild dogs. How fortunate that Monase and her sister had been requested by Punga and Cira as wives.

Cira. Monase glanced around for the isangoma. She must find out what monumental tidings the snake had brought to her and Cira's future home. She shuddered, rushing after the old woman. Why was the great Chief Shaka to be involved?

Trembling at the possibilities, Monase bit her lower lip as she struggled to mask her swirling emotions. She must concentrate, remember the proper protocol. Following the older woman's lead, she turned to face the armed guards. A tall wiry impi grabbed the old woman, stripping her of her hide shawl and her tightly clutched medicine bag. He then lightly ran his fingers over her body, making sure that she bore no weapons, and then with strong hands pushed her forward to her knees. She stumbled slightly, her old bones creaking in protest as she fell.

Monase gasped in amazement at such rough treatment. Only the guards protecting Shaka would have the audacity to treat an isangoma that way. She watched the woman crawl without complaint across the threshold.

She was turning back to the guards when she felt a rough hand jerk her upper arm. She cringed at the insolent leer that wreathed the impi's face. Unlike the quick patting-down that had been done to her companion, the guard ran slow, thorough hands along Monase's body, pausing often. When he reached the hem of her skirt, he paused again, then began moving his hands up underneath the fabric. Monase recoiled in horror. The guard's eyes grew dark and dangerous, his fingers biting into the soft flesh of her thighs, daring her to resist him. Drawing in a deep breath, she swallowed and turned her head away. With a cruel chuckle, his hands continued their upward movement.

"Enough." A deep growl vibrated through the tense silence.

The man halted, then hastily removed his hands from her skin. Monase turned thankful eyes to take in Cira's seething expression. His fists clenched and unclenched in rage. Trembling, the guard stepped a pace backward, throwing up his hands in protest.

"I was only doing my duty. Never can be too sure when it comes to Chief Shaka's safety."

Cira emitted a low warning growl, then grabbed Monase's wrist and pulled her after him into the dark coolness of the shelter. Falling to her elbows and knees, she dared not look back.

This time, unlike the day of her arrival, she was not so brazen as to look up and meet Shaka's eyes. Instead she trained her eyes on Cira's callused feet in front of her, hearing the shuffling and murmurs of the chief and his counselors as they assumed their positions on the raised platform. Only when she had cried her greeting did she dare to look up. She listened as the old woman and Cira sang the songs of praise to Shaka. She remained silent, knowing that she would not be asked to speak. Feeling rather than seeing, she knew no one was behind her, that her mother and sister had not been allowed to enter. She suddenly felt very frightened, and very alone. She turned her eyes to Cira's strong rigid back, hoping to draw some of the strength and comfort that emanated from him.

Shaka nodded as their voices fell silent. The guards around the platform where he sat moved forward, settling the old woman at Shaka's feet. The isangoma began to speak, her voice soft but strong, echoing through the great hall. She told of their ancestors and how they continued to surround the living, seeking shelter in the trees, the winds, and in the bodies of animals. She told of their wisdom and of their desire to warn and protect their descendants. As she had done a hundred times before, she gathered her audience under her hypnotic spell, drawing them forward, their eyes glazed in anticipation. Suddenly dropping her voice to a mere whisper, she raised her arms in a wide arch above her. In the silence that followed, she locked eyes with Shaka, lowering her entwined fingers to her head.

"Today I spoke with a great ancestor of yours. He came as a silver snake to the home of your brave impi Cira." The hairs on Monase's arms and legs bristled at the tone of the old woman's voice, and reluctantly she shifted her eyes from Cira. The woman continued, her hands, now folded, sliding to her sagging bosom. "He says that King Dingoswayo has been betrayed. Slaughtered like a trusting lamb."

At these words, Shaka bolted upright in his seat, his right hand clenching his bronze-tipped spear. Without faltering, the woman's voice droned on. "The greedy beast Zwide now turns towards you, my chief, to rid himself of your claim of succession to the throne."

When Shaka heard these words, his eyes closed in great pain as he slumped back in his chair. Dingoswayo, his mentor, had been more of a father to him then his own father had been. Gritting his teeth, he opened his eyes. Turning to Cira, he beckoned him to approach. Monase's hands twisted in the folds of her skirt as the reality of what had been said and what it meant for Cira sank into her disbelieving mind. Shaka then turned his angry eyes to the isangoma. She continued, her voice unwavering.

"Even as we speak Zwide comes forth, bearing an army of thousands. He plans to kill every Zulu man, woman, and child so that none will remain to claim your bloodline." Finished, the old woman bent, touching her forehead to the ground. Monase stared wide-eyed and horrified at the woman's bowed head.

Shaka turned toward his guards and whispered to two lean men, who were evidently messengers. Instantly the men touched their hearts and took off running. Shaka and his counselors then rose, and Cira followed them out the rear entrance, sparing not even a single glance for Monase.

Stunned, Monase sat staring at the isangoma. Outside she could hear the muffled movements and cries of men and women as the rumor spread like wildfire through the village. Inside, only she and the old woman remained. In silence, their eyes met.

The old woman's were surrounded by years of wisdom, pain, happiness, and sorrow. The young one's were bleak, innocent, and so very frightened.

Monase was only vaguely aware of her surroundings when her mother's arms wrapped around her, pulling her out of the palisade.

"Come, child. We have much to do. The chief has ordered that half his cattle be hidden in the hills, and the other half be slaughtered for food for his warriors." Niamani babbled on, more to herself then to Monase. "If Zwide overpowers us, Shaka wants the man to gain no booty."

She turned her eyes to Monase's blank face and gently touched her cold cheek. "Cira and his men are going ahead, to try to intercept Zwide and his army. Shaka has sent runners to verify the isangoma's words. But now it isn't necessary, a group of scouts from other tribes have arrived, confirming everything."

Monase felt herself falling. She watched her last hope—that the isangoma had somehow misunderstood her oracular promptings—crumble before her. She stumbled alongside her mother, clutching her arms. As they left the meeting hall they were stopped by the impudent guard who had accosted her earlier.

"I'll be seeing you around. Your Cira won't be coming back anytime soon." The man snorted, a crude animalistic sound. Then he turned to his partner, his hand never leaving Monase's arm. "If at all."

It was too much; the words and their meaning ripped through Monase's chest. Clutching her heart, she broke from his grasp. A high keening wail rising from her lips, she ran, blindly fleeing the hideous scene. She had to find Cira, to stop him, to save him.

As she hastened through the paths, all she saw were scenes of pandemonium. Panic permeated the village. Everywhere huge fires were crackling, and the women struggled to erect large spits above them. The air hung heavy with the smell of fresh blood and slaughtered meat. Despite the coolness, swarms of flies hovered, drawn to the stench. The frightened lowing of the cattle drifted eerily above the strained anxious cries of the people.

Ignoring the call to come and help, Monase ran toward the impi barracks. She vaguely knew which one was Cira's, and she moved in that direction with unrestrained speed. She was running so fast and with such desperation that she was unable to stop herself . . . and barreled into Punga's chest when he suddenly stepped from behind a barrack. The bone-jarring impact sent her stumbling.

"Cira?" was all she could gasp. Understanding, Punga mutely pointed to the hut Cira had built for her. Nodding her thanks, she took his hand and he hoisted her to her feet. A sharp cramp sliced through her side as she resumed running. In irritation, she pressed the offending place with her fingers, but refused to stop. She'd seen Punga; Cira couldn't have left yet. *Oh please, let him still be here.*

Outside the hut, Monase fell to her knees, taking in huge gasps of air. Her lungs rebelled, closing tightly against the onslaught, threatening to burst. She forced herself to slow down, to breathe slowly. Her heart knocked loud and painfully against her aching chest. After a few seconds she was able to crawl inside.

The interior of the hut was dark, and Monase felt a pang as she noticed the crushed and wilted coral blossoms lying strewn around the doorway, a painful reminder of a happier time. Reluctantly, she turned her eyes to the hearth; it was cold. The snake had departed, but, it appeared, so had Cira. Her heart plummeted; ragged sobs seized her. Cira had left; she wouldn't even be able to say goodbye, to say the words that he had never said to her.

"I love you." Her whispered words echoed emptily through the hut. Suddenly a small shuffle from the back of the hut caught her ear. She squinted into the darkness, afraid to hope. "Cira?"

A deep sadistic chuckle rose from the shadow. "You love me? Or perhaps it was your future, or maybe not-so-future bridegroom you hoped to meet."

Monase's eyes widened in horrified recognition as the large grotesque figure of Jama moved toward her, and she gasped, covering her mouth with her hand. Her stomach roiled in revolt. How dare this man desecrate her home? Jama moved closer, encircling her narrow wrist with his fat, stubby fingers. As always, his smell was overpowering. She jerked her arm back, hoping to distance herself from this beast, and heard him laugh, a low mirthless sound.

"Your betrothed, or is he your lover?" His eyes narrowed to black glittering slits. "He is brave, or just a fool." His hand released her, but his eyes held her with a demonic hold. Without releasing her eyes, he lit the hearth. "So now he leaves you, unmarried, perhaps with child?"

Monase felt a hot flush scourge her cheeks as she struggled to look away. Jama laughed again, the sound sending shivers down her spine. Never before had she heard such an evil noise.

"What will become of you? When your love doesn't return to make you his wife?" The word *love* rolled from his lips like a crude, sickly thing. To think she was almost betrothed to this hateful man; she cringed at the very notion. Again, Jama moved toward her, not touching, but close enough that his fetid breath fanned across her face.

"You must excuse me. I must go and find him before he goes." Monase scooted backward, on the balls of her feet, ready to spring from the hut, her hand braced on the dirt beside her.

Jama's voice cut across hers like a whip, raw and

stinging. "You will stay." When she didn't move, he grunted his approval. "We have much to talk about, if I am to help you save your . . . love?" Again he spat, the word distasteful in his mouth.

Monase hesitated. "You would help him?"

"Yes . . . I would help *you* for a price."

Monase lowered herself to the ground, folding her hands in her lap. She would do anything to ensure Cira's safety, anything. . . .

As the sun sank quickly behind the foothills, Cira breathed deeply of the crushed umsinsi blossom between his fingers. He welcomed the aromatic relief from the bloody stench filling the evening air. Before, the flower's fragrance had aroused painful memories. Now it brought Monase's beautiful face before him. He saw her smile, then her eyes, hooded with the awakening discovery of passion. She had not said she loved him, but that would come with time. She would be his body, mind, and spirit.

A frown pressed deep upon his brow. Time, if only they were given the time. He was no fool, he knew all too well the dangers he and his men faced. It was probable that at least half of them wouldn't return. This knowledge twisted painfully in his gut. He also knew that one of those men could be him. His stride quickened in response to these thoughts. He couldn't leave Monase to Jama. He recalled her eyes as she pleaded with him to save her from the man. He smiled as he remembered what had followed. He worried that he might have impregnated her, that she might be carrying his child. If he didn't return to marry her, she would be shamed, an unwed mother, perhaps even put to death. He had to get Shaka to bless the marriage, to make it binding before the formal ceremony, before he left.

His stride grew even faster. There wasn't much time; he had to hurry. Maybe he'd even have a moment to see her, and share the happy news before he left. A smile brightened his face. He thrust the impending journey from his mind, his thoughts only of Monase. He would not abandon her. She would be taken care of, protected.

Meanwhile, in the shadowy darkness of the hut, Monase listened as Jama spoke.

"Are you sure this man is worthy of you, my lovely one?" Jama licked his lips as his eyes raked her body. "Does he return your love, or just give you his lust?"

Monase lowered her eyes, unable to answer, and Jama smacked his lips as he shook his head. "Just as I thought. You are a fool. But I will help you. I will make a strong charm for Cira to protect him in battle. I will need potent medicines." He leaned forward, catching her chin in his fingers. "It will be very expensive."

Monase's eyes met his as the implication in his voice caused her to shudder. She responded, her voice coming out in a pitiful squeak.

"I haven't much, but what I do have is yours, anything to save him."

Jama released her face with disgust. "Very well then. What I ask is this. My medicines are strong. They rarely fail. . . . But like all medicines, sometimes they do." He paused, letting this information sink in. He studied her face carefully as he continued. "If Cira doesn't return, you will be mine." His eyes narrowed, small and pointedly black. "You are a used woman. I will not make you my wife, but I will allow you to keep any brat you may be carrying. I will protect both of you, and shield you from harm." Finished, he puffed up like a croaking river toad, pleased with what he felt to be a magnanimous offer.

Monase shook her head, her arms folding protectively across her middle. "I couldn't," she whispered as tears stained her ashen cheeks.

Jama's eyes grew wicked. A muscle twitched deep beneath the fat of his jowls. "Think carefully, Monase. Without my help, it is most certain that Cira won't return. Do not think only of yourself, but of him, and the child of his you may be carrying."

A small miserable moan rose from deep within her being. She could not be so selfish. Slowly she nodded her assent. Her eyes thick with tears, she did not see Jama's traitorous smile as he bent to sprinkle a brown-and-green mixture upon the flames.

With the gentle clicking of his tongue, like a mother reproving a recalcitrant child, Jama pulled Monase toward the fire. He forced her to breathe deeply of the sickly-sweet black smoke billowing from the hearth. He told her it would help soothe her, make her strong to face the upcoming ordeal. She coughed, and her eyes stung. The vapors wrapped around her, making her lungs and nostrils burn. Her heart pounded loudly in her ears, making her head hurt.

After an eternity, the pain lifted and she felt incredibly light. She turned; Jama was speaking to her, but his voice seemed to float to her from a great distance. She blinked as his beady eyes wavered before her. He was asking something about Cira, the medicine. He wanted . . .

Her eyes drifted to the fire. She watched the flame grow higher, casting dancing shadows on the golden flax of the wall. So beautiful, ever-changing like Cira's eyes. She sighed, oblivious now to the acrid smoke, and reached her had to grasp at the twirling gray plumes. Try as she might to seize them, they eluded her, slipping between her fingers, and a light giggle escaped her lips. The sound echoed loudly in her ears, causing her to giggle again. Somewhere, in the corner of her mind, a worry hovered, threatening to destroy the peaceful feeling that enveloped her. She struggled to hold on to it, but it evaded her, skittering off into the far recesses of her brain. She sighed, sinking into the delightful sensation she floated on, letting all other feelings go.

In her stupor, Jama asked her where she and Cira had lain together. She smiled, crawling across the furs to the one where she and Cira had made love the night before. She ran her fingers lovingly along the velvety softness. Jama returned her smile, his eyes sliding along her swaying body. Monase watched him as he gleaned Cira's and her bodily hairs and oils from the fur. He mixed these in a small wooden bowl, adding a foul-smelling liquid from a little clay flask he carried. Monase leaned closer, entranced by his actions.

All of a sudden, quick as a striking serpent, he

reached out, pricking the soft flap of skin between her forefinger and thumb with a long ivory needle. Too spellbound to cry out, Monase merely watched the warm crimson blood trickle down her hand as if she were observing the hand of another. Lifting her hand, she turned it, seeing, dazedly, the dribble pool into her palm. Gently, Jama took her hand, turning it so the blood dripped into his bowl. Softly, he muttered something about holding the spirit of her beloved.

When he released her, Monase pressed the wound to her lips, tasting the salty metallic taste of her blood. She watched as Jama studied her face. He then moved to the hearth, sprinkling more of the mixture on the fire. She noticed him turn his head away, placing a hand across his nose and mouth. Her fuzzy mind wondered why he didn't partake of the blissful happiness the smoke imparted. She giggled as she saw him jump suddenly, the rolls of flesh around his waist quivering like jellied animal fat. In triumph, he held up the dried snake droppings. Like a large rodent, he scurried over to his bowl. He turned to Monase.

"This is indeed powerful medicine. With the blood of your body and the droppings of Shaka's ancestor, I cannot fail."

Monase beamed at him, her mind grasping a glimmer of his meaning. She was vaguely aware that Jama was staring hard at her, his eyes hungrily caressing her gently heaving breast. The firelight cast sensuous shadows over her womanly curves.

A burning knot of jealous hatred raged through Jama's body. He placed the droppings in the bowl and moved closer to Monase. He reached out to take her wounded hand. Giggling, she let him. Locking his eyes with hers, he put his mouth to the wound.

Something warned Monase to pull away, but her muscles were limp, her body seemed to float out of her control. Jama pulled her closer to the fire, to the sweet curling smoke. Pulling her against his shoulder, he urged her to breathe deeply. He smiled into her eyes, telling her to trust him. He would protect her always.

Gradually she felt the final corners of her resistance curl up and fall to ashes. She couldn't remember why she had ever feared this man. He was so very kind. He would help her. He promised to make everything all right. She yawned, drinking in more of the heavy smoke. She felt so sleepy. She felt as if she was leaving her body, drifting away. His warm oily hands felt soft and soothing as they stroked her arms. She leaned heavily into the witch doctor as he lowered her across his lap. His hands continued their stroking over her shoulders down her breast. For a moment she stiffened, then the peaceful oblivion encompassed her again.

She wasn't aware as he untied the leather ties around her waist. . . .

She opened her eyes, as she rolled from Jama's warm lap. A distant roar echoed in her ears. She saw Cira looming above her. He was shaking Jama, screaming something at him. She raised her hand to protest, to tell him Jama was here to help him, but the words floated disjointed above her.

"Jama . . . no . . . stay . . . Jama." Her hand flopped back down beside her, like the useless wings of the ostrich. She watched as Jama grabbed his medicine bowl and fled. His threatening curses filling the hut in his wake. Slowly her eyes worked their way to Cira. She smiled, holding out a hand to him. The knot in his throat moved rapidly up and down. Monase stifled a giggle. Cira's eyes burned, sending a shower of golden sparks down upon her. In a bold, swift motion, he tore the leopard-skin headband that identified him as an engaged man from his forehead and flung it violently to the ground.

Monase's smile faded. Something was wrong. She struggled to sober herself. Standing above her, Cira's eyes reeled in pain. She stretched her arms out to him, unable to rise, beckoning him to come to her. He spat in disgust, dropping the fur band on her stomach. Then, tearing his eyes from her, he left without a word.

As the sound of his angry footsteps disappeared Monase grasped the leopard pelt. Something was very wrong. Again she struggled to rise. She blinked her eyes, she had to get outside, to the fresh air, to some cold water. She rolled to her side, the fog growing hazier. She must . . . No, first she must rest. She closed her eyes. Later, later she'd find him and explain everything. Her eyes fluttered in a final effort. A small voice echoed from far away, *There is no time.*

She felt a dark dull heaviness descend upon her, its weight dragging her down. She gasped for air. She was drowning, she felt hot tears streaming down her face. The weight pressed down, sucking her into a dark swirling vortex of nothingness. Exhausted, she surrendered to the darkness.

* * *

Late the next morning Monase awoke. A sleeting rain drummed steadily outside the hut. Her head ached, her mouth felt like dust from a windstorm had settled inside of it. Without opening her eyes, she moved. Her stomach roiled dangerously in protest. In an effort to moisten her parched lips, she ran an even drier tongue over them. She craved a drink of cool water, but even the water pot outside seemed too far away. She pressed her fingertips against her closed eyelids, staving off the memory of last night. She drew in a deep ragged breath and nearly choked. The acrid smoke from the strange drug Jama had thrown on the fire and his own putrid smell still lingered in the hut.

As if in answer to a prayer, Mkabuyi called tentatively from outside the dwelling. Monase croaked out a welcome and a plea for some water. A look of alarm creased Mkabuyi's brow as her gaze took in Monase's half-disrobed prone figure and the disheveled hut.

"What happened here?" the girl demanded, her voice quavering with fear. "Did Cira hurt you?"

Monase shook her head vigorously, then instantly regretted it. With a grimace, she grabbed the cup of water Mkabuyi had brought and drank greedily. Her stomach heaved, and she rolled to her back, her hands clutching the earth beneath her. Her fingers struck the thin strip of leopard fur. Slowly, the memories came flooding back as she stroked its soft hairs. Tears welled up in her swollen eyes.

"Oh, Mkabuyi, something terrible happened

here last night, but what, I'm not exactly sure. I think I've lost Cira forever."

Mkabuyi laid a cool gentle hand on her brow. "Is it really that bad? I ran into Cira last night when I went to say good-bye to Punga. He was very excited, and said he had some wonderful news to share with you. He was headed this way. . . ."

Her voice died as Monase extended the headband to her. Mkabuyi turned it over in her hands. "I was wondering what happened to this. You see, shortly after he came here, he returned. His betrothal headband was gone, and he was as angry as a lion robbed of his kill. Every Punga shrank from him. I would have come to you then, but Cira said something about if I wanted to maintain my honor, I should shun you. He then shouted at Punga to return to the ranks and forsake the evil temptation of women."

Stopping to take a breath, she turned worried eyes to Monase. "You know, I couldn't stay away from you, but what have you done? Do you think Punga will come back safely?" Mkabuyi then burst into tears.

Monase raised her arms, and her sister came toward her. Monase sighed heavily, burying her face in Mkabuyi's hair. Together, the sisters wept for the lovers they might have lost, and the love they might never know.

Somewhere amid the tears and sorrow, Monase drifted off into a troubled sleep. When she awoke, Mkabuyi was gone. Not knowing how much time had passed, she lay listening to the falling rain. The kraal was strangely quiet, and she wondered if it was nightfall already. In the silence, her stomach rumbled.

Feeling weak, but better than she had earlier, she gingerly sat upright. Her stomach rumbled again. She marveled at her body's craving to fulfill her baser needs while her heart lay shattered around her. Suddenly she smelled food. Blinking, she squinted into the almost nonexistent light of the hut. Just inside the door was a small basket covered with a woven mat. When she lifted the covering, her nose was assaulted by the delicious aroma of roasted beef, boiled pumpkin, and sweet banana curds. Hungrily, she delved into the small feast, silently thanking Mkabuyi for her thoughtfulness.

Once her hunger was satisfied, Monase stirred the cold coals in the hearth. She caught a spark and tossed a handful of dried grass on the ember. The remnants of Jama's magic drug caught flame, sending a last twirling plume of smoke upward. Monase gagged, hastily throwing a few dry sandalwood branches on the fire. The refreshing musky sandalwood scent wafted through the air, overpowering the other, ranker smell. Falling back on her haunches, she began to ponder her next course of action.

First she forced herself to retrieve all that she could remember of last night, and piece it together. Jama had tried to take advantage of her. He had drugged her. Cira had returned to find her half-undressed, in Jama's arms. Threatening tears stung her puffy red eyes. Angrily, she brushed them away, with a swipe of the back of her hand. She was finished crying. It accomplished nothing.

She forced her mind to return to the puzzle. Jama would be enraged at being thwarted. With sudden horror, she realized that Jama still possessed the powerful medicine he had prepared for Cira. He could now use it against him. She shuddered at the possibilities.

"Oh, Cira, will you ever forgive me for putting my trust in that man?" Her words fell unheard along with a tear, which sizzled and evaporated as it dropped into the flames. She turned to pick up the leopard headband again: a proclamation to the world that they were to become man and wife. She saw Cira's golden eyes, gentle and warm. His brilliant smile, the engaging dimple winking in his left cheek. His voice low and slightly off-key when he sang. The memories brought a pain so sharp that she fell backward, as if receiving an actual physical blow to her stomach. She couldn't let it go.

Suddenly she knew what she had to do. She would find him, explain, make him believe. She would risk everything. She would die trying if she had to. With a fierce determination, she began planning her strategy.

She glanced about the home that Cira had built for her. Her eyes followed the rounded walls as they curved gracefully above her head. Was there anything she would need to bring? As she looked on the empty hooks around the walls, her gaze fell on a small black bag hanging far from the fire. She rose, taking the bag back to the firelight. For a moment she held the heavy velvet weight in her hand. Then she opened it, spilling the contents into her lap. Two skillfully crafted spearheads clinked as they fell together onto her skirt. Fingering them gently, she recognized them as her father's work. Two of the many he had given Cira to give to Chief Shaka.

Quickly she replaced the blades, securing the small pouch around the ties of her skirt. She knew women were not allowed to have or carry a man's weapon, but she knew as well that she might need them for protection, or at least for the bartering power they might afford her. She then turned to rummage through the belongings that Mkabuyi had brought earlier that morning. She paused as she uncovered the two bronze bangles her father had given her. Bronze was rare and precious. Stroking the bracelet's cool smooth surface, she hoped her father would understand if she was forced to trade them. She slipped them into the pouch as well. Carefully, she tucked the small bag beneath the folds of her skirt; she wouldn't take any chances.

Next, retrieving a larger satchel, she filled it with an animal-bladder water bag, some biltong, a large cache of nuts and berries, and some millet meal wrapped in a large leaf. Securing the ties on the bag, she gazed around again, then hunched to place some flat rocks on the flame. As she bent to lift the rocks she stopped. Scattered along the crevices of the rock was a substantial amount of the dry grassy mixture Jama had used to drug her. Brushing it into a small pile, she scooped it onto another large leaf. She then wrapped the bundle tightly with some supple basket-weaving reeds that had been among her things.

As she bent to put it in the large bag, she suddenly paused. Changing her mind, she drew the small pouch from its hiding place. This medicine was much too potent to lose. She couldn't afford to lose it.

Slipping out of the hut, she was perplexed to see the kraal dark; only the smoke from the huts betrayed the presence of people. Already, they had become wary, preparing for Zwide's attack. The moon was full, casting ghostly shadows upon the hillside as the whispering breeze rustled through the long grass. Monase prayed silently to her ancestors, imploring them to allow her to return with Cira, to enter this hut once again, as husband and wife.

Reaching the gate to the kraal, she crouched in the darkness, listening to the sentries whisper about the atrocities of Zwide. As she waited the conversation turned to the departed impis. She listened carefully as they described the merits of the route Cira had chosen. When she felt secure enough about the direction, she moved along the thickly woven tree-trunk gate. Presently she came to a small notch in the wall. Picking up a stone, she threw it wide of the gate. It landed with a dull thud. She waited. The spooked guards came running, together. Just as she had expected, they had frightened each other so greatly that none of them dared go off alone.

Swiftly she ran back to the entrance while the men rooted through the tall grass. The two remaining men at the gate were intently watching their comrades, and so they didn't notice the thin shadow of a girl race soundlessly past them. She ran, not looking back, not stopping, until she reached the solitude of the dark line of trees leading up to the bush, and the way Cira had led his men. Pausing to catch her breath, she heard a sokone scops owl hoot in the darkness. A hyena bayed, followed by the screech of a low-flying bat. Suddenly Monase felt frightened, and alone. Clutching her satchel, she closed her eyes, her nostrils growing wide, and she inhaled deeply. She had to be brave, she had made it this far. There was no turning back now.

Thirteen

Cira and his men marched in silence through the tangled undergrowth of the bush. The thorny labyrinth smelled heavily of animal. The muddy air was filled with the grunts and groans of wild beasts. Cira slashed angrily at the vegetation snaring his feet, blocking his way. His men followed him without question, but at a safe distance. They watched their leader's muscles bunch and strain with unnecessary vehemence. They wondered at his wasteful use of energy. But still they followed, asking no questions. He had never led them astray.

As if reading their thoughts, Cira paused to draw in a labored breath. He knew he was expending too much of his strength in the job of clearing their way through the underbrush. He was also aware that his men knew this. He cursed at Monase, angrily ordering his mind to keep to the matter at hand. He had been charged with a very important mission, and his men's safety and lives depended on him. But try as he might, he could not keep his anger in check. He had been deceived again, he thought, bringing his knobkerrie club down viciously, again and again. How had he let her gull him into believing her story? He had willingly let himself be seduced. He had been unable to resist her beauty, her bewitching voice, and her feigned innocence. Confusion and doubt gnawed at the corners of his mind.

Monase had reacted to his lovemaking as if she were a virgin. Although she had responded with eagerness, it had definitely been the reaction of an inexperienced maiden. He recalled the pain flickering across her brow as he had entered her. Suddenly the intimate memories caused a burning knot to twist in his loins. Feeling his manhood tighten and swell, he again cursed his wife-to-be and his body's lustful betrayal. Snarling, he pulled his lips back against his teeth. Perhaps she had only been inexperienced in that mode of lovemaking. He had heard that Jama's taste ran to the bizarre, so perhaps she had shared other intimacies with him.

He shuddered at the image his thoughts conjured up before him. He had been right when he thought her a charlatan. He was sure Jama was somehow involved in this plot with her. Perhaps they had connived to bring about this marriage so that Monase would inherit everything after he was killed. What a boon that he had been chosen to go on this dangerous campaign; now the lovers wouldn't have to find another way to dispose of him. Anger, hatred, and pain wrestled alternately within his battered heart.

Cira was so lost in thought that he did not hear the warning silence around him. Suddenly the air was filled with the bloodthirsty cry of hundreds of warriors. They rose from the thickets, brandishing knobkerrie clubs, assegai spears, and even the short iKlwa spear Shaka had created. Caught by surprise, Cira struggled to pull his men into the bull-and-horn formation. Fighting off the fierce attackers, his men grouped, rushing toward the center of Zwide's army. Punga and a line of thirty men spread out to the side, forming the horn, wrapping around the army to catch them in their unprotected sides and back. The strategy would have worked, but the other side of the horn was cut down before they could properly align themselves.

Frantic, Cira scrutinized their attackers; something was amiss. It was then that he noticed that the enemy army was a mixture of young warriors, old men, and children. It could be inferred that Zwide, hoping for strength in numbers, had assembled an army using any male he could find.

But how, Cira wondered, did one fight a ten-year-old boy? He saw his men hesitate as old and young came at them with sharp spears. He saw a thin child leap on Punga's back while an ancient man came at him with a iKlwa spear, and for an instant Cira's eyes locked with his friend's. The gentle giant seemed to plead for advice, then he went down.

Cira whirled to help him, but it was too late: a

spear's tip grazed his right temple. He felt the blood, warm and stinging, flood his vision. As he raised his hand to wipe the viscid fluid from his eyes, he was hit from behind. His head spun as his stomach heaved. He staggered, then twisted, to plunge blindly with his spear. The spear hit resistance, then sank in with a dull tearing sound. A scream rang through his ears. His spear had found its mark. As he was struggling to retrieve it, all the while desperately clawing at the red haze covering his eyes, he felt the impact of a heavy object that had been hurled against the back of his knees, causing them to buckle.

Sinking to the ground, he clutched his spear and shield. A piercing sting ripped through his left thigh. He fell forward, his hands releasing their hold. He felt the thick hot drops of blood from his head drip onto his thumbs and fingers. He struggled to rise, pushing up on his weary arms. Sharp talons of iron scraped deeply across his calves. He had opened his mouth to cry out when a blunt club struck the back of his skull and shoulder. The thud was followed by the loud crack of breaking bones. He fell to his face, pain surging through every nerve, then felt nothing as a welcoming abyss of oblivion rose to engulf him.

Monase picked her way cautiously through the thick brush. During the day it was hazardous enough, but at night it was downright treacherous. Around her, fireflies flashed and glowed as bats flitted above her, their wings whirring eerily. She heard hyena cackle, then whinny in a high hysterical laugh. The sound was followed by a lion roaring in the distance. There was no doubt that the bush was alive and dangerous. She knew she had to keep moving, to cover enough terrain that the sentries would be unable to see any fire she might light.

She paused, looking around, eyes wide with fear . . . for Zwide's men. The tales of the horrendous tortures they had inflicted on their enemies still rang in her ears. Damn those guards, for making her so frightened. She pushed onward, her eyes darting about her, gauging, evaluating. Right now she didn't feel very much like a brave huntress; rather, she felt like the hunted. She dug into the pouch at her waist, withdrawing a long six-inch assegai blade. She curled her fingers around it, drawing some strength from the cold sharp metal.

For hours in the darkness, Monase followed the path Cira and his men had cleared. For every moment that passed without her finding Cira's slain body, she thanked her ancestors and continued to push wearily onward. Her muscles ached from the strain, and her ankles and calves were raw from the prickly thorns that covered her pathway.

As the sky began to melt into a milky gray, she rested. She started a small fire, thrusting her fingers toward the heat, hoping to ward off the chill in her bones. Even the early-morning call of the birds spooked her, causing her to draw closer to the weak flame. Perhaps she was just tired and hungry, she thought as she reached for her satchel with numb, trembling fingers.

Withdrawing a thin strip of dried meat and a handful of dried berries, she began to eat. She fought the urge to drain her water bag, and instead took a small sip, then retied the leather thong. Feeling a little bit better, she rose to douse the fire. She was fatigued and frightened, but she knew she had to push onward, that every second she waited could cause her to be too late.

Too late? Perhaps it is already too late. She cringed at the thought of Cira lying lifeless, never to return. Hastily, she swung her sack over her shoulder, kicked up enough dirt to extinguish the flames, and followed the trail once again.

Traveling during the day, even if the sun was diluted by the wispy silver-and-black clouds floating over, was infinitely better than traveling at night. The birds seemed to sing more brightly, and she even spotted a few familiar gray monkeys swinging from the branches. As the breeze whispered through the leaves and dry grass, Monase could almost believe a kindly ancestor walked beside her. A hornbill bird squawked happily from a nearby tree, and she laughed as it twisted its head to look at her. It was a good sign, foretelling of a pleasant night.

She hastened her stride, feeling sure she would find Cira by nightfall. Perhaps he would even welcome her into his arms, forgiving everything. A small voice inside her head cautioned her not to let her hopes get too high, but she brushed it aside and let her spirits soar. Still wary of the bush animals and the possibility of coming upon Zwide's men in hiding, she began to hum softly. This time the tune was cheerful and light, a Zulu carol the women of the tribe had taught her.

The day went by uneventfully. Twice she had

encountered the droppings of elephants, and moved quietly, and as far away as possible, from the open spaces where they liked to congregate. Once she stopped to scale a tree to watch a group of three male elephants, the oldest sporting thick curling tusks. The two younger ones' tusks were, in comparison, mere cones of white. Looking down at the powerful gray animals, she felt vulnerable and small. But the majestic beasts took no notice of her, intermittently flapping their ears and quietly feeding on the nearby bushes.

Toward evening, she spotted dried blood on the vegetation at her feet. Hunkering down, she studied the dark rust-colored spot. It flaked and fluttered to the ground when she touched it. The moisture from her hand dissolved what clung to her finger, leaving a rich brownish-red stain. She straightened, and looking around, she sniffed the air. The blood was not that old. She moved cautiously, following the trail of blood that threaded through the grass. For a moment she hesitated when the track diverged from the path. Deciding, she picked through the uncut tangle of leaves and thorny branches. She had to find out if it was animal or human blood.

As the route led her farther from her original direction, she paused, ready to give up, when the chatter of a monkey drew her attention to a fallen rhinoceros. It was a white rhinoceros, a rarity. She approached cautiously, not sure if the creature was sleeping or dead, but then noticed that its eyes were open while flies swarmed around a congealed gash in its side. Slowly, keeping her eyes on the animal, she picked up a rock. Rolling onto the balls of her feet, she prepared to flee as she tossed the rock at the unblinking eye. Her father had taught her long ago that the only way to be sure that a dangerous animal was truly dead was to throw a rock at its eye. Too many hunters had died when a wounded prey suddenly charged them.

The animal didn't move. Her aim had been true, and the rock hit the eye with a squish, and rolled off. The flies momentarily lifted, then resettled to their feast. Gingerly, Monase moved closer, and noticed the gaping hole where the horn had been. Her head flew up as she glanced around nervously. Men had been here, and not too long ago. Briefly, she remembered Cira and his men tossing the rhinoceros horn along the riverbank on the journey to Zululand. Silently, she prayed that it had been those same men who had killed the rhinoceros, but the small hairs on her neck bristled. She suspected that it had not been them.

There had been no blood on the clear trail, but only to the one side, and the rhinoceros's tracks had been on both sides . . . but not on the trail itself. This meant that the rhinoceros had been killed before the trail had been made. Monase moved farther into the forest; once she was past the carcass, she stopped short. She found what she had hoped not to see: sandal prints. Cira and his men were barefoot, as always. So, Zwide's men had been here first. She went back to the dead beast and studied its wounds more closely. They had taken nothing save the horn, a sign that they were in a hurry. She dipped her finger in the wound; the cavity was clammy and cool. The animal could have been dead for hours.

She moved back to the cleared path. The foot-prints there clearly were made by bare feet. Again she bent to study the hacked vegetation. Cira and his men had been there less than two hours ago at best. Her brow creased, then deepened to lines of horror as she realized that Zwide's men had been lying in wait for Cira. A strangled cry rose from her chest, startling the birds and monkeys around her into silence. Picking up her belongings, she tore along the path, no longer aware of the biting thorns. She had to find Cira, to warn him.

Oh, great ancestors, please let it not be too late.

Fourteen

The foul, rotting smell of carrion assaulted Cira's senses. With a struggle, he slowly, painfully opened his eyes. A lonely bird cawed in the distance. He struggled to move. His head and body protested vehemently as burning pain surged through him, leaving him drenched with sweat. Lying still, he opened his eyes again. They burned, and the right side was sightless. He gingerly touched the swollen slit of an eye. Tentatively, he plucked at the dried blood encrusting the lashes and lid.

Relief flooded through him as light and pattern danced across his retina. As both eyes slowly focused he moved his hand to the tender place at his temple, where he had been hit. The spot was sensitive to the touch, but scabbed over. All of a sudden a pointed pain streaked up his left calf. He turned his face, sending a jarring agony through his head. He spat as his lips passed through the dirt. The pain came again. He looked to see a large gray vulture, timidly venturing back and forth to peck at his leg. Gathering what little strength he had, Cira kicked vehemently, hissing in a hoarse, cracked voice. The threat echoed resoundingly through the silence, causing the creature to back up a step or two.

Cocking his beady eyes at Cira, the ugly bird waited, as if knowing his threats were empty. Again Cira kicked, weaker this time, his energy failing. The animal moved closer, its curiosity aroused. The Zulu attempted to roll over onto his back. When he shifted onto his side, a heavy thud sounded beside him as a weight fell from his back. He endeavored to look over his shoulder, but the movement was excruciating. Glancing down, he saw the bone of his arm jutting out awkwardly from the joint. The skin above it was pale, the milky brown of river water. Carefully, he eased himself onto his back. His chest heaved with pain and exertion. He would have to move slowly, carefully, so as not to lose consciousness. He turned wary eyes to the vulture.

The bird, unthreatened, didn't move. Cira looked around at the many other vultures ravishing the corpses that had once been his and Zwide's men. A great sadness and feeling of loss welled up within him, and he lowered his head as a sigh escaped his parched lips. He didn't know if he could, or even wanted to, go on trying. As if sensing his defeat, the gray bird hopped forward to perch on his body.The creature's biting talons brought Cira's eyes wide open. Snarling through clenched teeth, he screamed at the bird, so near that its fetid breath reached his nostrils. The bird flapped its huge wings noisily as it leaped from his chest.

Turning once again onto his stomach, Cira dragged himself with his good arm away from the persistent scavenger. He paused only to look at the body that had fallen from his back. He cringed as he gazed into the wide sightless eyes of a child, a boy no more than seven or eight. Somewhere a mother was grieving, never to see her son again. His heart ached for the unknown woman.

Then, gritting his teeth against the pain and anger growing inside, he hauled himself away from the battlefield. Damn Zwide, his impi old men and children. The boy never to be a man. Zwide thought nothing of enlisting every able—or unable, for that matter—body from six to sixty. Cira could not let that man win, to conquer Shaka. Shaka must become king. Halting a few paces from where he had fallen, he retrieved his shield and spear. He was a great Zulu impi and must never leave his weapons. There was no greater shame than to return without them . . . and he *would* return.

As he continued his painful crawl the vulture watched, following him for a few feet, then decided to go back to the young boy's body lying in the dirt. Cira wanted to scream again, but the spear was clutched tightly between his teeth, and he knew he had to save his strength; night was just ahead.

With a sigh, the wounded warrior finally reached his destination. A large craggy rock several hundred feet from the body-strewn battlefield. Hoisting himself against the cool shadowed underside of the boulder and pulling the spear from between his teeth, he swallowed, the saliva barely enough to moisten his dry mouth. Carefully, he removed his big shield from his good shoulder. The six-by-three-foot shield had proven too difficult to drag with his wounded shoulder, so he had slung it over his back, using the leather arm strap as a sling. Now he laid his flushed, rough, unshaven cheek against the slab and watched the sun, orange and round, like an incandescent medallion, sink lower and lower, until it hung half-submerged among the intricate weave of the silhouetted trees.

Cira closed his eyes, blocking out the gore and carnage all about him. This prey for the ruthless scavengers had been his men. His heart twisted painfully, and his stomach lurched. The pounding in his head threatened to overtake him. He had to resist, to hang on to something. As darkness descended the night predators would arrive to finish the violation of his— He stopped. They were no longer his men, he couldn't think of them that way. Their spirits had already departed to dwell with the ancestors. He wished he had the strength to open their chests, as custom demanded, but the vultures had already done that.

His eyes burned and his breath blew hot from his mouth and nostrils. He shivered. He had to make a fire, to keep away the night beasts and evil wizards. He wiped the beads of perspiration from his brow and upper lip and ran a thick tongue over his dry and swollen lips. He had to get water. He reached to his side, his hand grazing the thick coagulated gash in his thigh. The rim was puffy, and a thin stream of yellow puss oozed out of the side. Infection was setting in. Again he reached for his water pouch. It was gone. He groped for his food pouch, his hand brushing against hot fevered skin. Slowly, with a great effort, he retrieved, and placed in his mouth, a few dried bitter berries. The sour tang on his tongue filled his mouth with saliva. He swallowed, the moisture soothing his raw throat.

With heavy, feverish eyes, Cira scraped together some dry grass and twigs. Over and over he tried to start a fire, his left arm aching, protesting against the movement. Finally, after what must have been the fifteenth try, a small spark caught, licking hungrily at the brittle kindling. It wouldn't last long, but it would do for now. He was so tired, he just needed to sleep. The haunting melodious call of a hyena startled him awake. He must hold on, he must stay awake. The cry was answered by another, then another. The thieves of the night were coming: they had smelled the blood.

Cira's heart began to race. His breath came in short and desperate gasps. In the darkening bush, the fireflies began to blink, their lights like so many inflamed eyes. He clutched his spear, his mind clouding with feverish delirium. He thought of his wound, the men he had killed. He had to cleanse himself. He had to lance the wound, rid his body of the evil spirits, before the madness could descend upon him. His fading consciousness grappled frantically for something, anything to prevent the swirling darkness from devouring him.

As if in a fever dream or a vision, Monase's face swam before him. His mind reached out to grasp it. He opened his mouth, croaking out her name in a broken sound, the last syllable seeping out in a low angry hiss. Memories flooded his brain, like a torrential river of pain and hatred. The emotions surged, rising, threatening to consume him. She had betrayed him. By betraying him, she had caused his men to die, to be caught unaware. Her witchery, her collusion with that witch doctor, had succeeded in bringing the mighty Haze to its knees.

With a sudden swell of strength, he opened his eyes. Those demons would not prevail, he would return. If any of his men had survived, and been taken captive, he would find them. Monase would be . . .

Somehow, the thought of revenge did not inspire him. Revenge was not sweet. He closed his eyes and wept for all he had hoped for, and all he had lost.

The silence was broken by a small woodford owl, hooting a soft melody that sounded like *woz, woz, Mobengwana*. The eerie sound—*woz* meant "come" in the Zulu tongue—echoed through the sable blackness of the bush. The call broke through Cira's sorrow. A cold trickle of fear slithered down his spine. Again: *Woz, woz, Mobengwana*. The small owl was an emissary of the dangerous witch Mobengwana. The surrounding bush quivered with ghostly sounds and movements. A low moan of dread climbed up Cira's throat. His hot flushed body was covered by a thin sheen of sweat. His shoulders began to shake, and he grasped at the strongly rooted grass at his side. His eyes wide, he searched the blackness. He tried to resurrect his anger, willing it to give him strength. When that failed, he whispered Monase's name in a harsh chant, which seemed to rattle from his very core.

A gentle breeze began to blow, swaying the long gnarled fingers of the trees to and fro. Cira's tenuous fire began to flicker, grow brighter, then wane. The night became alive with a symphony of new sounds. A large specter of a moon rose over the silvery branches of the forest, and long black cobwebs of clouds floated past it, causing long dancing shadows upon the ground. Cira piled more sticks on the fire, moving closer to its warmth and protection. In the near distance, a leopard grunted. Decidedly nearer came the beautiful haunting call of the hyena.

It was almost more than Cira could bear, and he felt his resolve slipping. His bloodshot eyes scanned the bush again. Again the unearthly musical call. It came again, louder, then rose into a hideous high-pitched squeal of laughter. It lapsed, then his ears made out a slow uncanny gurgle. The hyena had vanquished its prey.

Cira turned his eyes back to the dying fire, willing himself to gather more sticks. His body would not obey. Pain and fear prevented him from leaving the small circle of light. He had depleted what had lain in that perimeter. Again, his eyes were drawn to the noisy bush, to the silvery-blue brightness, thrown into weird patterns by the erratic zigzagging of the bats. As he pushed the memory of his mother from his mind, it was filled with religious stories of the dreaded imkovu. These were the bodies of the dead, which the night wizards exhumed and converted to ghostlike apparitions with glowing eyes. The wizards were said to plunge their fiery nightsticks into the corpses' heads, setting the hollow eye sockets gleaming like burning embers.

What with the strain of staring combined with the heat of his fever, Cira's eyes burned uncomfortably. He rubbed them briefly, then opened them again. He started, then froze. A silvery-blue form emerged from the trees. Again, Cira rubbed his eyes. The figure moved silently toward the field. He watched in horror as the specter bent, turning the remains of a corpse to face it. A low moan wafted through the night as the apparition released each body, turning to another, searching. Cira clutched his heart with fear. The night wizard had come, to claim its own before the night predators arrived. A raw deep cry rose from Cira's lungs, rushing from his mouth before he could stifle it.

The phantom lifted its head and rose, turning slowly toward him like a creature from a dream, the moonlight gleaming on its wide eyes and leaving silvery streaks on its face. Cira cowered in terror as the figure stretched an arm out beseechingly toward him, crying his name. He knew he should look away, lest he be struck blind. Again and again the voice called to him. He must not respond, or the wizard would turn him dumb. Closer, closer, the image moved toward him. A strangled cry rose from his throat.

"Monase? No, not you." Again, he opened his mouth to speak, but no words came forth. Still the ghastly thing moved toward him. Monase was dead, and the wizards had inhabited her body. He clutched his spear. She was closer now, he could see her eyes, the silver tracks from her tears. The spear fell from his hand. Agony clawed unrelentingly at his body while fever devoured his sanity. It was all too much. With one last heroic effort, Cira struggled to stand. A vicious inferno blazed through his body. He twisted, and an explosion of lights erupted inside his brain. Darkness dragged him down into a deep pit of nothingness. Somewhere in the darkness, someone was screaming, a heartrending sound.

Weary in body and spirit, Monase's heart died in her breast when she came upon the bloodied, vulture-ravished corpses littered about the field. Tears had trickled slowly down her cheeks, making dark patches on the dirt at her feet. She was too late. When she found the rhinoceros, she had rushed down the hacked-out trail, only to find it disappeared a few hundred yards away. Even using all her tracking skills, she had wandered aimlessly for hours.

Only as the sun began its rapid descent over the trees had she discovered a thatch of white cow-tail hair caught on a thorny branch. Looking more carefully, she had spotted an occasional smeared heel- or toe-print. Then the sun had set, taking the last of its burnished glow with it. For a moment the sky was tinged with a red-and-purple haze, as if a vast fire had been lit below the horizon. The gathering clouds became rimmed with gold. Then all light was gone: the sky was shrouded in blackness.

Monase groped about her, frustrated, and impatient for the full moon to rise. She didn't have to wait long, but the time seemed an eternity, every second keeping her from warning, or . . . she couldn't think about it. The blue cool light of the moon fell welcomingly about her, slipping like silvery water over the branches to pool at her feet. She had frantically pushed forward, unaware of the awakening bush around her.

It was then that she had come upon the battlefield. In a daze, she walked past a low thorny bush, oblivious to the sharp points tearing across her legs. Silently, she stood looking down at the first body she reached. Unrecognizable, devoid of eyes and most of the nose. It smiled up at her with its deathly grin, its lips a mass of frayed skin.

Her stomach lurched. She turned, vomiting the little she had eaten onto the bloodstained dirt. Closing her eyes, she wiped her mouth with the back of her hand. She must go on, she must find Cira. Steeling herself for the ordeal, she turned back to the corpse. With an amazing force of will, she opened her eyes to stare back at the sightless cadaver. The pitiful remains of a man were not Cira. He was much taller than this. She moved on to the next victim. Bending down, she looked the large body over. The face was totally gone, the vultures having destroyed the tender flesh there. She felt her stomach clench and hastily backed away. Then she saw the sandals. This man was not Cira either. Again the tears streamed down her face as she glanced with despair at all the corpses strewn about the ground. Would she ever be able to find her Cira? And would she recognize him if she did?

It was then that she had heard the cry.

It was a weak, strangled cry, startling her with its anguished torment. Turning, she barely recognized the tattered bloody man propped against the rock. Slowly, as if in a dream, she moved toward him, a moth drawn to the flame, a flicker of hope burning in her heart. Then the man spoke, calling her name. The hope burst into flame. She lifted her arms to him. He cowered, screaming out in fear, rejecting her even among all the deathly silence. Refusing to leave, she raised her hands, palms upward, in a motion of surrender, her eyes pleading. Clenching his spear, glassy-eyed with terror, Cira tried to rise. She rushed to him, watching him fall, crumble into . . .

Surely not death. Not when she had traveled so far, searched so long. The spirits would not take him from her now. She knelt beside him, a scream of agony rising from her throat, torn from her very soul.

With gentle hands she bent over him, turning his beloved face toward her. She felt his hot, shallow, rasping breath eke out of his dry, cracked lips. He was alive. Thank the ancestors, he was alive. Both in exhaustion, and relief, Monase let her head drop to his chest, her tears rolling unchecked over her face, pooling in the hollow space beneath his breastbone.

How long she lay like that, Monase didn't know. She had been unaware of the gathering night predators, drawn to the smell of carnage. Suddenly a low, steady panting sound raised the small hairs along the back of her neck. Slowly, she lifted her head to peer into large luminous yellow eyes. Not daring to move her head or body, she slowly inched her hand toward Cira's spear. The large hunchbacked brown hyena moved stealthily forward. Monase swallowed hard, feeling her heart beating rapidly against her ribs. She knew the hyena was assessing his prey, judging when to attack. The South African brown hyena was a gutsy, vicious predator, this one measuring almost five feet in length. Only they would challenge the mighty lion for its kill.

Monase tried to swallow again, this time the moisture lodging in her throat, unable to pass. She knew she was no match for this beast's strength. Once it had gotten a hold of her, it would never loosen its grip. She had seen captive animals locked in the iron teeth of a hyena, screaming out in pain as their limbs were ripped from their joints. Quickly concealing a small shudder, she silently dragged the spear to her side. Her mind searched frantically for an idea.

The animal stopped. Its wary eyes flickered to her slow-moving hand. In response, it drew back its thin lips, revealing two rows of sharp jagged teeth, teeth that could crush through bone. Monase tensed her muscles, forcing herself not to shiver as she bore her eyes into those wild yellow ones. Gripping the spear tightly in her hand, she clutched it to her chest.

In a flash, she remembered the story of Shaka and the leopard that Punga had told on the journey, and a frightened, excited thrill whizzed through her body. The hyena's haunches bunched. The speckled hairs on its hunched shoulders rose stiffly. A shrill bloodcurdling scream issued forth from between those deadly teeth. In a response as old as time, Monase's adrenaline flowed through her veins, preparing her body. Her heart hammered savagely against the walls of her chest. The hairs on her limbs stood on edge. *Fight or flight, fight or flight.* The ancient chant echoed through every taut nerve in her body. Clenching her teeth, she pointed the spear's tip toward the beast. With a deep breath she braced herself for the animal's onslaught.

The hyena pulled back on its legs, then lunged forward, a blur of tawny fur, hurling its whole weight at Monase. The spear quivered, the tip glittering in the moonlight, then she thrust it forward at an upward angle, the handle gripped tightly between her white knuckled fists and rigidly locked arms.

The animal's screams tore through the night as the spear plunged deeply into its white-furred chest. The power of the hyena sent Monase sprawling on her back, its coarse fur grating against her skin. With horror, she found herself pinned to the ground by the heavy beast; she desperately pushed at it, trying to relieve herself of the weight that was so loathsome to her. Once free, she drew in short, ragged breaths.

Suddenly she was overcome by a fit of uncontrollable tremors. She closed her eyes, drawing in deep calming breaths. After a few moments she opened her eyes to look down at the still figure at her side. A white frothy foam slid slowly from its lips, swirling pinkly with a thick string of blood. She moved away with a jerk, when its long rough tongue lolled out of the deep cavity of its mouth.

Her eyes flew to its large yellow eyes. They stared unseeing into the darkness above her, their pupils growing larger, swallowing the pale yellow iris. As she watched, a milky-white film spread over the no-longer-moving orbs, as if summoning the beast spirit to a distant land.

A hoarse moan drew Monase's hypnotized gaze back to the unconscious man lying beside her. She then looked past him to the feeding animals. A large lion tossed its silvery mane in the moonlight, swiping a large deadly paw at a rambunctious cub that was trying to steal a— Monase gagged, then gulped back the bitter bile rising in her throat. She had to look away, she had known some of those unfortunate men. Now she had to keep Cira and herself alive. Quickly she rose and began to gather handfuls of dry grass and branches. Returning, she dropped them on the waning embers of Cira's fire. The coals began to smoke and hiss, then burst into flame, hungrily devouring the meager kindling. Again Monase threw some more tinder on the fire. The bright tongues reached high into the sky, startling the animals nearest them. Grunting in protest, the predators backed off warily. The lion and its cubs paused momentarily, their eyes gleaming a deep gold, in the reflected flames. Monase was reminded of Cira. She turned to his silent form; closing eyelashes damp with tears, she prayed to her ancestors to spare him . . . for her.

Monase spent the night alternately cradling Cira's head, his hot skin burning her arms, and gathering more brushwood to keep the fire bright. As she rocked him she sang the beautiful Zulu carol the women of the village had taught her:

U ya ngin tan daya, on gi tan da yo,
Un kulu unkulu, un kulu unkulu.
U ta ngin tan da ya, un sin di si-i,
Nalya pinda ngiti on gi tan da you.

I am loved by the Almighty,
Who loves me.
The healing is, I say again,
That I am loved and I love the Almighty.

Monase knew that Umvelinquangi, the Almighty, had only created the earth and its creatures, then had little to do with their day-to-day living, but she'd pray to him anyway. She figured that reminding Umvelinquangi that He loved her and she loved Him wouldn't hurt.

Just before sunrise, the animals began to leave. The battlefield was a graveyard filled with skeletons from which all vestiges of humanity had been picked clean. Monase hugged Cira's limp, feverish body to her chest. How easily one of those men could have been he. Turning a tender gaze upon him, she reluctantly released him. Their water was almost depleted. She knew that she would have to get more; now was the time when the night predators went to slake their thirst. If she wanted to find water in this unknown territory, she would have to risk leaving Cira. As if to wipe any hesitation from her mind, Cira gasped out a barely audible request for water.

After dampening his parched lips and flushed skin with a few leaves laden with morning dew, she fed the hungry fire. When the blaze burned brightly, she gathered her tired and worn courage, kissed Cira's brow lightly, and set off with their water bags. As she passed through the empty field she kept her eyes straight ahead, unwilling to meet the hollow-eyed skulls looking at her. Only once did she pause. Gritting her teeth, she bent to retrieve an abandoned bladder bag. She didn't know how far they would have to travel, but she needed to carry as much water as possible, and this bag would come in handy for that purpose.

Several minutes later Monase was sitting silently in the branches of a huge, gnarled baobab tree. Its lofty, heavy branches allowed her to watch the animals lap thirstily at a small stream from a quarter of a mile distance.

Slowly the dawn sent rosy orange streaks across the misty purple sky. All around her, on the ground, the morning dew glittered like liquid fire. Then, as if in mute agreement, the nocturnal hunters dispersed. Gradually, the whirs and cries of the night animals dwindled, becoming the quieter, friendly symphony of morning birds. Unnoticed until now, a family of gray, black-handed little monkeys chattered on the branches overhead. One little scoundrel ventured hesitantly down the trunk to get a better view of the large brown intruder. Sitting at the juncture of the tree trunk and Monase's branch, he tilted his head to one side. Monase followed his descent, meeting his small, bright, inquisitive eyes. A small tired laugh escaped her lips. The startled monkey bolted up the tree to safety, scolding her angrily. The weak laugh had even surprised Monase. It seemed like it had been so long since she had laughed that her vocal cords felt rusty. She smiled in apology to the incensed monkey and swung down from her roost.

Cautiously she made her way to the narrow rippling stream. She was glad it hadn't been as far away as she had feared, but her limbs protested wearily as she bent to scoop handfuls of the precious cool water. She drank greedily, careless of the crystal fluid running in fine rivulets down her chin. Submerging the water bags in the water, she filled all three. A small rustling sound at her elbow caused her to turn swiftly. Her bright-eyed furry friend had followed her to the stream. Smiling, she withdrew several nuts from the pouch hanging from her waist.

"Not so timid, are we?" Monase leaned forward, placing the nuts on her outstretched palm.

Sniffing delicately, the monkey sat up on its haunches, craning its neck to peer into her hand. Again Monase laughed, happy for the company.

"Come, little fellow. I won't hurt you. But don't take too long, for I must hurry."

The little black hands reached up to scratch its head, as if contemplating her words. The monkey then rubbed its velvety white stomach vigorously, waiting, not moving forward. Disappointed, Monase scattered the nuts on the hard ground and rose to leave. The brief laughter was gone. Lines of worry and exhaustion creased her face. Her sandaled feet slapped softly against the dusty earth as she hurried back to Cira.

Gradually, the open plain grew into low, scraggly, thorny bushes. As Monase picked her way through the narrow paths, she was startled by a sudden surge of birds rising from a dense cluster of bushes. As their wings flapped noisily within inches of her face, she clutched her precious water vessels, tucking her chin deep into the hollow of her neck. Just as suddenly, the birds were gone, leaving an unnerving stillness, broken only by a lone screeching call. Monase raised her horrified eyes to the skies, where several large vultures were circling in the distance. Then one swooped downward. Monase moved her lips in a mute *no*, then burst through the bushes and thickening trees screaming. The foul scavengers needed no other incentive. The large gray-brown bird who had landed near Cira's motionless form spread its wings and departed.

Sobbing, Monase set down the water bags and cradled Cira's head against her heaving breasts. Rocking back and forth, she whispered her apologies, her regrets, and her love.

Fifteen

All through the night, Cira barely moved, the fever sapping his body of all its energy. As the blisteringly hot sun rose into the sky, Monase continued to bathe his flushed body with water. Crooning softly to him, as a mother to a child, she lifted his head to pour a small portion of water down his parched throat. Some of the water dribbled down his chin. She caught it with her fingers, spreading it gently across his dry cracked lips. A small tear slipped down her cheek to see him so helpless, so weak.

As the day wore on, Monase's head drooped with exhaustion. Hours later she awoke to Cira's frantic thrashing and hoarse cries. Hushing him, she dampened his blazing forehead. Momentarily, he quieted, murmuring forlornly, as a tear slid down his hollowed cheeks.

Not fully awake, Monase turned her worried eyes to his inflamed wound. Laying his head down gently, she moved to examine the deep gash in his thigh. Infection had set in. With trembling hands, she removed one of the sharp blades from her secreted pouch. Touching the metal to the flame of the fire, she turned it slowly, until it was nearly too hot to hold. Turning back to Cira and the task before her, she steeled her nerves. Quickly, she lanced the yellow puffy scab that had formed.

The moment the blade sliced the skin, Cira's body arched in agony. A wild animallike scream rose from deep inside of his chest, and he thrashed deliriously, causing the bone of his dislocated shoulder to push precariously against the already straining skin.

Monase tried to subdue him, but he threw her from him, as if she were no more than an unwanted blanket. Helpless terror welled within her. She knew she had to do something to calm him. If she didn't drain the poisons from his wound, he wouldn't last the night. Frantically, she looked around her. Then she remembered the potent magical drug Jama had left by her fire. With shaking fingers, she withdrew the precious bundle from her hidden bag. Offering a silent prayer, she lit one corner of the bound herbs. While it was smoldering, she stealthily approached Cira.

In one quick, fluid motion, she stuffed the water-dampened hide she had been using to wipe his brow, into his mouth. Grasping his coiling locks, she dangled the smoking parcel beneath his flaring nostrils.

In a fight for breath, the delirious Cira drew in deep lungfuls of the drug. He bucked and bowed. Monase was tossed from side to side like a rag doll, but still she maintained her grip. The seconds seemed to drag on for hours until finally Cira's head began to loll and his struggles weakened to mere shrugging protest. Monase unwound her hand from his hair, a few strands remaining entangled in her fingers. Drawing in a ragged breath of relief, she removed the cloth from Cira's mouth. She quickly wrapped it around the remains of the blackened pouch. She didn't know whether she would need it again, but fervently hoped she would not.

Cira moaned softly. Monase stroked a stray lock from his sweat-glistening brow. Turning, she bent to the festering wound. With a deep breath she fastened her lips around it, drawing the bitter poison into her mouth. Nearly gagging, she spit the slimy substance out beside her. Again and again, she repeated this procedure, until the blood ran bright and clean.

Rocking back on her heels, Monase spat once again, then took a long draft from the water bag. Cira shifted slightly, whimpering like a child. Monase grew alarmed; perhaps the drug was wearing off. Hastily, she ran the blade through the fire again, this time allowing the metal to glow. Holding the knife with the hem of her skirt, she pressed the flat edge against the bleeding wound.

The smell of burning skin assaulted her nostrils as Cira's body began to shake violently. Dropping the blade, she stroked his temples, uttering words of endearment. This seemed to soothe him, and the shaking diminished to small tremors. Gazing down at the unconscious man's face etched in pain, Monase was loath to attend to setting his shoulder. Another whimper from Cira forced her to realize that his drug-induced state could be waning, and to wait might only mean more torture for him.

Running gentle fingers across his shoulder, she determined that the bone was dislocated, but not broken. Once, twice, she heaved, and pushed. Cira's good hand clutched aimlessly at the air, as if to fight off an invisible assailant. His cries of anguish twisted Monase's stomach. Then suddenly the bone popped, followed by a squish. The joint was in place. Monase fell back in relief. Exhausted, she slept again.

Sometime before dusk, rain began to fall, rousing her from her dreamless slumber. She woke with a start, disoriented and confused. Then she saw Cira's thrashing form, his body covered with a thin sheen of sweat. Running her hand along his burning flesh, she turned her dry lips to the sky to whisper thanks to the spirits for sending this cooling rain. As if in response, the heavens opened, sending a cool delicious deluge. After a while she propped Cira's shield against the rock, making a passable shelter above him. Then she lay down, uncovered, letting the refreshing water run over her body, its rivulets drawing the heat from her, soothing her parched skin.

The rain ceased around midnight. The moon broke free of the restraining clouds, sending weak streams of silvery-blue light across the rain-sodden earth. All around them the darkness came alive. With the whispering rush of wings, the reassuring chirp of the crickets, and the twinkling blink of the fireflies, another night began. Monase struggled to find enough dry brush to restart the fire. Glad for the short rest, she began her watch over Cira. Once she had a small flame blazing, she crouched down beside him and studied his wound. The skin puckered angrily around the new scab, but all signs of the previous infection had gone.

Cira tossed and moaned, rambling incoherently. Occasionally he called out for his mother. Then he wept, murmuring her name over and over, a cry of despair. Once he called out Monase's name, his voice heavy with anguish.

Monase sat upright in attention. "I'm here, Cira, I'm here."

Cira continued to moan, unaware that she had spoken. "Don't go. Don't leave me." The plaintive cry tore at Monase's heart as she gathered him into her arms. Weakly, he struggled, his voice crying out, "Don't hold me. I must go to her. She needs me. Please let me go."

Briefly, Monase was confused, then realized he was speaking of someone else. She loosened her hold, letting her fingers lightly stroke his soaked hairline.

"Mama, Mama. Don't leave me." The deep masculine voice took on the high whining tone of a child.

Monase grasped his hand, unable to stand the pain in his twisted face. "Shh, shh, I'm here, baby. Mama won't leave you."

Cira grasped her hand in an iron grip. "The

hyena, he's taking you away. Don't let him. Dadda's gone. He broke. I'm so alone . . . please don't leave me."

Monase's heart turned in agony for him. Her tears falling over him, as once again she pulled him into her arms. This time he did not resist, as her soothing words reached him.

"I'll never leave you. I'll always be here for you. I love you. I'll love you forever." He sighed, turning his face into her. Monase sighed, too, knowing he wasn't aware that it was she, but content to hold him. Softly, she began to sing her song of sorrow, of love. Lulled by the comfort, and the music, he slept.

As dawn neared, a soft beautiful voice drifted to Cira, unintelligible, distorted, as if from a great distance. The notes seemed to waver like the morning mist rising from the dew-laden earth. With difficulty, he opened heavy lids. The music was closer now; he could feel the singer's warm breath upon his face. He squinted into the dim light.

Monase smiled, and Cira was stunned anew by her heart-wrenching beauty. He squeezed his eyes shut tightly. He was hallucinating. He wanted to return to the dream. He was young again, his mother was holding him. The brutal slaughter of his men had not happened. Her sweet breath fanned across his face, then caught, as if she were waiting for him to open his eyes.

He refused to open them, trying to blot Monase's visage from his mind. The evil wizards were back, but they would not wrest his sanity from him. Soft, cool hands stroked his temples, the fingers gliding gently over his leaden lids.

Then he heard the singing begin again, the voice growing clearer as he caught the phrases of an ancient Zulu lullaby. The sweet words and melody washed over him in a welcoming wave, tugging him gently into a deep dark chasm. He struggled briefly. The voice melted into that of his mother's, and he moaned in surrender. In a torn whisper, he called out for his mother to come take his spirit with her. He then slipped into the murky depths of blissful oblivion.

Monase had nearly wept in relief when Cira opened his eyes. For a moment he seemed to recognize her, then she saw his eyes cloud over with an eerie glazed expression, more frightening than his fevered thrashing. With a shudder she recalled his cry to his mother to release his spirit from this world. From his rambling, delirious words, she had pieced together that his mother had been taken by a hyena, probably never to be found again. From what he had told her before about the love between his parents, she could only imagine that his father had fallen apart after the loss.

She wept for the poor abandoned child Cira had been. No wonder he had been so taken with the strong, paternal Shaka. She realized that it was his fears of being abandoned again that made him keep everyone at a distance. And here she was, hurting him again. He thought she had betrayed him, leaving him abandoned for a second time in his life.

"Never, never, my love. I will always be here for

you," she whispered to Cira's tear-stained cheek. The heat that rose from his skin against her made her realize that he needed help, more help than she alone could provide. But she couldn't leave him; she'd have to take him to a village. Quickly, her eyes flew around her, weighing, assessing.

She blocked out the doubts that gnawed at her mind. How could she carry a giant like Cira anywhere? How far? Over what kind of terrain? In what direction? The doubt sank to her stomach, twisting, rising to squeeze her chest. She heard the ever-present voice, demanding that she give up such outlandish notions. Traveling alone this far had been foolish enough, but to drag an unconscious, bleeding man would be an open invitation to all the carnivores of the jungle.

Weakening in her resolve, she turned to look down lovingly into Cira's ashen face. She couldn't just leave him. Yet she couldn't stay and watch him die. But how could she carry, or drag—

She stopped, her eyes glowing brightly as they wandered to the makeshift shelter. She *could* drag him. Quickly she placed the six-foot shield on the ground. With great care, she rolled his inert body onto the slightly concave surface. She then wrapped his ankles, which extended over the end, with a strip of hide she had cut from the hyena she had killed. She had saved it as a trophy, before dragging the carcass far from their fire. They had needed no other attractions for the ubiquitous flies, vulture, and night predators.

Building up the fire for what she hoped would be the last time, she set out to the stream she had found earlier. As she knelt to fill the three water bags, a familiar gray face appeared several yards away from her. She smiled ruefully at the little monkey.

"I've no time today. I'm leaving." The monkey cocked his head from one side to the other, then scampered off. Monase felt suddenly sad, and very lonely. Cira might not make it, and even if he did, he didn't want her. Her future looked very bleak. She slowly began slicing long supple reeds from the banks of the stream, forcing her mind to focus on the task at hand. These rushes she would weave into a sturdy harness. If she fastened them to the leather stitching in Cira's shield, she could loop them over her chest and shoulders to gain leverage.

Wrapping the strands across her neck, she trudged back to the rock where Cira lay. She was so engrossed in the construction of the travois in her mind that she was startled by the angry outburst beside her. She turned to see her little friend from the stream scamper past her, waving a frantic hand toward her feet.

Stopping, she froze and saw, coiled up less than a foot in front of her, a ten-foot deadly black mamba. Its lethal eyes stared unblinking at her. Monase shivered. Had the ancestors come to tell her something, or to call her to them?

Slowly, the snake began to uncoil and, with a dry raspy sound, started to slither from its skin. Monase waited, mesmerized by the hideous beauty unraveling before her. When the snake had sloughed off its skin, it slid off silently, leaving the dry brittle case shimmering in the sunlight.

Gently, Monase bent to retrieve the translucent

membrane. A few blue-black scales loosened and fluttered to the ground. With the utmost care, she wound the skin around her finger, the placed it in the pouch tied to her waist. When, and if, they reached a village, she would ask an isangoma what it meant.

Now that the snake had vacated the premises, the little gray monkey happily approached Monase. She extended a brown nut on her flattened palm. Without its previous hesitation, the monkey snatched the nut. This time, he didn't disappear, but followed Monase at a safe distance. As she walked he chattered contentedly, his cheeks bulging with the meat of the nut.

Once again, sitting beside Cira, Monase lifted his head so he could drink a little water. She then nimbly wove the strong supple reeds into a harness and fastened it to the end of Cira's shield. Securing the water bags to her belt, she slipped the harness over her shoulders, fastening the front with a few leather thongs she had cut from an abandoned shield lying in the field. Taking a last long look around her, she sighed deeply and headed east.

Sixteen

Days turned into nights, turned into days. Monase, Cira, and the still-present monkey stopped only at night, to build a fire and eat of their diminishing supplies. During the day Monase paused only long enough to hunt for nuts, berries, and succulent roots. Occasionally, she found safe water to refill their bags, but not often enough. Cira had few lucid moments, when he would look about himself and try to rise. But always, toward evening, the sinister fever returned.

One evening Monase ventured out to catch some small game; taking Cira's spear and a crudely made club, she set out into the tall surrounding grasses. Moving slowly through the grass, she beat through its dry brittle lengths. The movement caused a great flurry of activity. Raising her club above her head, she brought down the weapon with a lethal thud. At her feet lay a large shrewlike amavondwe. With only a slight aversion, she bent to slice off its rodentlike tail close to the body. With the tail gone, it looked less like a rat.

Her queasiness gone, she hastened back to the fire for a taste of freshly cooked meat.

After skinning the animal, she stretched its skin on a makeshift rack to dry. In the morning, she would fashion it into new sandals. Hers had worn clean through. As she skewered the amavondwe on the spit she had made, turning it slowly, the air around her was filled with the delicious scent of roasting meat. Her mouth watered, but her stomach had grown so tight that she was only able to digest a little of the beast. Finding an empty turtle shell, Monase mixed and warmed a little meat broth for Cira. Allowing him small sips, she tilted the bowl toward his lips. Although the food did nothing for his fever, his coloring seemed to improve slightly. Cutting the remaining meat into small chunks, she let it dry over the smoke from the dying fire. This meal might have to serve them for a long time.

The monkey was not at all interested in the meat, and was content to chomp on nuts and drink the sweet nectar from the umsinsi blossoms it invariably found. Monase was happy for the company, since Cira's only conversation was one-sided incoherent rambling.

Sometime during the fourth day of her journey Monase decided to name the furry little fellow Panza. Now, as she scooped up the cooling animal fat from the rocks around the fire and slathered it on her raw shoulders, she scolded the little monkey.

"You know, Panza, the harness wouldn't rub my shoulders nearly so raw if you'd pull your own weight. I don't remember inviting you to ride with Cira on his shield." As if understanding, the little imp covered his eyes with his hands and peered out between splayed black fingers. Monase laughed, and swiped at him. Prattling happily, he swung up on a tree, out of her reach.

By now, Panza was following Monase everywhere she went, but he curled up with Cira at night. Even though this made her a little jealous, she was happy to have this watchful guardian when Cira's frightening screams woke her. Once, a large hairy spider crawled up Cira's leg. Another time Cira's arm slipped off the shield as she transported him, and his knuckles raw and bleeding by the time Panza complained and she realized what had transpired.

On the sixth morning, Monase went a short distance to a small stream. As she knelt to rebundle the shredded hides around her feet, she chided Panza for having drunk some of the broth she had brewed for Cira. In his disgust, the monkey had dumped the whole batch on the ground.

"You know you were lucky that we came upon this stream this morning. The brew you spilled last night was nearly the last of our water. I should . . . what the . . ."

Her words were cut short as a dark shadow fell over her. Squinting up at the dark form haloed by the sun, she gasped. A large rotund woman, with a melon balanced on her head and a baby strapped to her back, loomed angrily above her.

The woman's voice was deep and surly. Her accent was heavy, making it difficult for Monase to understand her.

"Want you? . . . Trouble . . . Go."

Monase shook her head vigorously and pointed over to where Cira lay in the distance. "Man . . . Hurt . . . Needs help."

The woman seemed to understand, and raised a callused hand to shield her eyes as she gazed out to where Cira lay. Dropping her hand, she returned her eyes to Monase. "Old? Young?" The woman's voice held no softness, only a terse forbearance.

Baffled, then unsure, Monase responded hesitantly. "Thirty-two seasons." Uncomfortable with her submissive position, Monase rose to her feet. She stood a good four inches above the woman, who was now studying her slowly, from the feet upward. Monase shifted uneasily, feeling as if she were an animal for sale.

Again the woman's voice came brusk and demanding. "Your man?"

And again Monase hesitated. Should she say yes, even though technically he wasn't? What if questions were asked about Cira's missing headband? What if, when Cira was able, he laughed at her, denying any claim to her? Unable to meet the woman's intense stare, Monase dropped her eyes and mumbled, "No, he's my . . . brother."

The woman grunted, obviously satisfied. "Come. Bring brother." She then turned to head up the stream bank, evidently with no plans to aid the travel-worn girl. Hopping upon Monase's shoulder, Panza scolded the woman's rapidly retreating back.

Afraid she would lose sight of her, Monase fled back to the camp she had made last night. Looking down on Cira's weakened body, she was assaulted with the realization that for all his disheveled state, he still looked like a mighty Zulu warrior.

For a brief moment she pondered the situation. In all the days of travel, she had no idea how far north they had gone. She also didn't know whose protection the strange woman's tribe was under. If they had sworn allegiance to Zwide, they would surely kill her and Cira the moment they recognized him as a Zulu impi. A decision quickly reached, she grabbed Cira's spear and, with whispered apologies, cut the leather bands of cow tails from his arms and legs. She then removed the blade from the spear, hiding it in the pouch with the assegai blades.

Next, loosening the already ragged leather thongs woven through the shield, she stood to survey her work. The days of endless travel had worn the colored hairs off the shield, and it was doubtful that anyone would recognize it as an instrument of war.

Finally bending to remove the cowhide disks from Cira's ears, she placed a kiss upon his brow. "Not much longer, love. Surely the medicine man here will heal you."

Cira's eyelids flickered slightly as he willed his mind to comprehend. But only the word *medicine man* echoed painfully through his brain.

Seventeen

Nearly two weeks had passed since Monase told the ancient chief that she and her brother Cira were emDletsheni, and that they had been going to Dingoswayo's famous market up north when a band of marauding impi had attacked them. The chief pushed incessantly for details about the warriors. Repeatedly, she feigned ignorance, saying that she had been too frightened to notice much. Finally the chief relented, saying that his kraal had been attacked at night by the Ngwane. The ruthless impi had taken all their herds, killing and capturing most of their young men and women. Now they were just a remnant of the great Hlubis tribe they had once been. The chief then went on to say that he was impressed with Monase's stouthearted perseverance, and as it was obvious he needed young men, she and her brother were welcome to stay.

At the chief's welcome, the women of the tribe converged upon Cira, fighting over who was to have the right to keep him and nurse him in their hut. The women, either bereft of husbands or with widowed and single daughters, were anxious to get their hands on this young, virile, handsome man. With a twinge of regret, Monase realized she had done the right thing in saying he was her brother. If she had claimed Cira, she would not have been welcome here. Although Cira could have many wives, she would be viewed with jealousy.

As both Cira and the women disappeared, their angry squabbling being lost in the retreating dust, Monase felt the full impact of her loneliness. She was a stranger in a strange place. Just then Panza swung up to her shoulder, wrapping a long silky tail around her neck.

"I know, you'll miss him, too," she said. "Though I'm glad you decided to stay with me." She smiled up at the wizened gray face. Her eye caught that of the woman she had followed here. The woman studied her suspiciously from the shadows of the chief's palace. Their eyes continued to hold as the woman unstrapped the baby from her back. Swinging the infant across her hip, she held it out to Monase.

"Baby, you help."

Nodding, Monase took the child into her arms and followed the woman to a modest hut.

The pillaging Ngwane had destroyed all semblance of kraal order in the Hlubi village. Half the huts were burned, and what cattle pens had not been destroyed in the raid had been disassembled for firewood. For two weeks Monase worked and lived with the woman who had befriended her. She had learned that the woman's name was Ufudu, or Little Turtle. The big woman had proved to be generous and kindhearted. She had guffawed loudly when Monase questioned her name, saying that no doubt the ancestors had guessed at her future diminutive size. Monase smiled in shock when she heard the woman speak with bawdy irreverence about religion. But all in all, Ufudu and her baby were all that kept Monase going.

In the beginning, seeing Cira fawned over and flirted with, Monase felt hurt and jealous. As his health improved, and he seemed to flourish under the attention, she felt guilty for her jealousy. But try as she might, she could not fight the unexpected tears that stung her eyes as she watched sullenly from Ufudu's hut.

Unbeknownst to Monase, her guardian watched it all, with the seed of suspicion growing deep roots in her mind.

Now, as she worked side by side with Ufudu, she raised her eyes to seek out Cira one more time. He was now walking, with a serious limp, but able to get around unaided. Although she had watched him for some time, his face a smiling mask covering the excruciating pain, he never met her eyes. Instead he laughed and talked to the bevy of women constantly surrounded him. They seemed to find endless pleasure in helping him with the slightest task.

In irritation, Monase swung her harvesting ax

carelessly, cracking open a ripe yellow-orange pumpkin. Embarrassed at her clumsiness, she began to apologize as she lowered her eyes to survey the mess she'd made. The words never reached her lips as she stared at the slimy yellow pulp spilling out on the broad green leaves. The slow oozing strands caused her stomach to lurch.

Dropping her ax, Monase clasped a hand over her mouth and staggered backward. Her stomach churned again, and she fled. Bending over a small group of bushes, she retched up that morning's meal. Still shaking, she felt her friend's large warm hands on her shoulders.

"How many months?"

Still staring at the bushes, Monase shook her head, not understanding. "Months?"

A gentle laugh rumbled deep in Ufudu's massive belly. "Until baby come?"

Monase felt her head spin as she gasped. The idea had not occurred to her, at least not since that night when Jama—

"Baby? Me? No, no, it can't be."

A sudden knowing sadness swept over Ufudu's normally jovial features. She turned Monase to face her, her eyes bright with compassion.

"No husband. Gone . . . or never?"

Monase lowered her eyes, a flush darkening her damp cheeks. Without a word, Ufudu drew her into her arms, rocking her, as if she were a child.

The tears that came so easily now sprang to her eyes. Clutching Ufudu's ample frame, she collapsed into wretched sobs. What would she do?

Cira was careful to look away every time he felt Monase look toward him. He was confused as to why she stayed, as to why she had brought him here. But his anger outweighed the confusion when he recalled waking in a strange hut, surrounded by strange women. Although he smiled, pretending to enjoy it, it was really a nightmare. That was what he had liked about Monase. She had not fussed and fawned. She had not simpered and acted coy. He looked over at her now as she played happily with that fat woman's baby. What was it with her and heavy people? He let his mind wander to Jama, then squashed the memory of the witch doctor as surely as if it were an annoying pest.

Over a week ago he had opened his eyes to bright painful light. He remembered feeling as if a thousand particles of sand had blown into their sockets. At first, the faces had floated above him, vague and hazy. Then, one by one, they had come into focus, unknown, and speaking a strange dialect. It had hurt his head to concentrate; all he could remember, and think of, was Monase. He had managed to croak out her name, to be understood. In the vast fog that surrounded him, he heard a low feminine voice whisper that the name he was calling was his sister's. With his head throbbing painfully, he labored to open his eyes again, to tell them that they were wrong. But the words would not come; instead, he called for Monase again.

The same soft voice moved nearer, its warm sweet breath blowing across his neck. "You not move. I get sister."

"Sister? Sister?" Cira whispered, his energy waning. The women later told him that in those early hours of consciousness, he was still delirious, that he had even forgotten his own sister, the brave creature who had borne him for so many miles. Sure that the fever had destroyed his memory, they explained to him the whole story as it had been told to them by Monase.

He cringed when he found his cow tails gone and his shield and spear missing. But these were small things next to Monase's betrayal. He continued to let the women believe the story, watching, waiting to find out what plans Monase now had. There was time yet; he would learn her secrets before he returned with her to Zululand. But first he had to heal, to gain back his strength.

The following days had been hell. Frustrated, and in pain, he forced himself to hobble. Time after time he fell in exhaustion, once opening the wound in his thigh. After that, he had moved more slowly, allowing the women to help him.

He made it a practice, whenever Monase looked his way, to lavish attention and smiles on whatever woman was with him. This seemed to annoy Monase and gave him a small amount of pleasure, a very small amount.

As he grew stronger the women pushed harder and harder for his favor. He was often a guest at the chief's amakhanda. The old man made no secret of his desire for Cira to select some wives. He made it clear that for now there was no cost, and barely a limit on number. Cira tried to brush this offer off with laughter, saying he hadn't the strength yet for even one wife. The chief laughed with him, but his brown eyes were serious. He wanted to build up his tribe, and it had to start with children, many children.

Cira liked the old man, and wondered at his own reluctance to enjoy what so many men would die to have. It would be so easy to please the chief. The man had even hinted at a union between Cira and his only daughter. Of course, that would be later, when Cira had obtained some cattle and could make her his Great Wife. But the implication was still there. Succession to the chieftainship was his for the asking. Still, all the Zulu warrior could think of was home, and his duty to Shaka. Of course, there was the other matter of Monase and Jama, but he couldn't afford himself the luxury of thinking of that now.

Somewhere out there was a crazed chief named Zwide, who might or might not still be holding many of his men captive. With these thoughts, Cira's disabilities caged him, making him impatient and angry.

Another week went by, and Cira was up before dawn, pacing, working his legs and arms. As the burnt-orange sun rose up over the purple mountains, tinging the sky with a myriad of colors, Nyasha, a soft-spoken young beauty, touched him from behind. He whirled on her, agitated by the unexpected intrusion on his quiet time. Her eyes grew dark with fear as she backed away. Her sweet innocence reminded him of Mkabuyi, and of his friend Punga. Where were they now?

Uncertain of his reaction, Nyasha moved closer. When Cira smiled down at her, she grew bolder, asking him to dinner that night. Cira leaned heavily on a stick that he occasionally used as a crutch now. It was always the same. He was frustrated, weary of his captivity. In a flat tone he responded.

"Why?"

Nyasha was caught off guard. She had expected a yes or a no. She hedged, then lifted her face to meet him squarely in the eyes. She had felt that he perhaps favored her a little above the others, and had wanted to press the advantage. She hadn't the bloodline to be a Great Wife, but she was damned if she wouldn't be a first wife. She'd seen Cira go to the chief's house for meal after meal. Everyone knew the chief had practically given his daughter to his foreign guest. One day he would be chief, and she wanted to be a part of that. When his eyes did not waver, she responded truthfully.

"I want to win your favor, and become your wife."

Cira was unprepared for this baldly honest statement of intent. He rolled the words around his tongue, the taste bittersweet. Cursed women, he already had a wife and she had dismissed him. As always when he thought of Monase's treachery, a small niggling doubt tugged at the back of his mind. How had Monase found him? Why had she found him? He was unaware of the heated anger blazing from his eyes. Nyasha quickly regretted her truthfulness and fled.

"You awake?" A masculine voice startled Cira out of his daydream. Distractedly, he glanced around. Where had the girl . . . he couldn't remember her name. He turned his attention to Bakuza, the medicine man.

"Barely, I think. I just frightened off a pretty

young maiden." Cira laughed good-naturedly, his mask back in place.

"Ah, that I in your position." Bakuza sighed.

Cira looked at the man with mild surprise. He was young, one of few remaining men in the tribe. His father had been the medicine man before him, and had been slaughtered in the night raid. Bakuza had buried him and, with calm authority, had taken his place. Cira liked and respected the man.

Sitting on a low stool, Bakuza examined Cira's wounds. "I'm sure you have your pick of women," Cira said.

Bakuza laughed a low easy laugh. "Yes, those who want status. But none lust for me." His fingers gently, knowingly ran along Cira's collarbone. "Now, your sister, there is a woman. She did an incredible job with shoulder and wounds, considering. You owe her your life."

Cira bristled at the mention of Monase.

"Does it pain you?" Bakuza asked, genuine concern in his eyes.

Cira looked away, unable to meet the medicine man's eyes. "Yes . . . I mean, not much. I'll get used to it."

Bakuza laughed. "I suppose warriors do."

For a moment their eyes met, and Cira saw the wistful sadness in Bakuza's. For all his wisdom and status, he was a slight wisp of a man. Soft-spoken, he was timid, even frightened around women. Cira had grudgingly noticed him staring moony-eyed at Monase.

"My sister's just like the rest. She may be brave, but she has her sights set on power and wealth.

Don't let her fool you." Cira wanted to add, "Like she did me," but instead rose to his feet.

Bakuza smiled at him, nodding, then walked away, whistling. Cira had tried to warn him away from his sister, but instead had put the idea into Bakuza's head that he could have Monase if he was willing to trade his status and wealth. Maybe he'd just have to spend a little more time around her to find out the truth, Bakuza thought.

Too late Cira realized his mistake when day after day, he saw Bakuza hovering around Monase in the field, outside her hut, by the fire at night. It annoyed him, but he refused to admit it. Every beautiful smile she bestowed on the medicine man twisted his stomach in jealous knots. *How easily she trades one medicine man for another.* Instead of going to her, talking it out, he waited. Wanting *her* to come to him.

Both Ufudu and Bakuza were baffled by Monase and Cira's bizarre apathy toward one another. Although they claimed there was no rift between them, they never spoke, but only darted furtive glances at each other. Less baffling were Bakuza's feelings toward Monase. Ufudu could see that the medicine man was sweet on her young guest, and did everything in her power to feed the flames.

One evening, as Monase cleared the dishes, Ufudu confided Monase's condition to the medicine man. Afraid at first that he might denounce her, Ufudu was relieved to find that the knowledge only strengthened his affection toward her. Together, they surmised that possibly the father was what stood between brother and sister. Like two naughty children Ufudu and Bakuza contrived a way to get them back together.

So intent was Monase in watching Cira, but not appearing to do so, that she didn't really notice the additional attention she received from Bakuza. She just accepted his sweet brotherly overtures as she accepted Ufudu. Night after night Bakuza was invited for the evening meal. Afterward he would beg her to sing. At first she had been shy, unwilling, but as their friendship grew she at last complied to his request.

Sometimes, after she finished in the fields, the medicine man invited her to come with him to pick herbs. One day they came across Cira and a young woman emerging from the shaded forest. Both couples stopped in their tracks. Bakuza and Cira's companion greeted each other cordially, but Cira and Monase just stared silently at each other. After a while the silence grew uncomfortable. The young woman tugged gently on Cira's arm. Without warning, he pulled her into his embrace, leaning her back against him as he nibbled her earlobe. The woman blushed with delighted pleasure. In the depths of the forest, he hadn't responded to any of her overtures.

Monase felt her cheeks grow hot with shame, anger, and jealousy. She had seen Cira kiss women before, from a distance, but not right in front of her face. She placed a firm hand on Bakuza's forearm, then noticed the worshiping gaze he had turned to Cira. She dropped her hand in disgust. Cira's sultry voice drew her eyes back to his hooded ones.

"Doesn't your brother deserve a better greeting . . . *dear sister*?" The words were sickly-sweet, yet seductive. Before she could answer, Cira swept her up against him, her feet leaving the ground. She didn't have time to wonder at his regained strength before he let her slide slowly, tauntingly down the front of him to the ground. The current that ran between them sizzled in the air.

His eyes inscrutable, Cira held her to him a few moments before placing a cool chaste kiss upon her forehead. Reluctantly, she let her eyes meet his. Through his lashes, she could see, and feel, the molten gold heat coming from them.

Stumbling, she pushed away, only to be stopped by Bakuza, his brow creased in a frown. This was not the reunion he and Ufudu had imagined.

As Monase walked away with Bakuza she turned around to look over her shoulder. Again her eyes met Cira's. A wicked smile played at the corners of his mouth. She wanted to scream, so intense were the feelings that churned inside her. She wanted to run back into his arms and beg him to hold her again, to give her what his smoldering eyes promised. Yet, at the same time, she wanted to slap that cruel smile off his face, to create a small semblance of the pain he caused her. Instead, she smiled back, a brittle sugary smile, sweetly, but with no substance.

After that one encounter, the two peacemakers no longer sought to reunite sister and brother. Monase was sulky for three days, and Cira would not even see Bakuza. Ufudu and the medicine man decided it was better to let nature take its course, with no intervention from them. So, by the end of the fourth week, Bakuza began again to make his nightly visits to Ufudu's hut.

One night Monase was lying back drowsily against a thick log, alongside the outside fire, listening to Bakuza tell a wonderful story about a legendary being called the spiderman and his quest for stories from heaven. It had now been two months since her monthly flow, and she was fairly certain that she was pregnant. Ufudu had told her it was natural to be tired and out of sorts, and that she should count herself fortunate that she was only a little queasy in the morning. Monase liked not having her monthly flow, but knew that soon her protruding belly would show. She closed her eyes, contemplating, wishing it could have all been different. She wondered what Cira would say if he knew. As her mind explored one possibility after another, she began to drift off to sleep.

"Monase? Monase?" Bakuza had ended his story. Ufudu had skuttled away, saying she had to put the baby to bed. She turned meaningful eyes on Bakuza as she nodded toward Monase.

Groggy, Monase whimpered, opening her eyes reluctantly. Bakuza knelt before her. His eyes shone bright in the firelight. Shyly, he bent and placed a kiss on her cheek. When she didn't refuse him, he ventured to place a dry kiss on her lips.

Monase stiffened, her eyes opening wide. "Bakuza?"

With a sudden passion, Bakuza gripped both her hands to his lips. First kissing the backs of them, he turned them over, kissing her palms, then each fingertip. Monase curled her fingers inward, withdrawing them from his caresses.

"Monase, I love you. I know you do not love me,

but I will give to you anything, everything." His voice was raw with longing.

Monase turned her face away from his pleading eyes. She tugged at her hands, but he wouldn't release them.

"Bakuza, of course I love you. I love you as a friend, as a brother." Her attempt at a lighthearted tone failed miserably. Bakuza released her hands, his voice cold. It was this unusual iciness that caused her to look at him.

"Then you would show me brotherly affection you show your brother." His eyes glittered with a strange frigidity she'd never seen there before.

"I . . . there is more." She paused, looking miserable. "You see, I . . ." Monase's hands fluttered nervously above her lap, then fell to rest protectively across her waist. For a moment a spark of hope flickered in Bakuza's eyes. Tentatively, he touched her hand. She jumped, as if hit with a jolt of lightning.

"I know . . . Ufudu told me." His voice was incredibly gentle, lapsing into the heavy accent of his tribe. He had spent years traveling with his father and had developed an almost bland accentless tone. Monase ached to reach out and tell him that her condition was all that kept him from what he wanted. She cringed inside at the words that had almost spilled out so easily. Ufudu and Bakuza were her friends, they had opened their hearts and their lives to her, and she had lied to them.

Her silence seemed to empower him, giving him strength. "I wish to ask your brother for your hand. I've not many cattle." He gestured vaguely to the distant mountains. "The Ngwane impi took most. . . ." Then he turned fearful eyes upon her. "But I am young, able, I will make a good husband."

Monase flinched visibly at the word, and Bakuza retreated, hurt flickering across his face. Monase couldn't bear the pain; she reached out and took his hands, then as quickly released them. She shouldn't encourage him. Silence fell between them, amplifying the crackling of the fire, Ufudu's distant lullaby, and the melodic cries and whispers of the surrounding night.

Monase turned her head to gaze into the fire, a single tear shimmering on her lower lashes. It quivered, then slid silently down her cheek.

"Don't." Bakuza's voice was gruff with feeling. "It not your fault. I know your brother think it is, but I know those impis force you."

Monase's mouth dropped open, and Bakuza pulled her to him. "Those bastards."

Monase was shocked at the brutal words, and the force with which they were uttered. They sounded so strange coming from this gentle man.

Suddenly he tilted her face to his, his lips descending on hers with savage urgency. She could feel his burning passion and desire rippling through every muscle in his young supple body, but she felt unmoved, untouched, and so lost and alone. She was tired of trying, so very tired. Bakuza pulled away from her, his face wreathed in a triumphant smile. He was her champion. Throwing back his shoulders, he laid a hand on her cheek and then turned, marching off into the darkness.

Cira paced restlessly outside the hut he was occupying. Night after night he had heard the laughter, then the beautiful singing, drifting through the darkness toward him. He'd have known that voice anywhere, and he longed to go to her, to have her sing for him, only to him. Then he'd hear Bakuza's voice, and more laughter, as the medicine man told his tales. If Cira listened carefully, he could hear Monase's low laugh. If he closed his eyes, he could see her smile. Frustration and anger raged inside of him. He kicked a loose pebble at the fire.

But tonight, as the golden haze of the evening sun settled over the trees, she had sung his song. The song she had sung that day in the field. The day she had become his. It seemed like years ago, like a dream. But a dream that brought real pain.

Cira pushed a hand through his unruly hair. It was late, but there would be no sleep tonight. He again kicked at the loose stones. He would go find Bakuza, get him to mix him some of that potent brew. He knew that without it he faced yet another long tortured night. He needed to get his rest, conserve his strength. It was almost time to start the journey home, possibly with a very unwilling companion. With a menacing smile, he turned, and crashed head-on with the medicine man.

The impact sent Cira staggering and Bakuza sprawling. With a sheepish grin of apology, Cira hoisted the smaller man to his feet.

"I'm sorry, I was just coming to find—" Cira broke off as he noticed the strange pallor of Bakuza's face. "What is it? Monase?" The ashen young man looked up in shock at Cira's perceptiveness. Cira felt a heavy lump forming in his throat as Bakuza nodded yes. "What happened? Is she hurt?" The medicine man was surprised to see the genuine concern and fear distorting Cira's features.

"No, nothing like that." Bakuza took a deep breath, measuring out each word, as if he had only a few to spare. "I . . . We . . . Ask." He stopped in frustration, his hands curling into tight fists at his side. "I wish to marry Monase. I will pay fair lobala when I'm able." The words came out stiff, bland, with no accent or inflection. Then suddenly, as if the effort had cost him much, his shoulders sagged and his eyes turned pleading. "You understand?"

Cira stood frighteningly still. A dark ravishing fire spread through his eyes. He understood all right, only too well. Bakuza stepped back. Cira's eyes looked like the hot lava he had once seen spilling from the mountains up north. It was terrible, frightening. A low deep growl began from the center of Cira's being. It rose like a whirlwind, gathering force and speed, dragging in every hot-blooded, anger-infested nerve in his body.

Bakuza retreated a step further, cowering, waiting for the impact. Suddenly Cira's anger died as rapidly as it had started. The only sound he made was a loud deflating hiss. Bakuza, still in shock, was stunned further by the soft deadly word that followed in its wake.

"No." After uttering the single syllable, Cira turned and walked away into the darkness. All resemblance to the man the young medicine man had come to know had vanished behind this icy, untouchable facade.

Unable to believe or to accept Cira's answer without an explanation, Bakuza hurried after him. "But Cira, my friend . . ."

Cira whirled on him, his face a demonic mask, his lips curled in a barbarous sneer. "I know a medicine man that will pay a much higher price." Then he threw back his head, emitting a hollow unearthly laugh that sliced through the night, hanging ominously, then was swallowed with him as he disappeared into the darkness.

Bakuza followed him only with his eyes. The man was mad. The fever had done more damage than he had suspected. Tomorrow, he would get a blessing from the chief. He would broach the subject of Cira's madness carefully. He was a reasonable man, there would be plenty of time tomorrow.

Tossing restlessly among her covers, Monase repeated the events of the evening over and over in her mind. This evening she had sung the song that had brought Cira to her so long ago. She had hoped that perhaps its magic would work again. It had, it seemed—unfortunately, though, it had worked on the wrong man. Poor Bakuza; he was such a sweet caring man. He had offered to take her, even though he knew she was carrying another man's child. A child, which he thought was conceived by the same enemy that had raped him and his people of so much. She hadn't dared to tell him the truth.

Rolling onto her back, she gazed desolately at the tightly woven ceiling. She knew how it hurt to want someone badly and not have them return the feeling. Oh, how she wished Bakuza's kiss had fired passion in her the way a mere glance from Cira could. Laying a hand on her still-flat belly, she tried to envision the child lying deep within. A warm surge of maternal affection washed over her. She had to do what was best for the child. She couldn't risk subjecting it to shame and ridicule, or even death, if Cira were to refuse her. Her pride wouldn't let her crawl to him, beg him to take her. Conveniently, another option had presented itself. She could marry Bakuza and let Cira return to Zululand without her. For all the adulation Cira received here, she knew he was still the great Zulu warrior, sworn to Shaka, and he would return.

Having made her decision, she felt tears overwhelm her, for the family she would be losing, and the family she'd never have with Cira. The spirits had a strange way of deciding one's fate, and all she could do was accept it. Rolling back over, she buried her sobs into her arms so as not to wake Ufudu and the baby.

Eighteen

In the quiet of the night, strong hands wrenched Monase from her fitful slumber. She had opened her mouth to scream when large fingers clamped brutally over her mouth. A raspy voice hissed into her ear.

"Silence."

Immediately Monase's struggles ceased. Her heart started pumping rapidly. She knew that voice, would know it anywhere. Unable to control a few violent shivers, she allowed herself to be half carried, half dragged out of the hut.

Now, staring into Cira's strangely lit yellow-gold eyes, she heard him whisper, "Sister dear, obviously, we have stayed a little too long." The whisper then burst into a strangled laugh. She was frightened to see him look so deranged and tried to scoot backward, away from him, but he held her tight, his eyes glowing in the moonlight. Her heart skidded to a stop, then raced wildly, like a caged animal.

Scared, unsure, she bit down hard on Cira's hand across her mouth. He cursed loudly as she was pitched forward into the deep grass outside the Hlubi kraal. She struggled to rise only to have iron hands toss her to her back. Cira's hot barbaric lips crushed hers. She tried to turn her head, flailing wildly with her hands, but he gripped her chin to the bone with one hand and captured her wrist with the other, pulling her hands up and back over her head. In a panic Monase began to kick.

In response, Cira lowered his lung-crushing weight on her, pinning her legs with his own. The heat of his body was like a blazing brand, searing her flesh where it touched her. Completely a prisoner, she felt Cira's kiss deepen, his tongue plunging deep within her, without mercy. Whimpering, she fought; she didn't want it to be like this. She didn't want to succumb to his driving hate. But against her will, her body won out, responding to the onslaught of kisses he rained down upon her.

As Cira felt her weaken beneath him his kisses grew soft, even tender. The fingers holding her chin loosened their hold and began stroking the bruised skin, as if to wipe away the damage. Still he held her wrist, but the painful grip relaxed. He shifted his weight, kneeling slightly above her, and moaned her name as his lips slid over her chin, down the length of her throat, nipping at the collarbone, then dipping down to her erect nipples.

Moving rapidly from one to the other, his tongue lashed at their tips, enticing them to press further upward. As Monase groaned and arched forward, the hand restraining her wrist let go. Both of his hands cupped her full breasts, pushing them upward together. His mouth roamed greedily from one to the other, sucking, plundering, demanding.

Suddenly Cira raised his head, gasping for breath, the cold night air chilling Monase's moist nipples, making her yearn for more. She arched her back, grinding her hips into his. She could feel his manhood pressing hot and demanding between her thighs. Oh, how she wanted him, but he did not respond. Opening her eyes, she found herself staring into his cold glittering gold ones. Beneath the fine layer of ice she saw the molten heat, but the ice stood between them.

His sensuous lips twisted into a cruel smile. "What sisterly affection. Or did you believe I was Jama? Or is it Bakuza now?"

Wide-eyed with horror, Monase felt the passion that had risen within her traitorous body shrivel and die. She shrank back from him. His hatred was almost palpable in the darkness.

"Is your greed never satisfied? You use, then destroy men. You and Jama deserve each other." Suddenly a great weariness swept over Cira's face. He turned away, his voice distant. "I will keep my vow. Get up. Let's go." Pushing himself up, he began to walk away.

Monase rose, as if in a daze, and followed him, his final demand holding her as if his iron grip was still around her. As her mind began to focus she weighed her options. It had all seemed so simple last night, almost as if the decision had been made for her. But now, as she looked at Cira's slouched dejected shoulders, she wasn't sure.

After what seemed like hours, Monase began to stumble. Exhaustion, both mental and physical, dragged heavily on her limbs. When Cira turned, she lifted silent beseeching eyes to his shadowed face. Grudgingly, he stopped. As she dropped to the cold ground he started a fire and spread some hide covering around it; unrolling a small bundle Monase hadn't even noticed, she had been so tired, and deep in thought. Now she looked covetously at the soft hides. Without turning toward her, Cira tossed her one and a slab of biltong. He then rose to gather firewood for the night.

Tired and dejected, Monase chewed on the dried meat and contemplated running back to the Hlubi kraal. Quickly, she let that impulse go. Cira would return for her, his anger only stronger. He'd tell the whole story of their relationship, and then even Bakuza would reject her. Drawing her knees up beneath her, she curled into a fetal ball. The crackling fire, the chirping crickets, the effects of the long journey wove their spell, and she was asleep before Cira returned.

His arms were loaded with kindling, which he dropped unceremoniously near the fire. Alarm laced with anger flickered through him when he saw the hides around the fire empty. He whirled, his arms poised in a fighter's stance. Then his eyes rested on the small, huddled sleeping figure. He advanced cautiously, holding his breath, then releasing it slowly through his nose.

Close to the fire, Cira hunkered down, his shadow

covering all of the resting form. His eyes swept down the soft vulnerable face. Her eyelashes cast dark shadows on her tearstained cheeks. For the first time he noticed the dark smudges beneath her eyes. Concern creased his brow as he gently lifted her. As he straightened his knees she shifted, curling into his chest, her damp cheek nestling snugly against his warm skin. Again he caught his breath, a painful heaviness around his heart, which was soon swept away by a torrent of protectiveness. He released his breath in a heavy sigh and carried his wife to his bed.

Sometime after midnight, Monase awakened to a soft tickling sensation on her cheek. Opening her eyes, she stared groggily into black inquisitive ones. Panza sat in the curve of her chin and throat, stroking her cheek with his long tail. A warm smile stretched lazily over her lips, but froze and vanished when her gaze fell upon Cira's sleeping visage inches from her.

The minutes crept by as she watched him sleep. He, too, had been exhausted by the confrontation, and by the journey. Lying there asleep, he looked so young. His lips were moist and parted. Monase was suddenly seized with an incredible urge to kiss them, one last time. Raising a warning finger to her lips, she bade Panza to follow her silently. Carefully, she removed the possessive arm Cira had draped across her in his sleep.

Easing herself slowly from the covers, she stifled a sigh. Cira was taking her back to Zululand. There, he would denounce her, defer to Shaka's leadership by accepting another of his choosing. First her family, then the whole village would discover that she was an unwed mother. Perhaps Cira would even deny his paternity of the child. Who would doubt his word against hers? She would be shamed, her family would be shamed. She would probably be put to death. Or even worse, Cira would take the child and turn her, Monase, over to be Jama's mistress or one of Shaka's dead-eyed "sisters."

Imagining her child growing up, calling another woman mother, she felt a great sorrow grip her chest, making it difficult to breathe. She couldn't and wouldn't allow this. She had to get away. She could not return to the generous Hlubis. She would have to forge her way northward on her own. Jutting her chin out, steeling herself for the long loveless future before her, she turned to leave. For a moment Panza hesitated, his dark eyes studying first Cira, then Monase. Another rip in her tattered heart.

Monase stepped forward . . . and fell. Her arm flew outward, her mouth round with a silent scream. Cira rolled, releasing her ankle, and caught her falling figure squarely on his chest. His arms wrapped tightly around her waist, making it impossible to do anything but stare straight into his sandy-yellow eyes.

"Leaving so soon? So soon you forget Jama for the poor boy Bakuza. He only offers a handful of cattle for Jama's many." Cira's eyebrows raised quizzically. "Even I have more cows than Bakuza. But of course you knew that. Does he perhaps love you so well that you forget everyone else?"

Monase's hand came rushing forward and a sharp crack split the night as it made contact with

Cira's cheek. He rolled, crushing her beneath him, his eyes tawny and threatening.

"Tell me, Monase." The words hung, a menacing demand in the stillness. She would have raised her hand again, but he stopped it easily.

"You . . . you . . . beast, I hate you." Her sobs gushed out, despite his crushing weight above her.

Cira's eyes grew dark and dangerous, the last flicker of fire burning out, leaving only smoldering black coals. "Hate me? Maybe, but hate what I can do to you?" He answered his own question with a low sensuous chuckle. His warm breath cascaded over her face as the sweet musky masculine scent of him closed in around her. His right hand moved deftly up her rib cage, to mold and cup her still-sensitive breast.

Monase bucked angrily in response, which only seemed to excite him further. He wedged his knee between her thigh, forcing her legs apart.

"Tell me, Monase, did he have you? Tell me, is it only me who can arouse your body so? Or will any man with power or wealth do?"

The cruelty in his words contradicted the slow loving movements of his hands. She wanted to scream out in rage, frustration, and fear at her own body's betrayal. She wanted him still. His angry passion was exhilarating, yet frightened her beyond reason. She closed her eyes and moaned a desperate weak sound as he continued to spit his venomous hatred at her.

"If any man has touched you like this, I'll kill him. Tell me, Monase. Tell me now." The hate in his voice seemed to crack open, revealing the raw vulnerable pain in his voice. She turned her head away, whimpering.

"No."

The word was soft, barely above a whisper, and Cira bent closer to hear. Monase began to weep. It had all gone so wrong. Cira's next words were forced, no less cruel than before, but somehow lacking his earlier conviction.

"Do you wish it were he with you now?" His head bent lower, resting against her ear. When she didn't respond, he gently kissed the sensitive hollow below her ear. She shivered at the delicate touch. Encouraged, he rubbed his nose along the taut cord of her neck, then nibbled at her earlobe.

Monase squeezed her eyes tighter, feeling the burning tears stinging the raw tender skin at the corners. It seemed the tears just kept coming, a bottomless spring. Cira paused as one salty droplet met his lips. He drew in a ragged sigh as he rasped hoarsely against her temple.

"Tell me, Monase . . . I must know. Tell me."

His words ripped through her like a blunt blade, renting, mutilating, not clean and quick. She cringed as he repeated the words, the blade twisting, turning as the desperation of his plea registered on her mind. She could bear no more, and turned to him, wrapping her arms around him. She pressed him to her, her tears falling unbidden on his neck and shoulder.

"No, Cira. No, I love you, only you. I've never loved anyone else." She paused, choking on a sob. "Please don't hate me so . . . just let me go. Have pity on me . . . or at least my family . . . don't take me back to die in shame."

Cira remained where he was, unmoving, unresponsive. Then he pulled away from her slowly, his face in the shadows of the dying fire, his eyes dark, cloudy, unreadable. Unexpectedly, a lone tear slipped down his gaunt cheekbone. His hand touched first her cheek, then her lips, questioning. Then he threw back his head, his hands grasping her breasts, kneading them. With a howl of despairing agony, he buried his face in the side of her neck. His hips rose, then he plunged his hard blood-engorged shaft deep within her.

Monase was stunned as a sharp spasm of burning heat rolled through her, igniting the passion she was doomed to feel for this man. His body bucked uncontrollably above her, and she wrapped her legs around his waist to pull him deeper into her.

Exulting in her response, Cira cupped her bottom with his hands, gathering her closer to him. Over and over he pumped in and out of her, their bodies rising and falling in a dance as primitive and ancient as time.

Monase soared, small spasms bursting like lighting, ricocheting through every nerve, mounting to an intolerable intensity. Cira moaned against her throat, tasting the salty perspiration there. Monase grasped his back, her fingers sliding off his sweat-slick skin. She dug in her nails, making dark crescents in his flesh. He groaned, throwing his head back, as the moonlight cast shimmering silver shadows on the straining ropes of muscles in his arms, shoulders, and neck.

Suddenly Monase felt his body grow rigid as he released a deep, guttural, animallike sound, a cry of defeat, of victory, of surrender. Its echo rushed through her like a torrential flood through a canyon, carrying her to crashing heights. She clung to him, whipped by the storm that raged between them. Legs around legs, skin against skin, they melded, spent, drenched, exhausted.

Now, at last, their bodies were satisfied, but their hearts still remained battered and worn.

Nineteen

The next day dawned glorious, the sky azure blue with luminous streaks of amber and rose, shining over silver spiderwebs of frosty dew upon the grass. Drinking in the beauty with her eyes, Monase breathed deeply of the cold sharp air. Shivering, she pulled the covers up over her shoulders as she drew up her knees, creating a tight cocoon.

Soon she became aware of Panza crawling restlessly over her, and closed her eyes, feeling content and satisfied. She had had beautiful dreams, but they were just illusions: only her lovemaking with Cira was real. She willed the drowsy haze around her to stay, but with a frustrated screech, the monkey unceremoniously yanked the covers from her shoulders, baring her to the waist.

Her eyes flew open with a startled cry as the cold morning air seized her sleep-warmed skin. The cry became a silent gasp as her eyes met Cira's and saw the dark, sensuous expression within them. There was no mistaking the ardent embers glowing in their golden depths. Monase squirmed uncomfortably, her hand grasping unsuccessfully for the stolen blanket.

Leaning insolently, his back against a sturdy acacia tree, Cira raked his eyes over her body, pausing on the dark hardened peaks of her breasts. Bolting upright, Monase felt a wave of nausea crash over her. Bitter bile rose threatening in her throat. Gripping the elusive covers with shaking hands, she turned to retch, humiliated, in the frost-dusted grass.

Wiping the back of her hand across her pale trembling lips, she swung her eyes in a panic to Cira. She couldn't let him guess her condition. He'd never let her go then, and her life would become an empty loveless shell like her mother's. She knew last night had meant nothing to him, that he had merely used her to get his revenge. He had moved away from her, unable to meet her eyes when, after they made love, she had told him again that she loved him. He had laughed a brittle laugh, then told her to get some sleep. Now he was looking at her with lust, only lust. He'd make her pay for every bit of inconvenience she'd caused him.

Thinking such thoughts, she was startled to see tender concern flicker across his wide topaz eyes. He had shifted his body to stand upright, letting his hands drop from their defiant fold across his chest.

"Are you all right? Did I hurt you?" His fists clenched and unclenched as the anguish in his voice crushed down upon him, making his shoulders slump. Suddenly he looked so vulnerable, Monase couldn't help but be reminded of the lost orphaned boy he had been so many years ago.

Then just as suddenly, she *knew*, as if the blindfolds of pride and foolish innocence had been ripped from her eyes: he loved her, needed her, the way she needed and loved him. She wanted to run to him, to embrace him, to share her discovery with him. Still shaken from the impact of the realization, she smiled weakly at him and shook her head.

"No, I must have just sat up too quickly. I'm fine . . . now," she lied.

"Are you sure?" Cira sounded doubtful.

Again, Monase nodded. Then, taking a deep breath, she clasped her hands. "About last night . . ."

Cira's eyes turned suddenly cold, unyielding, as he stalked toward her, his voice silencing the morning birds. "Stop, no more talk about me leaving you behind."

Monase watched as his massive shoulders hunkered forward, the muscles rippling like a wild animal's beneath his rich dark skin. She didn't flinch, but trained her eyes on his. She'd teach this man that he loved her, and that she loved him. She wouldn't let him bully her into being frightened of him any longer.

Seeing the determination in her gaze, Cira stopped, reflecting on her unexpected forcefulness.

It was unnerving as well as inviting. A slow, lazy smile touched his lips as he recognized it as a challenge.

"I don't know what you have planned. But be sure I will not ever allow you to return to your grotesque witch doctor or your lovesick Bakuza. You are my wife." He moved closer to grasp her upper arms gently, pulling her toward him. "You are mine. Last night, today, tomorrow . . . *always.* Don't ever forget it." With these words, he released her, studying her reaction.

Monase was caught unprepared. Her mouth fell open, then closed, working soundlessly for several seconds. "But the headband? You mean you still want to marry me?"

Cira snorted. "I haven't much choice. Shaka gave his blessing before I left."

Monase's mind raced through fragmented memories of that evening, the days that followed. She grasped for hope, something to build on. Her hands moved in a complex choreography, much to Cira's amusement.

"If you are trying to communicate with me in a new sign language, I'm not following."

Monase turned wild eyes to him. "No . . . I'm your *wife*?"

Immediately Cira's smile faded as he stiffened, steeling himself for the answer to his next question. "Yes, is there something you regret having done?" His voice was a lethal whisper.

Monase floundered, shaking her head vehemently. She could only echo her own words—"Your *wife*?"—in a disbelieving cry. Abruptly, a rapturous smile wreathed her face, and a sweet, indefinable joy swept over her as all the pain of today and yesterday dissipated in the happiness of the moment. She was his wife, he had cared enough to protect her with his name. Her actions totally incongruous with the situation, she pulled him into her arms, showering his face, his shoulders, his chest with lilting laughter and kisses of exaltation.

Stunned, Cira stiffened for a moment, like a heat-parched man caught in a shower of cool, longed-for, but unexpected rain. He then relaxed, soaking in the caresses his body thirsted for.

"Oh, Cira, every word I said last night was true. I love you," Monase cried between kisses.

It was as if her words broke the spell. Cira's warm inviting flesh grew cold and rigid beneath her hands. Steely manacles encased her wrists, pulling them from his body. His ever-changing eyes glinted harshly.

"I have made my mistakes. Do not try to fool me again." His grip tightened painfully as his words gathered with a cruel force. "Do not speak of your love for me. Serve me as a wife does her husband, and I will ask no more of you."

He released her, but still her hand hung in midair, unable to move, or unwilling to be set free. Deliberately, he turned, his shoulders flexing, the massive shoulder blades pulling together, then lifting. "Come, we have a long journey ahead of us."

Tears threatened to engulf the last vestiges of Monase's pride. Valiantly, she fought them back, the effort burning harshly in her aching throat. Her lungs were constricted, wrapped in a python's deadly grip of despair. Drawing in a deep ragged breath, she released it slowly. It wavered, and caught, stumbling painfully over the lump in her throat. Monase drew in her bottom lip, biting down hard. Bright red drops of blood beaded along its swollen surface. She would not cry, she would prove her love for Cira. She must make him see, for to fail would destroy them all: Cira, herself, and the child they had created.

Twenty

The days and nights rolled by silently, emptily, a series of weary marchings, monosyllabic conversations, and exhausted slumbers. Food and water were scarce, but neither Monase nor Cira complained. Cira remained distant and aloof, not approaching or touching Monase. But his eyes followed her with an angry, frustrated yearning.

Monase was careful to rise slowly in the mornings and to tie additional bags and pouches around her waist to hide the now straining fabric of her skirt. She had all but forgotten about Cira's iKlwa spearhead until a few days ago. When she did remember it, she timidly presented it to him, and was moved when tears sprang to his eyes. He had fashioned a crude handle and brought back several small animals that very day. It was with these skins and bladders that she hid her growing pregnancy. For all the tension between them, Monase enjoyed cooking and caring for Cira. Sometimes she even hummed, or sang a little. Not looking at the man she loved, she knew he was listening. She could feel the anger soften as his eyes burned into her.

One evening, as Cira stirred the fire, he spoke in a stiff staccato voice.

"We are near. One, two days at most." A long silence. "Sleep. We leave early." Snapping a dry branch between powerful fingers, he then rose and walked off into the surrounding darkness.

Monase lifted an outstretched hand to his retreating back, then let it flutter uselessly to her lap, like the brittle scales of the snakeskin she'd found, she thought. This memory briefly distracted her from the despondency gnawing at the edges of her heart. Unfastening the pouch that she had kept concealed from Cira, she reached in and drew out the long coiled skin. The ever-present Panza screeched in horror and fled to a nearby tree. Monase gingerly ran her fingers along the scaly surface, wondering at its significance. She had been so absorbed in her own problems during her stay at the Hlubi village that she had forgotten to seek out an isangoma. Now she thought of the old woman in the Zulu village who had delivered her devastating news, news that could shatter her, Cira, and possibly the whole of the southeastern African world.

Replacing the skin, she reached out her arms to Panza. Welcoming the comfort of her arms and the disappearance of the frightful snakeskin, the monkey didn't hesitate, and was soon snuggling his head beneath her chin. Curling up around his tiny body, Monase fell asleep on her separate sleeping hide.

Something was wrong. Even sleeping, her hunter's sense came to her. She opened her eyes to the moonlight flickering among the trees' thorny shadows. She jerked away when Cira's face appeared suddenly, inches from her own. She opened her mouth to speak, but his gentle, firm hand molded snugly across it. His voice was low, almost inaudible, and she had to strain toward him to hear it.

"Don't move, don't speak. The Dlamini branch of the Ngwanes, one of Zwide's armies, has made camp on the other side of this patch of forest."

Monase trembled at the terror that both the names Zwide and the Ngwanes evoked in her. She had not forgotten the tales of the Zulu sentry, or the horrors wreaked on the Hlubi tribe. Now she and Cira were alone, a few yards from where these fearsome men had made their camp. All her life she had been fortunate. Her tribe had never been faced with a violently aggressive adversary. Facing a ferocious beast, she could be brave. An animal was predictable, primitive, ignorant, only interested in killing or being killed. But from what she had heard, Zwide was evil. He thrilled to the pain and devastation of battle, took pleasure in the cruel process of killing, not merely in the result.

Cira's soft voice broke through her morbid reverie. "Come with me quietly. I don't dare leave you here, unprotected, alone."

Briefly, the impulsive Monase felt the urge to remind him that she had passed through this same terrain weeks ago, by herself. But then she thought better of it. In truth, she didn't want to be left alone to wait . . . to wait for what? The possibilities sent icy shivers down her spine, making her hands cold and clammy. She nodded, and Cira removed his hand. For a moment he swayed toward her, and she thought he was going to kiss her, but he abruptly rose, doused the fire, then turned to her with a warning glance. As she rose he crept silently through the trees.

The Ngwane camp was alive with laughter and loud, arrogant bragging. Pushing Monase behind him, Cira surveyed the campsite from their hiding place in the dense bushes. Monase peeked tentatively around his broad shoulders, her hands sandwiched between his warm back and her soft breasts.

Suddenly the muscles beneath her fingers tightened, bunching and straining, like an animal ready to pounce. Looking at Cira's frozen profile, she followed his gaze to where a dozen or more bruised and tattered Zulu impi were bound to the rough trunks of trees. Looking down the line of shattered, defeated faces, she recognized Punga. The right side of his face was gashed and bleeding. His chest bore fresh burn marks. She shrank at the sight. The battle had been over for weeks, but still these beasts tortured their prisoners.

Turning her eyes to Cira, she watched frustration and helplessness grip his features. His jaw quivered slightly as a small muscle twitched below the hollow of his cheek. She felt the deep, jagged breaths he drew painfully into his lungs as he squatted, his fists clenched, making his knuckles a bright white against the darkness of his skin. These were his men, his family. They meant everything to him, and he had failed them.

At that moment, as if unable to bear the torturous responsibility and guilt, he raised his face to the waning moon. His mouth twisted, falling open to release a silent scream of anguish. Running his hands into his thick dark hair, he pulled it to the roots. Falling forward, his head pulled down by his clawed hands, he crumbled, tears streaming down his cheeks. He was but one, and they were so many.

Monase clutched her hands to her chest, horrified to see this fearless giant of a man reduced to weeping. Her heart ached for the pain and agony he must be going through. These men had trusted him, depended on him, and now he must watch them die, tortured, humiliated. He was being forced to do the one act he found unpardonable: abandon his men. And to be forced to such an act under these conditions was more than anyone should have to do.

Outrage flooded Monase's being. She cursed Zwide and his savage barbarians, feeling a cold impenetrable curtain come down around her. Silently, she turned and walked through the trees toward the camp. She knew what she had to do.

The boisterous Ngwane impis quieted momentarily as Monase's figure glowed like a bronze specter in the dancing firelight. Then the silence was broken by blatant leers and lecherous cries as she walked straight toward the man who was obviously their leader, standing outside the only shelter. Six guards rushed forward to stop her, but she fell to her knees before him. The men stood, suspended, waiting for a sign from their leader.

Steeling herself against her fear and revulsion, Monase looked up seductively at the man through lowered lashes, all trace of her previous loathing apparently gone. In a soft, sensuous whisper she began to speak.

"I am a shifta, a wanderer. I have been abandoned." Her voice dropped lower as the man bent closer to listen. "I roam the land learning the spirits' songs, stories, and dances."

She paused, then began again in her deep sultry whisper, her eyes rising to gaze deep into the leader's eyes, a slow promising smile curving her moistened lips. "And if you are brave enough, I will teach you the secrets of lovemaking they have taught me." She watched with concealed hatred as the man's eyes grew hooded with desire. Slowly, she rose, pressing the length of her body against him. She heard the guards gasp, but none moved forward to stop her.

Wrapping a strong arm around her waist, the leader gazed hungrily at her now voluptuous breasts, plumped high and full against him. Reluctantly, he raised his head, his eyes challenging any man to take her.

"This shifta will sing, dance, tell stories for you . . . but she is mine for the other." The women-starved impis' muted grumbles threatened to rise to a roar of mutiny. "Enough!" snapped the man who held her. "First she will dance."

These words were met with loud hoots and animal growls, but the men relented. Monase moistened her lips again, smiling a lush smile. She touched each man's arm as she made her way to the opening they had made by the fire. One man pulled out an ugumbu, a musical instrument with a long stick protruding from a gourd base, from his belongings while others made makeshift drums and clacking sticks. The music began.

Monase hesitated a minute as fingers of panic strangled her bravado. She closed her eyes, willing the cold blinding blanket of raging hatred to return. She breathed in deeply, welcoming the numbing folds of anger as they wrapped around her, transporting her from her normal self. Only the music remained.

With an easy grace, she slid forward, raising her smooth arms elegantly above her head. She turned her face to the misty moon and released a bittersweet, eerie note. Momentarily, the music stopped, the chord drifting above the crowd, almost seeming to shimmer in the starless night. Then slowly, Monase began to undulate her hips. The drums began again, followed by the steady beat of the ugumbu. First, her right arm dipped over her head, running seductively along her shoulder and the back of her neck. Her voice sang out the song of the spirits of the trees, the wind in their branches.

As her song grew stronger, she lost herself in the words. The world dissolved around her as she poured her heart into her performance. She was going to save the man she loved.

The haunting, piercing note startled Cira from his grief. Dark panic crushed in around him as he reached out for Monase. He knew he would not find her; he knew that voice too well. Crawling forth on his hands and his knees, he waited silently behind the concealing bush. Shock and disbelief flared across his face as he watched Monase writhe like an unearthly nymph among the fire's dancing shadows. Slowly, an all-consuming rage burned through the shock, disbelief, fear, and even grief. Every fiber of his being was ignited, threatening to erupt. What was she doing? What madness had possessed her? He watched in helpless fury. What had he done to deserve this? The ancestors must have surely damned him the day he set eyes on that witch.

The minutes passed slowly as the men drew closer and closer to Monase's bewitching figure. Always, she seemed to move just out of their yearning grasp. She could feel their hot, lusting breaths upon her as her energy waned. She knew she needed to set her plan into motion before her strength and courage deserted her. Moving toward the man who had claimed her, she draped a sleek, languid arm around his neck. Smiling again that slow sexy smile, she spoke.

"I cannot remember when last I've eaten. I'm also very thirsty." Again she smiled, encompassing all the men in her gaze. They hung on her every word as she ran her soft pink tongue around her lips, then pulled it in to suck seductively on her bottom lip. "And I must freshen up for my next . . . lessons."

Her eyes returned to the leader. Instantly he clapped his hands, and the men fell over themselves to do her bidding.

Watching in the shadows, Cira gripped the handle of his spear with one hand while the other clutched the dry, wheat-colored grass around him, as if to anchor himself to the spot. His mind fought frantically for control. Every nerve in his body craved to attack, to rip Monase from his enemy, whose arm was now encircling her waist. She was his. She was his wife. He watched as she slipped off into the trees, smiling, saying she wouldn't be but a moment. His mind raced, weighing the odds. Did he have time to move around and capture her before she returned?

Monase forced her feet to walk slowly through the trees while with every step she wanted to flee. Glancing nervously over her shoulder, she slipped silently through the darkness. As she approached the backs of the trees where Cira's men were tied, she pulled the two assegai blades from her pouch. With trembling hands, she sawed at the leather thongs binding the first man's wrist. "Wait," she whispered, pressing the blade into his freed hands. She then moved on to the next man, repeating each step.

As she approached the third tree she heard the start of an angry, questioning buzz emanating from the campfire. The voices rose in volume as Zwide's men waited for her return. Monase turned quickly, thrusting the last blade into a prisoner's open, waiting palm. Whispering an apology to him, she fled into the surrounding darkness. She had done what she could; she would have to trust these Zulu impi abilities. Panza leaped lithely from branch to branch, showing her the way.

Cira had caught the slight movement behind his

captured men, and his eyes widened in suspicious confusion, then understanding. The Ngwane leader barked an angry command to his men to find and bring back the woman. Through clenched teeth, he ordered her not to be harmed. Then a dark, demonic gleam lit his eyes as he continued.

"When she is found, she will teach each and every one of us the lessons of love. The man who finds her first shall be after me."

A deafening cheer rose from the men, sending a virulent chill down Cira's spine. His heart cried out, *Oh Monase, what have you done? What have I made you do for me?* With defeated agony, he realized that all that she had claimed was true. She did love him, with a love that was so pure and true that she had been willing to sacrifice everything, even her life, for his honor. Unwept tears swam in his eyes as he whispered in a soft, reverent voice that he would avenge her sacrifice. He knew, with a sinking heart, that she would never escape these vicious warriors.

With hopes for a share in the delectable prize, the majority of the Ngwane impi crashed recklessly through the forest. Reluctantly, a handful of guards remained to guard the prisoners and their leader.

Knowing that the time to act had arrived, the bound men, who had passed the blades, unseen, to the other prisoners, about fifteen in all, rushed toward the unsuspecting Ngwane guards. Cira jumped into the foray to help. His appearance seemed to bolster his men's spirits as they ruthlessly slit the Ngwanes' throats and crushed their skulls with stones. The hushed commotion, then the eerie silence drew the Ngwane leader from his shelter.

Hearing his approach, Punga raised a hand to stop his eager men from pouncing. Cira nodded as he stepped forward. His battered men flanked behind him, their eyes shining with jubilant pride. The silence was deafening as neither Cira nor the Ngwane leader moved. Suddenly Cira hunched, then lunged forward, his spear hitting its mark.

The Ngwane leader stumbled backward. A fountain of crimson blood gushed from his chest. Frantically, he pressed his hands against the flood of life draining from him, but the blood forced its way through his fingers, staining the ground where he fell. His eyes widened with horror as he raised his bloodied hands before his fading vision. Lifting his face to the heavens, he cried out to his ancestors to come for him. A haunting silence stilled the night. The forest was quiet; even the ever-present whir of the insects had ceased.

Cira's men crowded around him, watching with horrified fascination as their captor's face grew still, and bright red blood bubbled from his lips. Then their eyes turned to Cira, waiting, questioning. Cira stood silently, still clenching his blood-soaked spear.

"Release him, Cira."

The words, spoken by Punga, tumbled over him like a distant song. Then Punga's frightened voice came again.

"Cira, release his spirit. He has the right to go."

Still, Cira did not move, the tormenting image of Monase's abused and wasted body swimming before his eyes. This man had ordered a fate worse than death for her, let him be damned. Punga's plea became lost in the torrential pounding in his head. Waves of rage and loss washed over him.

"Cira, please." Punga's words echoed urgently now as he grasped Cira's arm.

Dazed, Cira turned to his friend. For a moment his face hardened, then it crumbled. He couldn't do it. He wasn't like that. He couldn't sentence any man to eternal damnation. Yet, just as surely, he couldn't be the one to free this man's spirit. Not after what he had ordered done to Monase. Broken, he handed the spear to Punga. Relief swept over his men's faces. Punga bent, dragging the blade cleanly down the man's chest and abdomen. A heavy cloud seemed to rise from it depths.

Looking away, Cira lit a torch from the fire and began igniting the solitary hut, then the Ngwanes' weapons and supplies. His men quickly followed suit. Cleansing flames leaped high into the night. Sparks jumped restlessly to the trees; their glowing embers, like so many fireflies, showered down around them. Confused, bats flew erratically above the brightness, soaring then diving, only to be consumed by the burning heat.

In minutes, Zwide's men returned to the clearing, horror reflected in their fire-lit eyes, a cowering, frightened Monase in their midst. They surrounded Cira's small band of men.

Seeing the woman he loved, Cira turned gentle, sorrow-filled eyes to her, silently begging her forgiveness. Shimmering tears welled up in her eyes as she forced a brave smile to her lips. Cira drew in his breath at the courage and magnitude of the gesture. He knew she was not ignorant of the ordeal that faced her, that it would be more brutal and horrifying than any he and his men would ever face.

As if reading his thoughts, Monase raised her chin defiantly, her smile quivering ever so slightly. Wrenching a hand free from her captor, she placed it protectively upon her abdomen.

Cira's eyes flickered from her face to that telling hand. Understanding loomed dark and treacherously above his tenuous hold on sanity.

Suddenly the forest came alive as thousands of Zulu impi crashed through the branches. Their blood-chilling war cries echoed through the night. A horde of running bodies separated Cira from Monase. As he searched desperately for her the air was filled with the dull thud of spears entering the bodies of the surprised enemy and the groans of dying men. The sound of a savage cry close beside him awakened him to the extremity of his situation. In a mindless daze, he fought with superhuman strength.

Aware of the hopelessness of the situation, the few remaining Ngwane fled, or begged to be allowed to swear allegiance to Shaka.

Realizing the tremendous defeat they had dealt to Zwide and the irrefutable claim of their chief, Shaka, to be the new king, the Zulu impi raised a terror-inspiring cry of victory. Gradually, the men broke up into little groups, assuming their responsibility to release their victims' spirits, and at the same time garnering any treasures they might find among the fallen men's possessions.

While this was going on, Cira's dark, haunted eyes searched frantically among the death-strewn clearing. Monase's name caught painfully in his raw throat. He didn't hear the men around him tell of the defeat of Zwide, how Shaka had chased him from Zululand to Bopeli with every intent to kill him, only to discover that Zwide had done the deed to himself, dying, it was said, of a broken heart. For he had seen his mighty tribe scattered and destroyed in a single day. They told how they had been returning home when they had seen the flames; then a half-crazed monkey had led them here.

Frustrated with Cira's apparent apathy, the men finally moved away. It was then that Cira saw her. Their eyes met briefly, then her eyes flickered to the side, growing round with terror. Her mouth formed a silent no. Confused, unwilling to tear his eyes from her, Cira turned around.

There, before him, was Jama, his face streaked with white clay, wearing the feathers and adornments of the Ngwane, rising out of the bushes. A wild unearthly scream issued from his bared yellow teeth. As if in slow motion, Cira saw him leap, his massive weight barreling toward him, a glittering blade pointed directly at Cira's heart.

Just then, Monase screamed, and Cira turned his eyes toward her. He watched in horror as her lithe body flew through the air, her arm wrapping around his neck. For that instant time stood still. Their eyes locked, her gaze speaking eternal love, deeper than the oceans, unquenchable by death. Then pain clouded her eyes and her arms fell away. Cira felt her body falling, slipping out of his grasp, as she collapsed to a heap at his feet. Then

Jama's body, perforated by a hundred iKlwa spears, fell lifelessly upon her.

Cira bent, staggering backward, as if he'd been hit. An anguished cry tumbled from his lips. Reality rushed back, the sounds, the threatening silence, the crumbling heap of Monase's body. Like a man possessed, Cira wrenched Jama's body from Monase's. Falling to his knees, he lifted her still, limp body. Hugging her to his chest, he wept a torrent of tears, his grief released in primitive cries of tortured agony that seemed to be ripped from his core.

Punga struggled to take Monase's body from him, to assess the damage. But Cira only glared at him with red-rimmed, unfocused eyes. Punga tried to tell him that they had made a stretcher for her, that she needed to be taken to a healer. That she needed to go home.

"Home." Cira echoed the last word in a hollow voice.

Punga nodded, and watched as Cira began walking through the smoldering bush toward Zululand.

The troops marched for hours, their progress slowed by the wounded. Only Cira trudged onward, unfailing in his strength, unaware of the flies swarming over his open wounds and of Monase's blood congealing on his arms and hands. He marched without stopping, his eyes straight ahead, unaware of his cramped muscles as they maintained their unyielding embrace of Monase's body. He didn't hear the whispers of the men, doubting that she would survive the night.

Twenty-one

A weak, gray light announced the dawn of a new day. The tired troops picked up their speed as they saw the glowing fire of their kraals in the distance. At the welcome sight of the lush, green pastures dotted with white-and-black cattle, many of the men dispersed to hastily cleanse themselves of the deaths of their enemy.

Cries of relief echoed up the hillside as families spotted their loved ones returning. Monase's mother broke free from the crowd when she saw the limp, unmoving form of her child. Her face was masked in a silent agony as she approached Cira.

Punga hesitated, unsure if he should intervene. By this time the others had arrived, and Mkabuyi placed a gentle hand on his arm, pulling him back.

"Come, Cira, bring my baby home," Niamani whispered wretchedly. Then she turned, heading back down the hill.

Cira nodded, the blank vacant look still in his eyes as he again echoed the word *home.*

Niamani led him to his bridal hut. Only then did Cira relinquish his hold on Monase's body. Both the inyangas and a witch doctor had been summoned, and they fell to work on Monase, eyeing Cira nervously, afraid he would snatch her back into his arms at any time. They had been told of his refusal to let her go, and were thus relieved that they hadn't had to wrest her from him.

Cira didn't interfere, but sat staring into the fire. Punga tried to convince him to come away, to attend to his wound, but Cira had sat unheeding, immovable. Mkabuyi came and offered him food and water, but it remained untouched.

After cauterizing the deep gash in Monase's back, the inyangas made a potent paste out of moss, white clay, and herbs. They plastered it over her wound, then wrapped it tightly in strips of soft tanned hides. Taking a bronze amulet from his pouch, the witch doctor laid it on her chest. Soon the isangoma arrived, emptying some small animal bones onto the floor beside Monase. A broad knowing smile creased her wizened features.

"She will recover. The spirits protect her. She is a brave impi."

The witch doctor cast a scornful glance at the old woman and cleared his throat. "Cira did well to hold her wound so tightly. He saved her life. The pressure he placed on the wound clamped shut the blood tube, preventing her spirit from escaping."

Then, turning concerned eyes to Cira's bent back, he roughly patted his shoulder. "Watch her carefully; the fever could still take her. I will return tomorrow. Guard her from the evil spirits of the night. Do not answer if they call to you from the darkness."

With these final words, the people in the hut departed; only Monase, Niamani, and Cira remained.

Gently, Niamani stroked her child's sweat-beaded brow. Closing her eyes, she sang the sweet haunting melody of the Zulu lullaby.

Memories flooded Cira. It was the same melody his mother, then Monase, had sung to him. Giant sobs racked his body. He turned, and crawling to Monase's side, he laid his head gently on her thickening stomach. In a small voice, he pleaded, "Do not take her from me. I could not bear it. I am not strong enough."

In their grief, neither mother nor husband noticed the faint fluttering of Monase's eyelashes.

As the night grew dark, Ugebula came to escort Niamani home. Reluctantly, she rose to leave. Clutching Cira's hand in hers, she begged him to protect her little girl. Her words sliced like a sharp blade through his battered heart. Some protector he was. Wearily, he nodded his head. A watery smile quivered on her lips as she promised to return in the morning. Weeping, she allowed Ugebula to pull her into his arms as they left for the night.

Tirelessly, Cira maintained his lonely vigil by Monase's side. As the moon rose, a hyena called close by. Monase moaned as her temperature rose. The fever had come. Cira bathed her flushed face and sweat-glistened brow. By midnight, she was thrashing deliriously.

Going to the fire, Cira stirred the boiling brew the witch doctor had made from some cannabis leaves. He then poured the brew into Monase's wooden bowl. The steam wafted above his head, creating a light-headed sensation in his already sleep- and food-deprived brain. Monase whimpered in protest as he poured the hot liquid down her throat. Then she quieted. She had only touched a small portion of the drink.

Beginning to feel dizzy, Cira threw the undissolved leaves and remaining brew on the fire. It sizzled and popped, emitting a familiar sickly-sweet scent. For a moment the memory of that aroma tugged at the back of Cira's mind, then Monase cried out. He hurried to her, oblivious to the strange billowing smoke rising from the fire.

Cira's gentle hands soothed her as she turned her face into the palm stroking her cheek. He fought the exhaustion permeating his body, struggling to stay awake. The smoke burned his eyes, and his vision began to blur. Food, he thought. I need some food. He glanced around for the food Mkabuyi had brought earlier. It was cold, but he ate it with a ravishing hunger. He waited for energy to surge through his body, but it didn't. He coughed at the overpowering smoke. A small throbbing had begun at the base of his skull, and the space above his eyes felt tight and achy.

I must get some air, some water, he thought. As he moved toward the hut's opening he heard heavy breathing coming from outside. He froze as the panting came closer. Suddenly a shrill unearthly laugh ripped through the night. Little shivers ran over Cira's body, like a thousand squirming snakes. Frantically, he clawed at his skin.

"Cira, Cira, come to me." A haunting feminine voice seeped in under the door covering. Recalling the witch doctor's words, Cira backed way from the door, refusing to answer. Again he heard the words, this time low and gurgling. "Cira, Cira." Now, the voice changed, becoming sweet and high, a voice from his past. "Cira, it's me, come to me."

Cira's heart lurched; he was a boy again. He had prayed so many times for this very thing. The ancestors had heard him. His mother had returned. He opened his mouth to cry out, but instead drew in a lungful of the thick pungent air and heard Monase moan loudly. He turned his eyes to her, confused. Then a warning voice screamed through his mind.

Beware the night voices. Don't talk to them. Don't go to them. Don't let them in. You must protect her.

He squeezed his eyes shut. The voice outside called again, louder, this time joined by a low masculine one.

"Cira, please. We are cold, lonely. Let us in. Please don't abandon us." Cira swallowed hard, a tight burning sensation in his throat. The walls around his heart crumbled, and the small lonely boy inside cried out for his long-lost parents, for the years of lost love and affection.

As if hearing that silent plea, the voices grew more urgent. "Come to us, baby, weep no more." Then his father's mellow voice cried out, "I'm sorry, forgive me. Come home."

Cira crushed the heels of his hands into his

aching eye sockets. He breathed harsh, shallow breaths. It hurt so much.

"Cira? What's wrong?" Another voice, weaker, vaguely familiar, drifted to him from far away. "Cira, my head hurts. My body hurts. Hold me, please."

The words rolled through his clouded mind. He started to turn toward Monase, when the other voices beckoned again. Cira raised his hand to his head, covering his ears, his red eyes glancing around with fear and confusion. He heard weeping. It wasn't coming from outside. Frantic, he squinted into the smoky darkness. His eyes locked with Monase's. The voices outside grew still louder, angrier, more insistent. He reached out his hand to Monase. She took it. He clung to her like a man adrift in the ocean clings to a floating piece of timber. Her grasp was weak. She closed her eyes with a sigh, letting her dry, hot fingers slip. He groped desperately for them. The voices outside broke into the hideous high-pitched squeal of hyenas.

Crawling to Monase's side, Cira willed her to open her eyes. There was scratching at the door. She opened her eyes and looked up at him with a weak smile. His dry eyes welled up with tears as he fell exhausted upon her chest, burying his damp face in her soft yielding flesh, breathing deeply of her deliciously feminine, real flesh. The beating of her heart drowned out the sounds of the night. The voices outside ceased their torment.

The scene played itself over and over in Monase's fever-ravished mind. Jama's face twisted with jealous hatred . . . the light glinting off his spear . . . Cira's bewildered eyes . . . her body leaping to protect him, screaming, then falling, falling into dark fathomless nothingness.

As once more the images passed before her, she struggled to change the ending. Never, in her dreams, did she quite reach him. Always, she was just an instant too late. She fought to terminate the nightmare, to relieve herself of its hellish torment. Once, she had opened her eyes to see Cira's pained, desperate face. He had reached out to her, dark eyes pleading with her to help him. She had held out her hand to him, but the demonic dreams had clawed at her, dragging her back to their murky depths. As she felt her fingers growing numb and the blackness settling in around her, she struggled to rise, to break the surface, to face reality, to know for sure.

Strange swirling patterns of light danced across the translucent skin inside her eyelids. Monase tried to open them. Slowly, heavily, they lifted. A soft hazy light floated above her. Turning, she focused on a bright splinter of sunlight filtering through a narrow chink in the ceiling. After a while the pure intensity became too much, and she had to look away. Closing her eyes, she felt the stinging tears. In this brief respite, she realized a heavy weight was draped about her waist and legs. She opened her eyes to gaze down at Cira's sleep-softened face.

His strong arms were wrapped loosely around her hips while one long leg bent over hers. She raised a hand to stroke a stray lock of hair from his cheek, when severe pain jolted through her head and back. She dropped her hand with a loud, agonizing hissing intake of air.

Instantly, Cira's eyes popped open, bleary, red, and concerned. Monase forced a weak smile, her effort causing small beads of sweat to form on her upper lip.

"If this is the heavens, they must do something about this pain."

Cira answered her with a warm, tender smile. He moved to cushion her head on his lap. As he bent to kiss her forehead she tilted her face upward, catching his lips squarely on her own. He smiled again, the dimple in the left side of his face deep and welcoming.

"For this I'd suffer." She sighed.

At this remark, Cira threw back his head and laughed a weary, relieved laugh, which ended on a choking sob. When his eyes returned to hers, they were wet with tears.

"You are alive. My Monase. The spirits have not taken you from me." His hands ran over and over her hair, her face, her throat. "I was a fool. Can you ever—"

Withstanding the pain, Monase raised a finger to his lips, silencing him. He kissed the tip, and then kissed each finger in turn, his eyes dark, passionate, loving. Monase felt herself melt in their golden depths, her pain receding to a dull, bearable ache. She ran her tongue over dry, yearning lips. Lowering her hand, Cira cupped her face and kissed her deeply. As his warm breath filled her she felt a small tingling of new life in her womb. Her hand strayed to the roundness of her belly.

Noticing the movement, Cira withdrew from her

mouth. His eyes flickered to her hand, and then back to her face. The question was there, unasked, fearful, yet hopeful. Monase nodded and smiled, her lips pressed tightly together to prevent her from crying with happiness when she saw the joy on Cira's face.

Cira gasped a small gulp of air, held it, then expelled it in a disbelieving gush of sheer exultation.

"Please love me," Monase cried out, unable to contain her love and desire.

"But I do. I have loved you from the moment I laid eyes on you. You have driven me to madness with jealousy, grief, and longing. My sweet Monase, I only pray that you still love me in return. Although I am not worthy of it, I will surely die without it. I love you with all my being, and cherish you as my greatest prize."

Now tears of rapture streamed unchecked down Monase's cheeks. Cira watched their dewy descent as she nodded vigorously.

"Cira, that you could know what happiness you give me," Monase choked out between sobs. "I love you, I want you, I need you. . . ."

The last words died as his mouth slanted down to devour hers, and he lay down beside her, gently drawing her into his arms. Then their hips joined as one, rising and falling to the primitive dance of their ancestors, their bodies soaring to the glorious heavens, their hearts beating amid the shooting stars.

In the warm, sleepy aftermath, Cira hand-fed Monase the food that had, as if magically, appeared inside their doorway. Together, they laughed at the poor surprised soul who had stumbled upon their tumultuous lovemaking, when in all probability, he or she had been expecting to find a suffering invalid and a brooding attendant.

"Blessed are they that feed us lusty creatures." Cira beamed as he placed a bright red berry on Monase's tongue. She giggled as the juice of the ripe berry slid down her chin. Gallantly, Cira bent to lap it up. Their laughter melted into a soft sensuous kiss.

"Surely you have bewitched me. Who could have thought this hardened soul could know such happiness?" Cira tentatively placed his hand on Monase's stomach, his eyes sparkling as her hand covered his. He turned his hand to grasp hers. Then he threw back his head and roared in triumph.

Suddenly, the door covering flew open. Several concerned faces peered in.

"I'm to be a father," Cira announced, then turned to Monase, his eyebrows arched in a question.

"The baby is due in early summer, I think," she murmured shyly, afraid of disapproval, since surely no one knew of her secret marriage to Cira.

She was wrong; the people tumbled in to congratulate her and Cira on their marriage and the impending birth. It seemed that when the chief . . . king had been told of Monase's heroic act, he had smiled, saying that a wife should do no less. Shaka then told his people of the secret marriage.

Rising, Cira pounded savagely on his chest, his coiled locks whipping violently about his face. The men laughed, slapping him on the back, while the women looked on with mock disapproval.

"Come, let us celebrate your victory . . . all your victories!" Punga cried out amid the men's crude laughter.

Cira turned to Monase, with a concerned look on his face. Smiling, she sent him off with a flutter of her hand.

"Please go. I need my rest. Enjoy your barbaric revelry somewhere else." The women laughed and nodded in agreement, anxious to be rid of the men so they could hear the real story.

As the last man exited, the women burst into a garble of excitement and congratulations. Longing to breathe in the fresh air and feel the warm sunshine, Monase convinced her mother and sisters to help her outside. A cool wind whipped her rumpled skirt around her, threatening to reveal her naked body beneath. Her mother frowned and hurried off to find her some heavier—and larger-sized—clothing.

Twenty-two

Day by day Monase grew stronger. A week after she had returned, she was sitting outside her mother's hut drying some dyed seeds and shells with the other women when she looked out at the training grounds. Cira's old battalion was cavorting around him in a wild, demonstrative dance. Suddenly one man stopped in front of Cira to undulate his hips in a suggestive fashion. This brought a heated flush to Monase's face, when she recognized the man as one of the captive impi she had released from the Ngwanes.

She was about to look down in embarrassment when, across the distance, Cira's eyes met hers. Pride and love shone from their golden depths. A hearty slap on his back from one of the men brought his gaze back to the mocking impi. The man began to speak, gesticulating wildly as he did so, and the group broke into rowdy laughter.

Cira grinned. Turning back to face Monase, he placed his feet shoulder-width apart, hands on his hips. Monase's hands stopped their sorting as Cira beckoned her to come to him. Again, she blushed. Giggles erupted behind her as the woman pushed her forward, chanting.

"Choose, choose, the one you love the best."

Embarrassed at this public display, Monase lowered her lashes over burning cheeks and approached her beloved. Then, in fun, she wiggled her hips saucily when she stood before Cira. Cira laughed and swept her up into his arms. Then he dipped, cradling her against his left elbow, kissing her soundly.

The crowd sent up a roar of approval. Smiling shyly, Monase melted against him.

Suddenly Cira's body went rigid. Silence enveloped the small gathering. Monase looked up to see King Shaka a few feet away. Hastily, she pulled away. Smoothing her skirt, she lowered her eyes respectfully and slid three steps backward.

"I hear you are to present me with a new impi this summer. Congratulations."

Cira nodded a clipped nod, pride shining from his eyes. Moving closer, Shaka extended a hand, placing it on Cira's shoulder.

"I'm pleased with your victory against the Ngwanes." The great man's eyes momentarily flickered to Monase, a small smile twitching at the corner of his mouth. "You are a valiant impi," he told Cira. "To honor you, I allow you the privilege to take a Great Wife." An admiring murmur rippled through the crowd. "And . . ." Shaka continued as he turned to face his waiting people, "the lobala shall be of my own personal herd."

Shocked disbelief spliced the silence. Then a roar of approval and clapping rang out resoundingly through the air.

Monase swayed slightly. Her stomach lurched, and a dark, numbing despair hung around her. Biting her lip, she chastised herself for being so selfish, for believing she could keep Cira all to herself. She knew there would be others; she just hadn't expected it to be so soon. She tried to take solace in the fact that the man she loved had repeatedly professed his love for her over the last few days.

While Monase fought to stay calm, silent, expecting eyes turned toward Cira. Fathers and mothers with marriage-age daughters rubbed their hands together in anticipation. Monase's mother stepped closer to her, entwining her finger with hers. Monase let out a small, measured, wavering breath as she smiled at the small comfort this gesture offered.

"My king, I am honored at your generous prize. It is with pleasure that I serve you." The crowd nodded their approval of Cira's elegant words. "I would ask your majesty to accept my nomination of my treasured wife, Monase, as my Great Wife."

A stunned silence fell in a hush over the people. Then, turning to face her, Cira gently grasped Monase's shoulders with his hands. "I nominate you, Monase, as my Great Wife, bearer of my heirs. My only wife, mother of all my children."

Stumbling slightly, Monase would have fallen if

Cira had not pulled her to him. Sharp intakes of breath could be heard rippling through the crowd as Cira turned back to Shaka. The two men's eyes locked, a dark scowl flickering across the king's forehead.

Then, suddenly, Shaka erupted into hearty laughter. Wagging a finger at Monase, he admonished her. "In that case, you had better beget him a mighty brood." Again he laughed, this time the relieved crowd laughing with him. "Don't think you are so sly, my Cira. The lobala still goes to the father, not the husband."

Cira removed one hand from Monase to press it in mock innocence against his heart. Shaka laughed again as he waved a hand to his guards to fetch twenty-five of his cows to be presented to Ugebula.

The king then turned to Cira again. "Are you certain?"

Cira nodded. "As I've said before, women are too much trouble. One is so much more peaceful"—he looked at Monase—"I hope."

Monase smiled back at him, tears in her eyes. Quickly she wiped them away. How this man had a way of making her cry!

Feigning indignation, Monase pushed against him. He pulled her tighter, and she pushed again, their bodies sliding against each other. Suddenly the pouch at her waist broke loose, spilling a few nuts and berries to the ground. Panza scampered down from his perch in a nearby tree and stuffed the delicious morsels into his mouth. Pleased by the laughter he elicited from the audience, he reached into the pouch to get more. Pulling the rolled snakeskin from the bag, he screeched, flinging it upward in an arc, then scurrying onto Cira's shoulder.

The skin unrolled, fluttering gently to the ground, glittering translucent along its blue-black length. Fearful, the crowd moved back. With great care, the isangoma, who had foretold Dingo-swayo's death, lifted the ten-foot skin. Approaching Monase and Cira, she told them to follow. When they stood beneath a nearby tree, she draped the skin over a low-hanging branch. A slight breeze lifted the ends, the only noise the dry rattle of scale against scale.

Suddenly a cold wind snapped through the branches, and a dense dark cloud blocked out the sun. A small rustle in the grass made everyone turn to see a thin black snake slither down the side of a rock, where it had been sunning itself. Monase watched in apprehension as it made its way to a small hole in the ground and then disappeared. Clutching Cira's hand in dread, she turned to face the old woman. Removing the dry snakeskin, the isangoma wound it around Monase's abdomen.

"A great ancestor has spoken to me," she answered. Monase held her breath, her lungs aching.

"You shall bear many brave impi, and dutiful daughters," the old woman continued. "Even now, in your belly grows the beginning of a great warrior." Pausing, the old woman cocked her head, her eyes narrowing in deep thought. This time, with her voice barely above a whisper, she said, "They also tell of a strong daughter, dead to our world, sailing across the oceans to a strange new land."

The isangoma's face then relaxed into a crinkled smile as she shrugged her shoulders. Removing the binding skin, she placed a small, bony hand upon Monase's stomach. "Be happy, rejoice. Love is good, eh?"

Nodding his head vigorously, Cira joined in with the cackling laughter of the wise old woman, all but the joy of the moment forgotten. Taking Monase's hand, he led her to their home, to celebrate in private.